W9-BRG-289

these
GENTLE
WOUNDS

HELENE DUNBAR

flux
Woodbury, Minnesota

KENNEBUNK FREE LIBRARY

These Gentle Wounds © 2014 by Helene Dunbar. All rights reserved. No part of this book may be used or reproduced in any manner whatsoever, including Internet usage, without written permission from Flux, except in the case of brief quotations embodied in critical articles and reviews.

First Edition
First Printing, 2014

Book design by Bob Gaul
Cover design by Kevin R. Brown
Cover image by Oliver Charles

Flux, an imprint of Llewellyn Worldwide Ltd.

This is a work of fiction. Names, characters, places, and incidents are either the product of the author's imagination or are used fictitiously, and any resemblance to actual persons living or dead, business establishments, events, or locales is entirely coincidental. Cover model used for illustrative purposes only and may not endorse or represent the book's subject.

Library of Congress Cataloging-in-Publication Data
Dunbar, Helene.
  These gentle wounds/Helene Dunbar.—First edition.
    pages cm
  Summary: "Fifteen-year-old Gordie is trying to build a new life after tragically losing his family, but when his abusive father returns, Gordie must confront the traumas of the past."—Provided by publisher.
   ISBN 978-0-7387-4027-0
  [1. Brothers—Fiction. 2. Emotional problems—Fiction. 3. High schools—Fiction. 4. Schools—Fiction. 5. Stepfathers—Fiction. 6. Hockey—Fiction. 7. Child abuse—Fiction. 8. Fathers and sons—Fiction.] I. Title.
   PZ7.D79428The 2014
   [Fic]—dc23

                                                          2013044138

                              Flux
                    Llewellyn Worldwide Ltd.
                     2143 Wooddale Drive
                    Woodbury, MN 55125-2989
                        www.fluxnow.com

            Printed in the United States of America

In memory of my mother, Carol Baker,
who shared her love of books.

To my father, Harold Baker,
who told me I could do anything.

And to Suzanne Kamata, who said to do this.

With Love.

ONE

The last thing I saw before the car hit the water was an eagle pasted against the sky.

And what I remember is this: his tapered wings filled the width of the dirty window; the air held him up with the promise of magic; he looked free.

I used to dream about that bird.

But I don't have dreams anymore.

All I have are memories.

———————

My arms are pinned. Water rushes past my ears, and the kids cry in the backseat as they start to wake up. My mom's hands are wrapped around the steering wheel as she prays, saying words that make no sense but sound something like poetry.

I've left the car window cracked open and the river takes that as an invitation to pour in. At first it feels good against my hot skin. Cool. Cleansing. The sound it makes is music to Mom's words.

But suddenly there's only water. I throw my shoulder

against the window, trying to break the glass. I hold my head up to catch the little bit of air left in the car and gasp for as much as my lungs can hold.

"Gordie," I hear. "Ice. Hey, Ice."

The sound belongs to my brother, Kevin. My brain wraps around it like a kid around a security blanket. His voice climbs into my head and replaces the crying, the praying, the water.

"I didn't die." My mouth forms the words easily enough. It's harder to get my mind to accept them.

One part of me knows I didn't drown, but another part of my fucked-up brain thinks I did. Just like the kids in the back. Just like Mom meant me to.

My brother holds my arms down on the bed, thinking he's keeping me safe now like he couldn't before. My jaw is sore from clenching my teeth to stop myself from repeating the words. But part of me is still in the river, and Kevin knows that.

"You're okay," he says. It isn't a question.

He doesn't trust me enough to release my arms immediately. But once he does, they automatically fold up around me, stiff and sore like the broken wings of a gull. It hurts worse than after a hockey game where I've fended off a ton of shots on goal. Worse than it did on That Day, when it actually happened.

My eyes take a minute to focus, but when they do, it's on the bashed-up wall next to my bed. The blue paint is chipped. The edges of the holes in the plaster are tinged with blood stains that we've given up trying to wash away or paint over.

That's what happens when Kevin isn't around. I try to

claw my way out of the car and to the surface. The wall, the lamp, my own skin: all of them have been bruised at some point from the dream that is really a memory.

Without either of us saying anything, Kevin pulls the sweat-damp blankets off me and replaces them with fresh, dry ones from the closet, just like he's done hundreds of times. And just like I've done hundreds of times, I wrap up in them and try, unsuccessfully, to stop shivering.

"Sleep," he says. "You have practice tomorrow."

Tomorrow. School. Hockey. It seems a million years away, but I nod. We both know it'll be hours before I'll begin to trust my brain not to do this all over again.

Kevin sits down at my desk and pretends to read. He'll sit there until I fall asleep, however long that takes. I watch him and remind myself that because he's here, I'm safe.

You'd never know we're only half brothers from how close we are or from looking at us. If it weren't for the fact he's sixteen months older, with the inches to prove it, and that my eyes are green and his are brown, you might think we're twins.

But it wasn't our eye color or height that was the really important difference between us. See, though Kevin and I had the same mother, the fact that we have different fathers is what mattered. Having different fathers meant that Mom planned for Kevin to live. And planned for me to die when she drove the car into the river.

TWO

It's a shoot-off. Six-ounce disks of black rubber fly toward my face as, one by one, the best scorers on our team barrel toward the crease from the blue line and fire pucks at me.

This is why I love hockey. Pucks don't care that my mom tried to drown me 1,822 days ago. They don't care that I'm running on two hours of sleep. They don't care that, inside my glove, my right hand is twitching like an animal caught in a trap. Pucks don't care that I haven't felt this shitty in months or that I'd just let myself start to hope that maybe, *maybe,* I would end up normal and not like ... well, like me.

All a puck cares about is getting through to the goal, so all I have to care about is not letting that happen.

Focus, focus, focus, I repeat under my breath, narrowing my vision so all I can see is the blackness of rubber against the ice. I ignore Kenny Campbell when he tries to fake me out and I don't fall for Mitchell Strazynski's showboat moves when he tries to shoot backward between his legs.

The only thing I can't ignore is the hum in the rink that builds with every shot I block. So it's impossible not to notice that the rink goes quiet when Cody Bowman lines up in front of me. He's the largest defenseman on our team, since he was held back a grade, and he's leading the league in penalty minutes. Even Coach, who's at the back of the box having a heated discussion with Assistant Principal Warner, seems to have problems reining him in.

I take a deep breath and, for a minute, my hand stops shaking. Cody comes at me. I think he's planning to barrel right through me but I hold my ground. As he gets close, instead of shooting the puck, he changes directions and plows around the back of the net.

"Come on, freak," he snarls, quietly enough that no one else can hear but vicious enough to turn my stomach to jelly. "Let's see what you've got."

"Just shoot the puck," I say, trying to act like he's an annoyance and not someone set on making my life hell.

"Or what?" he asks, skating in front of me. "You going to have your big brother break my nose again?"

I actually might, if I thought Kevin could get away with it this time. But I'm not stupid enough to say that out loud so I just roll my eyes, which he probably can't see through my mask, and wait.

"Bowman, are you shooting that puck or dancing with it? We don't have all day here." Luke Miller is the captain of our team, our starting center, the god of Maple Grove, the one everyone else wants to be. Since Luke works with Coach to determine the lineups for the games (aka who will get the most ice time), he's also one of the few people that Cody will take orders from.

"Later, water boy," Cody says, slapping the puck vaguely in my direction.

Normally it would be easier to blow Cody off. Normally my hand wouldn't be this shaky, and I wouldn't have spent hours lying awake after a spin thinking of how it's been almost five years since everything happened and how I still don't really know what I'm meant to be feeling.

I try to stretch out the tightness from my shoulders as Jamie Walker, our senior goalie who can't hit the side of a bus with a puck, whips one at me. My legs each decide to go in a different direction and before I know it, I'm crumpled in a twisted pile on the ice.

"Geez, Allen, what's with you?" Walker skates in slow, choppy circles in front of the crease and I try to untangle my legs.

I shrug. No way am I telling him about last night. It's bad enough that he knows my whole life story, just like everyone else in Maple Grove. At least the school's been cool enough to let me use Jim's last name, "given the circumstances."

"I'm fine." I get back into my crouch in front of the net. I take a deep breath, but inside my glove, my hand starts to tighten. Spasms are one thing, but when it gets really bad, my hand cramps up to the point I can't move it. *Crap. I don't need this to happen in the rink.* I stand up, pull my glove off, and lift my mask to take a drink of water. But I can't even feel the surface of the bottle.

"You're looking green, Gordie," Walker says. "Go sit down."

I want to tell him again I'm fine. That I'll be good to start tomorrow's game. That I stayed up too late doing homework, or jerking off, or drinking beer pilfered from the fridge when Kevin's dad Jim wasn't looking. Any of the normal reasons for being fifteen and exhausted. Anything other than the truth.

"No...I..." is as far as I get.

A couple of the other guys gather around to see what's stopped Walker in front of the goal. The numbers on their jerseys blur in front of my eyes. I try to rub the fuzzy digits away with my sleeve, and my water bottle goes crashing to the ice.

Walker retrieves it, but when he holds it out to me, his expression changes from one of normal annoyance to that stupid, sad look people get around me all the time. The one that says he thinks he should go easy on me because, ultimately, we both know that Cody is right. I'm a freak.

I grab my bottle back and turn away so I don't have to see that look. My chest tightens and the tingling in my hand feels like it's on a direct course to my brain. I don't want to practice anymore. All I want to do is disappear.

I skate away from them, stepping off the ice and slamming the gate behind me. Coach is nowhere to be seen, so I make a quick break for it. My skates take a while to come off because of my hand, but then it doesn't take me long to throw them in my locker and stalk through the door to the parking lot. It's cold out and I forgot to grab my coat, but I don't care. I wish I didn't care about anything.

"Hey."

I wasn't sure if any of the guys were going to try to stop me, but this voice is definitely female, so I keep walking. It must be meant for someone else.

My head is a mess of needy thoughts. I need to get back to the house. I need to see my brother, although he's only going to give me a hard time. I need to forget about last night, and the anniversary that's coming up, and that I'm such a loser I can't even hold it together through freaking hockey practice.

As I cross the parking lot, a clomping sound, kind of like a two-legged horse galloping, breaks into my thoughts. I glance over my shoulder and the girl stops in her tracks—a large camera draped around her neck, a black bag over her shoulder, and high black boots that explain the sound. Her hair and clothes are black too, but not ripped and stagey like the goth kids. She looks...like someone I should know.

"Hey," she says again. This time I'm sure she's talking to me.

"What do you want?" I shove my hand deep into the pocket of my jeans even though I know it won't completely hide the shaking. With any luck she'll just think I'm cold.

"I just..." She lets out a deep breath, reaches out a hand, and then takes it back. "Are you okay?"

There's no way for me to answer her question. No one who asks this really wants an honest answer anyhow. Jim, the school shrinks, the kids at school—all they really want to hear is that everything is fine and that there's nothing they need to do. If I stay under the radar, keep my grades up, and stop the pucks, they'll all go away. So I just try to be quiet, paste a smile on my face, and act normal, hoping they won't notice that I'm not.

"Yeah, I'm fine," I say to the girl. I turn back around and start to walk off.

"Gordie, wait," she says, and I stop again, like her voice is changing the ground to quicksand.

"Who are you?" I ask over my shoulder, even though I should know better. All I want is to get far away as soon as possible, and starting a conversation with this mystery girl isn't the way to do that.

She leans on one leg and smiles. "You don't remember me?"

If I was Kevin, I'd say something mouthy along the lines of "If I did, I wouldn't be asking." But as I'm me, I don't say anything at all—until she holds her camera up to her face.

Now I get it. Last summer, I played in the city hockey league and I saw her taking pictures at all of our games. It turned into one of those stupid athlete superstitions. I had to see her, parked behind that camera, before I stepped into the crease or it nagged at me all game.

All I know is that her name is Sarah and I've probably just doubled the amount of words I've ever said to her. Talking to her was never part of my plan. But knowing who she is confuses me even more than not knowing.

"And?"

She lets her camera fall against her jacket and looks a little embarrassed. "Molly and Stephanie…" She pauses, waiting for me to say something, but I have nothing to add about the captains of the cheerleading team.

"They'reworkingonafundraiserandtheywantmetotake yourpicture," she spits out in one word.

"What?"

She takes a deep breath. "Look, I know this is weird, but

they're paying me and I'm saving up for a car, so ..." She looks me directly in the eyes and I'm kind of frozen to the ground. "They're putting together a calendar of pictures of the cutest boys on Maple Grove's sports teams, so I wanted to know if I could just use one of the photos I took of you last summer. You know, one without all of your padding on. If you say it's okay, I'll let you pick out the one you like best."

"They're paying you ..." I repeat back. *Now I get it.*

"No. Wait." Her shoulders fall and she bites her lip. "I mean, I want to talk to you anyhow. I've wanted to since last summer, but ..."

I shiver. This has got to be a joke. "Look, today really isn't a good day." I cut her off, but really, I wish I could shut up because I know I'm not saying anything interesting or useful or ... why do I even care?

"Today is the first day of the rest of your life." She sounds like an old bumper sticker, and I kind of laugh in spite of myself.

Far off in the distance, a yellow balloon rises in the sky. Some kid must have let go of it. I wish so badly I could catch the string in my hand and let it pull me away.

"I have to go," I mumble to both of us.

She puts the camera into the bag and my hand clenches. Despite what I said, I actually *am* curious to see her photos, but now I've missed my chance because she says, "Okay. Maybe some other time then." She sounds disappointed in a way that makes me feel disappointed too.

"See you in class," she says, and then does the worst thing of all. She turns away, leaving me to figure out what in the world she means by "in class" because, as far as I know, she doesn't even go to Maple Grove.

I watch her get smaller and smaller as she walks away without looking back. All at once, the exhaustion and frustration I'm feeling is eaten up by a huge emptiness. Like I've lost something I didn't even know I had.

THREE

"Allen, what the hell happened to you last night?" Walker shouts at me across the crowded hall. I know I'm going to need to do damage control with the team; missing practice is an automatic game suspension. I was just hoping not to have to do it right now.

I lean against a row of lockers and close my eyes while I let him catch up.

"Nothing," I say after he reaches me. "Nothing happened. Sorry." It's a total lie, but Walker is only smart on the ice.

I open my eyes and watch him try to figure out what he wants to say.

"Don't let him get the upper hand. The team needs you more than we need that douche."

It takes me a second to realize that he thinks I left because of Cody. "You're right," I say, playing along. "Sorry."

He slaps my shoulder with the back of his hand. "Dude. Seriously. You're going to be invincible next year. Just watch."

I nod. Next year. Maybe everything really will be different then. Cody will have graduated. No one else will care much about me spazzing out because I'm going to be starting goalie on a champion hockey team. Or maybe the spins and everything will have stopped by then and I won't have a reason to keep trying to hide in the shadows. Maybe next year I'll be normal.

"Gordie?" Walker stares at me and the pity starts to seep back into his expression.

"Invincible," I parrot back, needing to escape. "Yeah. Sure."

I push off the lockers and head down the hall.

Mr. Brooks is blocking the doorway to his classroom, his back to me. But that isn't what stops me cold. What does that is a flash of short dark hair so raven-black it's almost blue. It seems to fill up the hall.

I half-close my eyes and keep walking, hoping I can slip in unnoticed. Instead, Mr. Brooks stops me with a hand on my shoulder.

"Gordie. Just who I wanted to see." He smiles. "Sarah is joining our class today and since the two of you know each other, I hope you won't mind taking her under your wing and getting her up to speed on the assignments."

I narrow my eyes and stare at her incredibly sincere face. She doesn't look like someone who's just stretched the truth so far it's about to snap.

"We don't really . . . " I begin, but the hand on my shoulder tightens.

Unlike Sarah, Mr. Brooks really does know everything about me. I used to talk to him all the time when he taught at the middle school, and for a while he was the only one who didn't treat me like I was nuts. I kind of owe him.

"Yeah. Sure," I say, giving in just as the bell rings. Mr. Brooks ushers us in and I manage to hiss at Sarah, "Why did you ... " before she walks off without answering to take the only open seat, a few rows away from me.

Mr. Brooks starts talking about *Moby Dick*, which I read a couple of years ago. That's just as well, because the chance of me being able to pay attention to class is exactly zero. Instead, I have to fight the urge to keep twisting around to look at Sarah. Her eyes are as dark as her hair, which falls straight down to just the tips of her ears like one of those 1960s models on the old album covers that Kevin's dad has hanging in the den, and it's as shiny as newly laid ice. Her smile is really wide, and it makes her eyes light up.

I don't want to care, but my fingers tap a rhythm on my jeans as I stare at the clock. This is a double period, with a break in the middle that can't come quickly enough. I'm already halfway out of my seat when the bell rings and everyone pushes to leave.

In the hall, I call her name, trying to give my voice that air of nonchalance most kids seem to have perfected by high school, but the word kind of knots around my tongue.

"Me? Are you actually talking to me?" she asks with something resembling a smile.

"Yeah, but ... " She shouldn't be the one asking the questions. Besides, I could probably come up with a pretty long list of reasons why I wouldn't normally start a conversation with a girl outside English class. Why I never have before.

"Why are you so quiet, Gordie Allen?"

I press back against the wall to keep from walking away and get to my real point. "Why did you tell Mr. Brooks that we knew each other?"

"Wishful thinking?" She laughs. When I don't laugh back, she shrugs. "It isn't totally untrue. I mean, you recognized me from last summer, right?"

I want to explain to her that knowing that someone is taking pictures isn't the same as actually *knowing* them, but I have a feeling it won't matter to her.

"Look, yesterday. I mean ... can I see your photos?" I ask. My stomach rolls over as I remember her saying something about "the cutest athletes at Maple Grove." Now I'm pretty sure that I imagined the whole conversation, but if I could see the photos ...

Control it, Kevin would tell me. *Just because you think you need something doesn't mean you do.*

Easy for him to say. Not like he's so great about taking his own advice.

Sarah smirks, holding in a smile. "I didn't bring my camera."

I'm not sure how she can do this to me. My thumb twitches a million times. I don't know why I'm so bugged about it, but she's making me crazy.

"If you want to go get it, I could tell Mr. Brooks you'll be right back." I realize, as I say it, that it's ridiculous. I mean, however desperate I sound, it isn't even half of what I'm feeling. But if I was going for nonchalance, I've just fallen flat on my face.

"I meant I left it at home," she says, and my stomach sinks. Kids are streaming back into class like rivers going into dams and I have to hold on to the wall to avoid being swept away with them.

"Gordie?" There's something about her saying my name that sounds nice. I can't put my finger on it, but I'm surprised to find how much I like hearing it come out of her mouth.

And then she says it again. I look up, surprised to feel a rush of hot blood to my cheeks.

"You need to move out of the way. We have to go back in," she says.

Without thinking, I do what she says. She walks past me into the room, followed by the other kids who were log-jammed behind her. I stand there with my mouth hanging open, trying to figure out what the hell just happened.

I have no idea how I'm going to be able to stand being in class for a whole second hour listening to Mr. Brooks ramble on about Melville. I drum my fingers on the desk and say a prayer under my breath, hoping there will be a pop quiz or some sort of in-class assignment, something I actually have to think about, something to take my mind off of her.

Instead, what happens is this: we're splitting into groups. I cringe as I listen to Mr. Brooks explain that each group is expected to present a retelling of *Moby Dick* in some creative way that doesn't involve writing it down. I can't help but position myself five people away from Sarah, figuring that we're going to count off. I'm right. Still, it freaks me out that I'm doing this. I mean, what difference does it really make if

I'm working on this stupid assignment with Sarah? But even though I can't explain it, I know that I want to. I have to.

And so our group is the two of us, Andrew, and Scott. I listen as they start throwing ideas around. Andrew says, "Puppets," which is horrible. Scott says, "A poem in iambic pentameter," which is just as bad. Before I even think the idea through, I toss out, "Photographs."

This gets Sarah's attention, and she whips her head around to look at me as Andrew asks, "Photographs?"

I try to pull the idea together quickly so I don't sound like a total wacko. "We can take photos of ideas hidden in the book. And since Sarah's a photographer"—I pause when I see the expression of pure shock on her face—"we'll have an edge."

I realize, as I say it, that it's probably the longest sentence I've ever uttered in class. My hand shakes as I rub the back of my neck, so I jam it under my leg.

Andrew and Scott nod in unison and we all turn to look at Sarah, who blushes. I have to look away because looking at her is making me feel warm and cold all at once, like I have a fever or the flu.

"Yeah, sure," she says to the group. I can tell she's happier than she's letting on. "Thanks," she mouths directly to me, and it makes me feel even more feverish.

We start discussing our plans. I offer to take notes because it will give my hands something to do. I write down everyone's ideas in neat little columns. Andrew is going to the aquarium to photograph the whales. Scott is going to handle the "river as a place of transition" shots. There's no chance in hell of me doing that.

Which leaves me and Sarah.

Some really, really freaky urge makes me volunteer to do something on prophesy and harbingers of doom. It would be funny if it wasn't a subject I already knew too much about. I'm the poster child for things that can go wrong.

Sarah says she's going to tackle the bigger issues, all the "blasphemy" and "insurmountable tasks" stuff.

By the time we sort all of that out, the bell rings. I'm buzzing hard from what I've just done (initiated this), from what it might mean (spending time with Sarah, who all of a sudden I want to spend time with), and from trying to figure out what comes next (no idea).

I don't even know that she's standing next to my desk until I finish packing up my backpack and almost walk into her.

"I'm impressed," she says.

I feel a smile dance across my lips and then stop it in its tracks. I don't want to let her get to me like this. But at the same time, I do. And that confuses the hell out of me.

"Why?" I keep my head ducked down and fiddle with the buckle on my bag, hoping she can't see my face.

"That was a really good idea you had. I didn't think that would be your kind of thing."

I know it's a good idea. That part doesn't surprise me. And I knew she'd think it was one too, which is why I brought it up to begin with. But I can't overlook the subtext—that she'd even bother to wonder whether it was my kind of thing or not.

I don't know what to say. Any words that come to my mind float right out as soon as they get there. "I don't have a camera," I blurt out.

Sarah has a funny look on her face, like she's trying to figure something out. Like she's trying to figure *me* out, and it makes me feel really jumpy.

"So why did you suggest a photography project?"

This whole conversation is reminding me why I avoid having them.

"I..." The words are getting stuck again and I'm having problems thinking straight. My bag is packed and I don't know what to do with my hands so I shove them into my pockets.

She watches me for a second and then reaches out and puts her hand on my arm. All I can focus on is her touch. Everything else flies out of my head. So I just shrug.

She smiles, and I wonder if her fingertips are burning the same way my arm is.

"It's okay," she says. "You can use my camera, but I'll need to go with you. It was a gift from my brother and he'd kill me if I let it out of my sight."

A million objections race through my mind at once. I don't know if I can spend time with her outside of school. I mean, school is broken into all of these neat little boxes of time: class, break, class. And so on. All regimented and ordered. And class isn't exactly social. I can sit and do whatever. But just hanging out with her? I'm not sure if I know how to do that. What would we talk about? What if she realizes that I'm really fucked up? What if I start spinning?

"Earth to Gordie."

"Yeah. Sure. Great," I say, although really I'm terrified and my stomach is turning into jelly.

"Good. I have to get to Chem," she says, and I'm suddenly aware that the kids in the next class are streaming into the room and I'm in major danger of being late to French. She rips a piece of paper out of her notebook, writes on it quickly, and then thrusts it into my hand.

"Here's my number. I'm not going to be in school tomorrow and Friday because my mom..." She rolls her eyes. "Never mind. Just call me and we can figure out when would be good."

Then she turns and walks away. I'm left with too many questions, just staring at the alien piece of paper in my hand and at the empty space where she'd been.

FOUR

Kevin is in detention. On its own that's nothing new. But just like I hadn't had a spin in a while before the other night, he hasn't picked a fight with anyone, or mouthed off to a teacher, or whatever it was he did this time, in a while. It's kind of hard to believe that these two things have nothing to do with each other, and it sucks that I'm the one left feeling guilty because he decided to do something stupid.

Besides, I really need to talk to him about this crazy girl.

With him at school and Jim at work as usual, I have the house to myself and no one to yell at me for missing tonight's hockey game. Even though I got a game suspension for missing practice, I'm supposed to be there. But there's no way I'm just going to sit and twitch on the bench.

I flip through the mail for lack of anything better to do. I'm not looking for anything in particular. Half of it is for Kevin anyhow. College catalogs. As a sophomore, I have another year before I have to worry about things like college. Another year before I have to figure what to do with my life. And honestly, I'm really in no hurry.

I have an urge to dump the catalogs, with their shiny covers and fake smiling people, straight into the trash. I know that won't keep Kevin from leaving. I know he needs to get out and do his own thing. But it doesn't mean I have to like it. It doesn't mean that just the thought of him leaving doesn't make my damned hand start up again.

I bury the catalogs under a cooking magazine filled with recipes for things I'd never eat and take them all upstairs to the bedroom we share. When I dump the pile on Kevin's bed, a stiff, formal envelope falls out of the stack. It's for Jim, and I wouldn't normally give it a second glance except for the return address: *Child and Family Services.*

Usually they don't write. Once or twice a year, someone shows up and asks me questions off a sheet while all of us stare at the door and wait for them to leave.

I hold the letter up to the light, but they've used one of those stupid security envelopes so I can't see anything. I put it down on Kevin's bed and try to walk away, but that twisting feeling in my stomach starts, and I have to turn back and grab it to keep my head from starting to pound too.

Screw Kevin and his "learn to control it" crap.

Downstairs, I fill Jim's old copper teapot with water and hold my breath as I watch, waiting, waiting, waiting for the water to boil. Then, once it's really going, I hold the envelope over the steam and open it.

I'm wired, excited even though I know whatever's in the letter is going to suck. The page shakes in my hand as I scan the words saying that my father—the one who disappeared five years ago, the one who made my mom do it—is petition-ing to see me.

It feels like there's an electric eel in my brain trying to get out. My right hand is totally out of control, and the walls of the kitchen feel uncomfortably close. Everything is too bright. I rub my eyes and try to breathe, but I can hear myself gasping like the air has been sucked out of the room. This can't be happening.

This can't. This can't. This can't.

Before I know it, I'm stumbling upstairs and into my bedroom closet, panting, with my head in my hands. Time slows down. The universe spins around me. I let it. Hours pass. Years.

It doesn't matter how long it's been since I've needed to do this. It doesn't matter that it isn't something I can control.

Freak.

Freak.

Freak.

I replay the day—That Day—over and over in my head. I used to think I did it to see if there was anything I could have done differently. Some way I could have saved Mom or the kids.

But really, I know that isn't the reason.

Replaying That Day is like watching a familiar movie. I know how it starts. I know how it ends. And I know every single second in between. And fucked up as it is, there's some-thing comforting about that.

———

I'm ten, Kayla is three, and the twins, Sophie and Jason, aren't even a year old. Kevin is twelve. But he's at his dad's. At Jim's.

When Mom opens the door to wake me, I jerk up like someone's fired a shot into the room. She doesn't ask why I'm sleeping on the floor.

Mom had good days where she'd wake us up in costume, as a princess. Or a fairy. Or a cat with whiskers and a tail. She'd make us sandwiches shaped like hearts or stars. But when it wasn't a good day, she was sad, stuck in a place that meant Kevin would need to feed us, and one of us would need to skip school to watch the kids. But Kevin isn't here, and I know this is a bad day. The worst.

I get dressed in my blue shirt because it's dress-up day at school and they're taking photos and I haven't given up hope that I'll make it there. I'm just buttoning up when the smell of food meets me halfway down the stairs and surprises me. I didn't think Mom was okay enough to make breakfast, even though it's only oatmeal.

"Feed the kids," she says.

I glare at her tired eyes, which stare at me, unblinking. But I dish out the oatmeal. I always do what I'm told.

The kids eat and then settle down quickly, strangely quiet.

Mom is everywhere, all at once. She makes sure they've eaten everything and urges me to eat as well, even though she knows that food in the morning makes me feel sick.

She stands over me with a bottle of orange juice. Her voice is odd, harsh. "I'm going to watch until you finish this."

I know better than to argue. I guzzle some down, the acid forming a lump in my stomach. When she turns around, I spill the rest down the drain.

She tells me to get the kids into the car. I'm pissed at Kevin for leaving me to do this on my own and pissed at Mom for a million different things.

"Are you taking me to school?" I ask.

She doesn't answer. In fact, she doesn't say anything until...

She takes back roads, but I don't know which ones. I'm too tired and angry to notice.

She stops the car.

She looks at the kids in the backseat and then at me.

She puts her hand on my head and starts her prayers. Then she drives us straight into the water.

———————

A part of me knows I'm sitting in the closet like a dumb little kid. If I stretch my left hand a bit, I can feel my winter boots and the bottom of a hockey stick. My shirts drape down on metal hangers that clank together as I move. Goose bumps form on my arms. I can feel my right hand clenched around a cheap plastic pen.

Click. Click. Click. Click.

My thumb hits it over and over, echoing each frantic beat of my heart.

Mom is in front of me, making oatmeal and insisting that I drink the orange juice.

The car smells of leather and animal crackers. On top of that there's the air freshener that's meant to smell like cherries. The kids breathe, quiet, in the back. Then they cry, drowned out by the poetry of Mom's prayers.

The car goes into the water and I'm staring at that eagle overhead, pushing out the window, grasping for the sky. I'm cold, wet, sure that if I reach up to touch my hair, it will be soaked with river water. I can smell that horrible scent of fish, and seaweed, and dead things.

"Ice? What is it?" Kevin's voice circles through the dark like a rope to pull me out.

He's called me "Ice" as long as I can remember. Mom said it was my first word. No surprise—my father was only interested in me because he wanted a kid who could play hockey and finish what he'd started and fucked up.

But Kevin wasn't in the water. He wasn't … it takes me a minute to realize he's real and in front of me.

I hold out my hand with the letter clenched in it and watch my brother's face as he starts to read.

"That son of a … " Kevin stops himself and holds out his free hand to help me up. I force myself to take it. After the closet, the room is too bright for my eyes and Kevin closes the curtains while I throw myself onto his bed and press my back against the cool, hard wall.

"Don't worry," he says, like that's a realistic option. "We'll talk to my dad when he gets home. This"—he looks down at the letter and I can see his jaw tense—"is not going to happen."

I want to believe him. Kevin is great at sorting shit out, but at the same time, this is official stuff. Government stuff. I don't think even he can take care of it.

He moves the stack of catalogs over without looking at them and sits down, then picks my arm up and dangles it like it's a piece off a mannequin and not something attached to me. "Man, Ice, I thought you'd stopped doing that. At least stick to ruining your own clothes."

The gray fleece is Kevin's, really, but since I do the laundry in the house, I get dibs. I run my fingers over the bottom of the sleeve, which is frayed and wet. Half of the time I don't even know I've been chewing on something and anyway, I can't control what happens during a spin.

I grab my arm back and dry the shirt off on my jeans. I can feel my heart beating, the blood pounding in my ears so loud it's all I can focus on.

Kevin knocks me on the leg. "You aren't breaking our pact, are you?"

The pact came after That Day, and the spinning, and everything else. The pact was that Kevin would always look out for me. And that I would trust him to. I'd only have to tell him about Cody being a dick at practice and Kevin would go after him. He'll fight anyone and anything to keep me safe.

He doesn't know that I'm the one he should be beating the crap out of. And I can't tell him, because I can't handle him hating me.

So I shrug while he picks up a catalog and absentmindedly rifles through it, trying to look like I haven't just freaked out. I pretend I'm outlining a paper for school and make a list in my head of the things I know.

I know that my mom did it all to get back at my father for The Night Before.

I know that afterward, he didn't want us. Me, I mean. Because I was the only one left. Kevin wasn't even his kid, so Jim got stuck with me too.

I know that having one of your parents try to kill you and the other one not want you wrecks something inside.

And I know that even though all they really did was annoy me, I should have tried harder to save the kids.

Once everyone agreed I should try to go back to school, my hand would start spasming when I was stressed, or tired, or thinking about the wrong things, and I needed to keep moving all the time. Then the spins started. Sometimes they spun me back to That Day, sometimes just to some stupid memory that's locked in my screwed-up head.

I don't know if there was something in the water, or if I inherited something from Mom, or if it's my punishment for being so bad and selfish.

Perhaps all I really know is that I wasn't like this before. And I am now.

FIVE

It's called acrophobia when you're afraid of heights, but I'm not sure what it's called when you can't get enough of them.

Jim's house, the one he inherited from his parents, the one we're living in, has a widow's walk—kind of a walled-in area on the roof that goes around the whole top floor. Kevin and I have been climbing out our bedroom window onto it ever since we started living here.

That's a lie.

I've been climbing out. Kevin has been following me to make sure I don't jump.

I'm not stupid. And I'm not suicidal. I don't want to jump to my death any more than I wanted to die by drowning. But the urge to step off the wall—to free-fall through the air, to fly—is painfully hard for me to resist. I know I can't fly. I know it would end badly, with me crumpled in a bloody and probably dead mess. But sometimes I want to take that step so badly it hurts. My stomach clenches and for a minute I believe the only thing that will help is to go over that edge.

Even Kevin knows his lectures about control won't help when I'm feeling like that, so it's only his grasp on the back of my sweatshirt that stops me.

I know it's wrong, but I can't keep from going up there. The one concession I've made to both common sense and my brother is that I've promised I won't go up there alone. So far, this is a promise I've kept.

But now everything in my head is clumping together. Memories of my mom, fear of my dickhead father, confusion about Sarah, that freaking letter . . . all of it is making me feel like I'm going to explode if I don't get out.

So I head to the window, but Kevin calls me back. "Don't you have a game tonight?"

"Walker's starting," I mumble. I hope he isn't going to grill me about it, because I'm not sure I can deal with one more thing tonight.

I must look desperate, because Kevin shifts gears and says, "Hey, I almost forgot. I have something for you."

I take the brown paper bag he holds out. It rattles as my hand shakes and I wait for an explanation.

"Mark is finally trying to quit smoking," he says.

I'm not sure what that has to do with anything. I know his friend Mark a little, but I've never smoked. My father smoked. The smell still makes me gag.

"He wears one of these on his wrist and snaps it whenever he wants a cigarette. He says it distracts him or something," Kevin explains.

I stick my hand into the bag and pull out two stretchy circles of leather. They're kind of like rubber bands only they look cool, braided and dark with patterns of color running through them.

"I thought they'd work better than the pens," he says.

Now I get it. Kevin hates the pens.

I usually have one with me in case my hand starts acting up. The clicking annoys the crap out of him.

But I never do it for that reason.

Well, almost never.

Mostly I do it because it calms me down. And sometimes it keeps the spinning at bay.

I put one of the bracelets on and snap it hard against my wrist. It doesn't hurt, but it's a sharp jolt that seems like it will keep me where I need to be, in the moment.

"Thanks," I say. I mean it, but my head is already somewhere else. I reach under my bed and pull out the screwdriver I took from the tool shed the last time Jim forgot to lock it. I push it against the window frame and start to jimmy the lock open. Ever since I climbed onto the walk in my sleep one night, Kevin holds the key hostage. I get tired of begging for it or trying to steal it when he isn't watching.

My brother crosses his arms and shakes his head while I work at the window.

"Can this wait?" It's clear from his expression that he has other things to do. He probably should have thought of that before getting detention.

I want to make things easier for Kevin instead of always being a complication. At the same time, the thing that lives in the pit of my stomach is almost forcing me to push myself through that window. I feel like a little kid who thinks he'll die if he doesn't get a certain toy. It's stupid. But my heart is pounding hard and I can't resist the pull of all that air and free space.

Kevin grabs the screwdriver and holds it up in front of my face, trying to look tough.

"Fifteen minutes," he says, looking at his watch. "You can pay me back by helping me with this damned paper for English." That really means he wants me to write it for him, but it's a small price to pay.

I snatch the key out of his hand and am halfway out the window before he finishes speaking.

"...and when he gets home, we'll talk to Jim."

————

We sit on the roof side-by-side. One of Kevin's hands is wrapped around the bottom of my sweatshirt, pinning me to the shingles. If I really wanted to, I could pull away, but I let him hold on to the illusion that he's protecting me. He doesn't say it anymore, but he thinks that if he'd stayed home, he could have stopped Mom. So I let him feel like he's keeping me safe now, even though the things that can hurt me are mostly inside.

From up here I can see the tops of all the bare winter trees in the neighborhood. I can see the whole parking lot over at the elementary school. Closer to us, there are birds in the heated birdbath of the house next door, and the stars are just starting to come out.

"Remember our bird?" I ask.

Kevin sighs and nods. He hates when I talk about stuff from before.

When we were little, Mom bought us a bird. It was a parakeet, I think. Green and yellow. Every morning Kevin and I would make sure it had food and water. Sometimes we'd let it out of the cage and it would fly around my room, always landing on the highest spots: the curtain rods, the shelves. After a while it even learned to come back when I whistled for it.

One day we came home from school and it was gone. The cage wasn't even there, and when I asked Mom about it, she just looked at me and shook her head. "Sorry, sweetie. He thought it was making too much noise."

I never had the courage to ask what happened, whether my father killed it or let it go. But I like to think of it flying free, perched happily in a tall tree somewhere. Maybe it's even one of the birds I can see, although you don't see a lot of parakeets sitting in trees in Michigan.

"Why do you think he's showing up now?" I ask, hoping Kevin will have some insight. In all the time I spent in the closet, I couldn't come up with a reason that made sense. It isn't like my father stuck around after Mom and the kids were gone.

Kevin sighs and pulls his jacket tighter around him. He has more reason even than I do to hate my dad. "I don't know. Maybe he's got a girlfriend or something and thinks he can handle a kid? Maybe he just misses you?"

Something about the thought of my father missing me makes me shiver. I catch myself bringing my sleeve up to my mouth and force it back down again. Before all this, things had been cool for a while. *I'd* been cool—maybe not totally normal, but good. Now I'm back to being a mess.

"I wish I knew what Mom was thinking," I say to the darkening sky. I try to pretend, even to myself, that The Night Before never happened, that I have no idea why she did what she did.

Kevin doesn't know about that, so he just knocks his shoulder into mine. "That's a puzzle we're never going to solve. You know that. Whatever crazy-ass idea she had in her head was her being screwed up. Don't start blaming yourself again, okay?"

I nod again, because that's what he wants me to do. If I'm not careful he's going to start getting angry and irritated with all my questions. So I ask the real one that's on my mind.

"Do you think Jim will make me go? I mean, you're..." The word "leaving" gets trapped deep in my throat. I can't even say it, so I snap the band around my wrist. I'm not spinning, but that little bit of pain feels better than thinking of Kevin going off to school somewhere and leaving me alone.

He looks away like he's afraid of his own answer. "We have over a year before I go to college, if I go away. Who knows, I might stay here and commute. State has a good culinary program. Or maybe Mr. Meyers will give me that sous-chef job he keeps hinting at."

I pull my sweatshirt free and walk over to the railing. I put my arms out and spin around. When I close my eyes, the whole world feels like nothing but air and I'm floating in the middle of it, one of those fluffy bits you get when you blow a dead dandelion; the ones you're supposed to catch and make a wish on.

"Anyhow," I hear him say, "I don't think my dad is going to send you anywhere if he has a say in it."

My lips press together. I don't answer. Jim is a good guy, but who knows? Maybe he'll see this as his opportunity to get rid of me once and for all.

Kevin's feet scramble against the shingles as he follows behind me. I kind of wish I'd never told him how badly I want to step off.

"Ice?" he calls from somewhere, but I don't open my eyes to find out where. As I'm whirling around, it sounds as if his voice is everywhere at once.

"Yeah?"

"It'll be okay." There isn't one note of doubt in his voice. Kevin has always been able to get what he wants. Somewhere in the soup of our DNAs, his dad's must have made all the difference. He thinks telling me it will be okay will actually make it okay, like he has some direct line to the universe. I know it isn't true. Saying it doesn't just make it happen, not even for Kevin. But sometimes it helps to know he thinks that way.

It's part of what makes Kevin my best friend. My only friend, if I'm honest. The guys on the hockey team are okay. I don't think it's that they like me. But they like that I can stop the pucks that come flying toward me. They'd put up with almost anything for that.

"Come on, time's up," Kevin says, waiting for me to go back through the window first and locking it behind us. I know he's never going to take a chance that I'll turn around and do something stupid.

I flip through the book that Kevin's supposed to be writing about for his class, but my head isn't really in it. "Focus," he keeps telling me, but it isn't that my mind is wandering off; it's that I keep waiting for the front door to open and for Jim to come home and sort everything out.

Finally, finally, finally, I hear the door. Kevin and I look at each other and grab the paperwork, flying downstairs.

"Man, today kicked my ass," Jim says when he sees us. "Anyone want to grab me a beer?"

He does some kind of office work for one of the auto companies, but he comes home looking like he's been hauling car parts all day. Usually he takes a shower before he even wants to speak to us.

I can feel the weight of Jim's eyes on me. They're brown, like Kevin's. They both narrow them, like Jim is doing, when they know something's up.

I dart into the kitchen to grab him a beer, holding my breath when I open it. Beer always smells like the old house. Like my father.

I can't afford to spin now.

I lean against the door frame, trying to listen to what they're saying in the other room. Kevin's voice is tense and quiet, so I know he's telling Jim about the letter. I snap the band on my wrist a couple of times, take a deep breath, and walk back to the living room.

They stop talking when I walk in, and their deliberate quiet hurts my ears.

I hand Jim his beer and sit down next to Kevin on the couch, waiting for someone to break the silence.

"Sorry, kid," Jim says, holding up the letter in his calloused hand. "I think I need to give DeSilva a call tomorrow."

Amy DeSilva is the lawyer who dealt with everything five years ago. I was hoping this wasn't the sort of thing we'd need her for. I was hoping Jim would say, "I won't let them take you," or "I'll fight tooth and nail to keep you here," and we'd be done with it. But he isn't saying anything. I squeeze my eyes shut and scrunch my hands into the spaces between the cushions on the couch.

"It doesn't matter though, right?" Kevin asks. "I mean, he left. Doesn't that terminate his rights?" He's fishing for the words I want to hear. I guess maybe he wants to hear them too.

"Hell, I don't know," Jim says. "I don't think so. But ..." I open my eyes just as he holds his empty hands out. "I'm not a lawyer. Let's see what she says."

I don't know if his "I don't think so" is in reference to it not mattering or to my father signing his rights way.

Kevin's jaw works like he's got one of those hard candies in his mouth. I recognize the signs of him trying to contain his anger, like the counselors at school taught him to a couple of years ago after he broke Cody's nose for pushing me into a locker and writing "spaz" on the outside.

It might be wrong, but I'm jealous that Kevin can just get pissed, punch something, and get it out of his system. Most of the time I turn into a black hole. All of the stress concentrates in one tiny place in my stomach and twists and turns until it feels like it's going to flip me inside out.

"In the meantime, we still need to eat. How about something easy? Pizza?" Jim asks, looking at Kevin. Then he adds, "Or ..." and looks at me.

I get it, given that I have kind of a strange thing with food. I always have, but Mom made it way worse by deciding to use oatmeal and orange juice as her sedative delivery system. There's no way I'm ever going near either of those again.

I sometimes wonder if that's why Kevin became such a good cook. He's always trying to find something I'll be willing to eat. But now I just shrug. I don't really care. Eating isn't really high on my priority list.

"Pineapple," Kevin says, because he knows it's my favorite right now. His expression dares me to put up a fight.

While they wait for the pizza, I charge upstairs hoping to find some way to keep the pain in my stomach from crawling up to my brain.

I try the window in case Kevin left it open, but of course he didn't. For a very short second, I think about breaking the glass. But Kevin would be pissed, and I don't want to get Jim mad just when I need him to step in and solve things.

I grab my backpack and dump my books, a couple of pens, and a half-eaten candy bar onto my bed.

I used to wonder what I'd grab in case there was a fire and I had to get out of the house. Now that practical list escapes me and, as I toss things into my bag, I realize the stuff I'm packing isn't the really useful stuff. I mean, clothes might be more important than a book of poetry that used to be my mom's or a hockey puck, but I don't care. I'm not worried about useful stuff. I'm worried about escaping; not being here when they come to take me away. I'd rather figure out how to live on my own than live with my father.

The door to the bedroom opens, then closes. Kevin leans against it with his arms folded.

It takes a while before he says anything. I'm almost done packing, except for the twenty dollars hidden in my sock drawer.

"What are you doing?" He sounds tired, like we're having a conversation we've had over and over, just with different words.

"I'm leaving," I say. "I thought that was obvious."

"No, you aren't," he counters. He looks like he wants to laugh, but he bites his lip and holds it in.

I wonder how far he'd go to stop me. Or how far I'd go to prove it.

When I reach for my jacket, he comes up behind me and I try to take a swing at him. He grabs my wrists and wraps my arms around me, under his, like my very own damned straitjacket.

I want to shake him off, but I can't move my arms at all and kicking backward isn't getting me anywhere. "Get off me." I keep struggling, but can't get any leverage.

"Nope. Not until you tell me that you aren't going anywhere," he says. I know he means it. If I don't say what he wants, he won't release me and we'll stay here all night. I've learned the hard way that Kevin is even more stubborn than I am.

It would be easy enough to say the words and then leave anyhow, but I've never really lied to him, not even when we were little. I'm not sure I could.

"I'm not going with that son of a bitch," I say. Kevin, of all people, has to understand that.

"No one said you were."

I don't understand how he can be so certain of this. He doesn't have any more information than I do.

"They aren't going to let me stay here. They're going to send me back to him. You know that," I say as I keep struggling against his grasp. "I have to get out of here."

Part of me is pissed that he has me physically stopped like this. Still my stomach unknots just a little, knowing that

Kevin hasn't loosened his hold at all. This pretty much sums up our relationship.

"If you have to run away, we'll go together. But you aren't leaving now. Seriously, Ice, get a grip."

I didn't really expect him to say that. That he would go with me.

"Oh." My bag falls from my shoulder. The tension drains out of me so quickly that I go limp in his arms as he lowers me to the ground.

"Say it." He takes a step back and stands over me with his hands on my shoulders.

I stay there, exhausted, on my knees, snap snap snapping the leather band.

Finally, I'm able to force the words out of my mouth. They feel like barbed wire as they work their way around my tongue. "Fine. I won't leave before we find out what's going to happen."

He lets me go and I sit there, out of breath, twisting and twisting the stretchy leather around my wrist, wondering what it would take to break it.

Kevin stands in the doorway and I think he's going to say something else, but then he shakes his head and goes back downstairs.

I get up and put my backpack into the closet next to the hockey stick, the winter boots, and the memories. And poke at the sore spots on my wrist until I'm sure I'm here to stay.

SIX

"Don't even think about it," Kevin says as we get to school.

Of course I'm thinking of skipping. Who wouldn't? I pause in the doorway, halfway between then and now, not knowing what comes next.

Kevin slaps my shoulder with the back of his hand. "Ice." His voice is tense and stretched and his teeth are clenched together.

"I just..."

"Nothing," he says. "You just nothing. Go to class. There's nothing you can do. There's nothing either of us can do until she calls."

I don't get how anyone can go on with their day while we're waiting to hear back from Ms. DeSilva. How is Jim going to concentrate on work? I'd at least expect Kevin to get it, and it ticks me off that he doesn't.

But then I see how he's flexing his hands, into and out of fists. It makes me realize that he's more pissed off about my father's letter than he's letting on, and I know better than to be on the wrong end of his anger.

"Fine," I say. "But...can you try to get home on time? I mean, don't double your detention or anything."

One by one, his muscles relax, his hands stop moving, his shoulders lower. He grabs my arm. "We'll sort this out, promise." I'm pretty sure he's trying to convince himself as much as he is me.

We stand there, frozen, as kids start shuffling in around us. We're stuck, neither of us knowing what to say. Or if we should say anything at all.

"Bryce!" Kevin yells when his friend appears and tugs on his arm. He turns back, looking relieved, and points his finger at me. "I promise." And then he's swept off with the tide.

Without Kevin's constant lectures and advice I'll be able to hear myself think, and that's the last thing I want. But right now my head is buzzing like it's been invaded by a swarm of bees and my thumb won't stop twitching, which sucks in a whole different way.

For a fleeting second I think about going to the counselor's office, but I fought hard to stop seeing him. If I tell him how I'm feeling, he's just going to drag me back into some stupid therapy sessions and pump me full of the same drugs that never did anything to help in the first place.

Besides, I know the drill of running through calming techniques and all of that.

The problem is, the only thing that will calm me down is to hear that I'll never have to see my father again, that there's a restraining order against him or some other way of keeping him away from me.

No one is telling me any of those things.

I walk to my locker like a reject from some zombie movie. I spin and spin the dial on the lock until I hit the right combination and then watch, transfixed, as something flutters out.

When it hits the ground, I pick it up and look at the black-and-white image. It isn't one of the pictures from hockey practice. It isn't of me, or of hockey at all. Instead, it's an eagle, wings spread against the sky at sunset.

It shakes in my hands as I flip it over. *One of my favorites*, it says. Then, *S*. Just *S*.

It makes me feel like she's inside my head, which should freak me out. Instead, it makes me feel, for once, like I'm not alone.

———

After school, I try to call Jim, but it goes to voicemail. I call again and the same thing happens. I sit there with the phone on redial. I probably call him two hundred times, but he doesn't pick up. I call until Kevin comes home and grabs the phone away from me with a look on his face that I'm pretty sure means he wants to ram it down my throat.

"You've been sitting here doing this for an hour?" he asks, flipping through the phone's memory.

I shrug. Time was the last thing on my mind.

"Come on. I need your help," he says, dragging me into the kitchen. He peers into the fridge and takes out a bowl of green stuff that looks frighteningly like that slime we used to play with as kids.

"What the hell is that?" I'd like to say it's the first time

I've asked this question when Kevin's cooking, but actually, it's pretty much the opposite.

"That, little brother, is what, with your help, I'm going to turn into pea balls."

I look into the bowl. "I didn't know that ... "

" ... peas had balls," we finish together.

"Yeah, whatever." Kevin laughs. Instead of cooking normal things, Kevin is into this weird mix of science and food called molecular gastronomy. It would be cool except that while Kevin is a great cook, he isn't a great scientist, so I'm pretty much in charge of keeping him from blowing the house up.

He throws a packet at me. Sodium alginate. It makes things thicken like jelly. At least it isn't something that will explode. The frosting he used on my birthday cake last year had some sort of super pop rocks in it and Jim made him throw it out before I even tried it.

"Boil that with water," he says.

I get out a pot, fill it, and drop the powder in. I wonder if Kevin thinks this is going to distract me from everything that's going on. He should know better. But it isn't even mainly the stuff with Jim and my father that's preying on my mind right now. There are other thoughts I'm having a hard time shaking off too, and no amount of weird science is going to clear them out of my head.

I sit and watch the pot, waiting for it to boil, while Kevin pulls a sieve and a handheld blender out of the cupboard.

"How come you don't have a girlfriend?" I ask. I've wondered about this for a while now. I mean, Kevin is seventeen. Even if he isn't a brainiac, he works hard in school. He doesn't even get detention as much as he used to. He's got the whole bizarre cooking thing going. He has friends.

Also, I've heard girls whispering in the halls about him. They stare as he walks by, then laugh. But I don't think they're laughing at him. Sometimes I think they're trying to get his attention. They don't realize all the other stuff that's in his head, like trying to make sure I don't go over the edge and controlling his temper. I wonder if he could have a normal life if it weren't for me.

Kevin puts everything on the table and runs a hand through his shaggy hair. "Why? You know someone?"

"Just wondering."

"Well…" I hear the pause in his voice as he chooses an answer. "First off, none of our parents made relationships look very attractive. I mean, what if all girls turn out to be like Mom?"

People tell me I should be angry at Mom for what she did, but I'm not. Instead, thinking of her makes me feel empty deep inside, like an important part of me has been removed.

"So you're gay?" I ask, wondering why we've never talked about it before.

"No." He pours in the peas and turns the blender up to high. It's so noisy I have to wait until he's done to ask anything else.

"So what then?" I ask as soon as he hits the off switch.

"Crap, Ice. It's not like I really have time. Between school and…you…I mean…" He doesn't finish.

"Well, you have all the time when I'm at practice or a game," I say.

He stares at me. "I don't think it works that way. Not

many girls are going to be into a relationship scheduled during my brother's hockey games."

I guess that's something else I should hate, that he's given up so much for me. But I don't. It's just the way it is. I don't know what I'd do without him.

I pull the boiling pot off the stove and Kevin shoves another pot, filled with ice, underneath it.

"What about you?" he asks.

The bubbles explode on the surface of the water. Pop. Pop. Pop. Pop. "What do you mean, 'what about me?'" I answer, distracted.

"Ever thought about getting yourself a girlfriend?"

His question freezes my brain like when you eat ice cream too quickly. He's got to be joking. I mean, really? If he's using Mom as a reason not to let any girl get close, what the hell does he think is going through my head?

"You're out of your mind," I say.

"Maybe you should. Maybe it's just what you need." Then he gives me that know-it-all look that makes me wonder if he's heard me getting off in the middle of the night. "Maybe that's why you're asking me."

My stomach twists at the direction the conversation is going and suddenly the kitchen is way too small for us and this vat of green gloop. I look at the door, wondering how pissed he'd be if I just left. I wonder how long the house would be standing if I did.

"So what's her name?" he asks.

I consider pretending I have no idea what he's talking about, but I brought this up. At some level I must want to talk about it, right? That's what the counselors at school would say, not that they really understand anything about me. But Kevin does. He can see through me like I'm made of tissue paper.

"It's not like that," I say. Do I believe it? I don't even know. I twist and untwist the band on my wrist a million times.

"Then what's it like?" He's baiting me, and I can see by the glint in his eye that he's enjoying watching me squirm.

I sigh. Now I wish I hadn't brought it up at all. "Nothing, it's stupid. There's just this girl. In English."

He pulls out the bowl of green stuff from the refrigerator and mixes it with the stuff I boiled earlier. Then he pulls out another bowl from the fridge. This one is filled with calcium chloride, which is the stuff that comes in packets to dry things out. It's also the thing that guarantees I'm not going near this latest experiment. I don't care how well he thinks he can wash the stuff off—I'm not eating it.

I sit down and run my thumb over the peeling Formica on the table. I should have known better than to think that Kevin wouldn't push this conversation. I guess I sit there a while, because when I look up I recognize his impatient expression. It means that he's been talking to me and I have absolutely no idea what he's said.

Instead of asking him to repeat it and admitting I haven't been paying attention, I throw him a bone. "Sarah. Her name is Sarah. She's a photographer. She was the one taking pictures at the games last summer."

"And?"

"And nothing. She just got put in my English class."

"And you like her, don't you?"

"Never mind," I say. I don't even know the answer to that question. I don't know her. I don't...

"Too late." He's stopped dropping the green balls into the calcium bath and is actually smiling now in a way that's making my heart race.

I push the edge of the Formica under my nail until I can feel it, sharp against my skin. "She's..." I look down, hoping the table will tell me what she is. Annoying? Mysterious? Crazy?

I know that Kevin doesn't need to see my face to know there's something up. "Is she pretty?" he asks.

My right hand clenches, and unclenches, and clenches again. I get the whole snapping a band thing, but I really wish I had a pen. I look around, but all I see are sharp kitchen things and chemicals.

"Come on, Ice. Describe her."

"I don't know. She has really dark hair and eyes. Happy?" The words explode out of me. I get up and stand in the doorway, which makes me feel a little less penned in.

Kevin sets a timer and heads toward me.

"If you're so interested, I'll introduce you," I say, remembering that I need to work myself up to calling her.

"I'm not the one she's been taking pictures of," he says, squeezing my shoulder.

I pull away. "This is what it's like for everyone else, right? I mean, this is how brothers act when there's nothing else to talk about?"

Kevin just laughs. "I've never been anyone else. But if you're worried about being too normal, I wouldn't stress out about it."

Jim's car pulls into the drive and by the time he comes in,

we're waiting by the door like two hyperactive puppies who haven't been let out all day.

He looks tired, like he wishes he could turn back the clock and never meet Mom, and never have Kevin, and definitely never get saddled with me.

"What's that smell?" he asks Kevin.

"Pea balls," my brother answers. Jim shakes his head, like his son's weird cooking is one more cross he has to bear.

"Can I get ten minutes to myself before we do whatever we're going to do here?" Jim asks. I can hear the hope in his voice, but I can't wait any longer.

"No," I say.

Jim looks at Kevin to save him, so I look at Kevin ten times harder. I'm going to blow if I have to just wait here.

Kevin wrenches his eyes away from mine like it takes a lot of effort. "Dad..."

Jim takes one look at me and sighs. We all move into the living room. Jim and Kevin arrange themselves on various chairs while I stalk back and forth behind them, waiting to hear what's going on.

"Ice," Kevin demands. "Sit."

I glare at him, but I do as he says. It isn't worth the fight.

"I know you boys want something definitive, but I don't have it. Ms. DeSilva says she'll review the papers. But it sounds like your dad..." Jim winces. "By law he's entitled to see you."

"No. No he isn't. He can't be." I launch up again. I'm sure Jim must have misheard her, or maybe she's wrong, or... Kevin comes up to try to stop my pacing, but I wrench away.

"Dad?" he says. "There must be something—"

"She's going to get in touch with his lawyer and get back to me." Jim cuts him off. And then he's right in front of me with his big hands on my shoulders, stopping me. "And you, just stay out of trouble and let us handle this. Do you hear me?"

Jim pretty much lets Kevin deal with me. But I've learned that when he gets to the point where he puts his foot down about something, he means it.

"Gordie?" he asks softly. "Are you listening?"

What a ridiculous question. Of course I'm listening. It's my whole freaking life we're discussing. How could I not be listening? All I want is for him to take a stand and to tell me that he's going to fight it. That he agrees my father has no right to be anything in my life.

"Hey," he says again, louder this time.

I look up and see Kevin standing behind him. He's clenching his jaw and nodding his head, urging me silently to say something.

"Let me hear it, kid," Jim says.

I give up. "Handle it, then," I say. "Just handle it." I run upstairs, because I know there's nothing else he can say to me tonight that matters.

I slam the door harder than I need to and lie on Kevin's disheveled bed. It used to bother me that he's such a slob, but now I kind of envy him. I wish I could stop caring about everything being in its place and making sense.

His side of the room is littered with dirty jeans, scraps of paper with his indecipherable writing on it, and a couple of wooden spoons, although I'm not sure I want to know what those are doing here.

The only thing that's neat on his side of the room is the stack of college catalogs on his desk. *Figures.*

I get up and throw the whole stack across the room, which isn't as satisfying as I would have hoped. Then I flop back down and let my mind go.

And of course it goes to my father. I have no choice about that.

My father worked with contracts or proposals or something that meant he collected piles of paper and got paid for it.

Most office guys come home at night, I think. But he'd disappear for months at a time.

I have a few memories of him.

Him beating Kevin with the leather belt Mom made us save up to buy for him for Father's Day.

And watching him and Mom throw empty liquor bottles at each other, the glass shattering all over the living room floor.

And him at the funeral, not looking sad, but pissed, like Mom had finally gotten one over on him. As if killing the kids meant she'd finally gotten the last word. I watched him all through the service to see if he would cry, but he never did.

I guess that's where I got the crying thing from. I don't cry anymore. Ever. Not even at the funeral, although I was sad, not pissed. Pissed came later and left a whole lot of nothing in its wake.

Honestly, there are times I want to cry. Times, like now, when I think it would feel good to let everything seep out of me. But I can't.

I think maybe I've forgotten how.

Or that all the water in the river washed my tears away.

SEVEN

The trick to being a good goalie is to focus on the puck. I mean, what the hell else would you focus on when you're in the crease and people are shooting six ounces of hard rubber at your face?

But it's amazing how many things there are in hockey to be distracted by. The other team. The fans. Your coaches. Dumbass defensemen baiting you for fun. The insipid music they play during stoppages. How hot it can get under the padding.

I'm pretty good at ignoring it all. But during our pre-game, Walker flits around the crease like a mosquito, like there's nothing else on the ice he needs to be doing.

"You're gonna stick around today, right?" he asks as I brush the ice from his snowplow stop off my legs.

"Yeah," I say. "I'm here." I dive to my left and barely catch a shot I would have nailed if he'd been off practicing himself.

A whistle blows as I pull myself up.

"You two want to stop coordinating your prom outfits and play some hockey?" Coach yells.

I don't answer him. I just get back into my crouch, ready to go.

Walker does one more slow circle around the net. "Keep your head in the game, Gordie. We need the win tonight."

I sigh and avoid telling him that if he'd go away, my head would be plenty in the game. I know that with him, it's nothing personal. He just cares about winning more than anything.

He starts to skate off and I sense, more than see, something flying toward me from the right. I leap up and bat it away. Walker spins around with a goofy grin and gives me a nod like he's just remembered I'm actually pretty good at this.

I succeed at reminding him of that a few more times as we shut out one of our closest rivals, the Cougars. Then I stumble home to collapse.

Aside from all of the other things I love about it, hockey is great because it makes me so tired I swear the memories can't get in. And that's always a good thing.

But tonight something pulls me out of a deep sleep, and I don't know what. I don't think it's anything inside me for once, but the room is somehow too quiet. I keep my eyes shut, hoping I'll fall back asleep without starting to think too much, or spinning off somewhere. But the switch in my brain is clicked to "on" and there isn't anything I can do about it.

I open my eyes to see Kevin standing next to our bedroom window. He looks like he's still asleep, but I'm the sleepwalker, not him.

"You're awake," I say, to test out my theory. I wrestle out of the cocoon of blankets I sleep under and sit up, rubbing my eyes.

It takes him a minute, but then he sits down on the edge of my bed. "When did you get so observant?"

I let his sarcasm float up into the air and out the window with the breeze. "What's wrong?" I ask. "You look strange."

"Move over," he says, pushing my legs away. I sit up and draw my legs up. Kevin scootches fully onto the bed, forming a right angle to me, and leans his back against the wall. His legs hang partially off the end.

I wait for him to say something else, but he just sits there looking like he's a million miles away. I wonder if that's what I look like when I'm spacing out—like it's only my body on this planet.

It scares me. I nudge his leg, hoping it'll bring him back to our room. My stomach is starting to feel tangled. I don't think I can handle him spinning off somewhere, because then who would be here to bring me back? I've never really thought about the possibility that it could work in reverse.

He turns and I can see from his eyes that he's really here. I exhale as he asks, "You win tonight?"

I nod. "Yeah. Shutout. But I think Cody Bowman might get suspended for an illegal hit."

Normally that news would bring a smile to his face, but Kevin doesn't really react. "I have to talk to you about something." His low and breathy voice gives away his stress.

The snake in my stomach coils tighter.

"Your dad..."

He really couldn't have chosen two worse words to start a sentence. That alone makes me want to be somewhere else instead of listening to anything about my father that has Kevin this upset. I push against the wall and feel it press against each vertebrae through the soft fabric of my T-shirt. If I push hard enough, maybe I'll come out on the other side, where I can walk through the air and breathe without this horrible pressing feeling in my chest. Without my stomach spinning around like a carnival ride.

"Ice?" Kevin grips my bare leg hard enough that I can't spin off even though I sort of want to. His fingers dig into me like a vice. "We can do this in the morning if you want. I shouldn't have woken you."

I want to say that yes, we should put this off, but I know I'll never get back to sleep without knowing. "No. Tell me."

I hold my breath and wait for words I'm pretty sure I don't want to hear. It's like I can feel every molecule of air that's jostling inside me for space. I hold them all in until it hurts my lungs and I'm slightly dizzy. It isn't until I exhale that Kevin finishes his sentence.

"He didn't sell the old house. He's back. He's living there."

Everything freezes. Everything. Time itself shuts down. I didn't think anything could be worse than having to see him, but they will have to tie me up and drag me there to get me into that house. And even then, I promise that it will only be my body that makes an appearance because I, the part that is me, am not going to set foot in that house ever again.

Even after That Day, I didn't go back. Kevin and Jim went and got my stuff. We all assumed he'd sold the house. I thought he'd be in California, or the Antarctic, or on the moon by now. Not one person ever said to me that they thought he'd keep the property. That he'd live here ever again.

Kevin squeezes my leg, hard enough this time that I might have a bruise tomorrow.

"Stay with me," he says.

If I cross the threshold of the door to that house, I'm going to drown like Mom wanted me to.

Kevin's fingers chain me. I try to pull away, but I can't. There's no way he's going to let me out of this conversation now.

"What's going to happen?" Even to me, my voice sounds shaky and broken. *Fuck.*

Kevin takes my question literally. "He's coming over here tomorrow to talk to Jim."

I jerk hard and my leg pulls away from under his hand.

It's amazing how many different kinds of silence there are. I mean, the room is totally quiet. Kevin is, I think, holding his breath, waiting to see how I'm going react. And I'm listening, listening, listening, to see if anything makes sense. But all I hear is stuff from outside, like a distant car alarm and a bird that must be blind or something and doesn't know it's night because it's screaming right outside the window.

And then Kevin's voice comes blazing through it all. "My dad promised you wouldn't have to see him while he's here. But it's good they're dealing with this head-on, right?"

I know Kevin is trying to make this better. And maybe he's even right, but it's like someone telling you that whatever it is that scares you the most—giant spiders, or zombies, or guys with saws for hands—will be in your house, right under your room, and there isn't anything you can do about it.

I don't realize I'm shivering until Kevin throws a blanket at me.

"I'm sorry, Ice. I really am."

We spend a lot of time apologizing to each other. I'm pretty sure that's not normal brother behavior.

I should tell him it's okay. That I know it isn't his fault. That I appreciate everything he's ever done for me. I should tell him that I know I'm really lucky he's my brother, that I don't know what I'd do without him.

I should tell him all of those things. But I can't.

All I can do is to sit here and think about next year, and about being normal, and try to pretend none of this is happening.

EIGHT

I learned a long time ago that you can hear whatever's going on in the living room through a vent in the upstairs hall. The voices coming through the floor are so loud I wouldn't even have to lie flat on the metal to hear them, but I do anyhow.

Their words circle like birds. Kevin's is an eagle—strong, clear, and determined. Jim's is more of a seagull, grasping at scraps and not knowing what he's getting until it's in his mouth. My father is the vulture, dark and rumbling with an agenda all his own that serves no one but himself, looking to destroy anything and everything in his path.

I have to focus really, really hard to keep the voices straight in my head, to keep them from carrying me away with their sharp claws. I hook my fingers onto the metal of the vent and hold on tight. The harder I squeeze, the better my chances are of staying focused.

"It doesn't matter what you think. The law says I'm entitled to see him," I hear in raspy vulture tones. There's no point in trying to keep my other hand from seizing up at my side. Instead I focus on breathing and trying to keep my brain from seizing up too.

"I swear to God, if you lay one hand on him—" This is from Kevin, who's cut off by Jim, although I can't hear Jim's words.

I must miss something else, because my father's answer isn't to Kevin.

"Jim, this has nothing to do with you. You've stepped in and given him a home and I'm grateful. But he isn't a child anymore."

Kevin laughs, but it isn't his funny laugh. It's sad and kind of mocking. It's the kind of laugh that's gotten him into trouble at school. He says the words "trust fund" and then there's a sharp "shush" from Jim.

We don't talk about the money that people sent in after they read about what happened. I don't really understand why they'd do that, anyhow, and Jim has barely mentioned it except to say that I'll be able to go to college if I want to.

"Look, that boy's been through the ringer. You and Ava—"

Jim has done the unthinkable. He's mentioned my mom, and even though I've heard nothing from my father since the funeral, I know that isn't going to go over well.

"Are none of your business." The vulture voice shuts things down and all is silent.

I hold my breath expecting to hear a slap, expecting him to beat the hell out of Kevin like he used to.

I press the side of my face into the vent until it hurts. I can feel each horizontal strip of metal pushing into my cheek like lines on a grill. But all I hear is nothing; if nothing has a sound.

"Look, you haven't even seen him in five years. What the fuck would you want with him now?" Kevin shouts. I hear stomping and Jim saying something. Then laughter swirls through the grate and around and around in my head. This laughter isn't funny, either. It has razor-sharp edges, and teeth that bite and claw at me. I press my face harder into the grate, but not even the pain is helping. My breath is coming in little gasps. I want to float off to someplace else, but I'm just stuck here with this painful laughter in my head.

Something tugs on the back of my shirt and I struggle because I'm sure it's the vulture, coming to carry me back to the house. Kevin would understand, but I'm here alone and the bird's claws are deep in my skin and pulling at me. I'm not sure I'm strong enough to fight it off, but I'm trying, trying, trying. Scratching at whatever I can reach. Kicking with my eyes closed at anything I can hit.

And suddenly I'm slammed back against the wall. "Damn it, stop."

From out of nowhere Kevin is there and I'm breathing so hard I think I might pass out.

"What the fuck?" he asks, and then runs his hand down my cheek. I reach up and feel the creases from the grate in my skin. In one place I feel sticky wet. I bring my fingers away and see blood.

"Are you an idiot?" he asks. "Or just trying to torture yourself?"

I don't have an answer for him.

"Room. Now," he says and stalks off. I follow, resting a hand on the wall to steady myself.

I fall into my chair and bend over with my head between my knees, trying to catch my breath. A drop of blood falls onto my jeans and I drag the bottom of my shirt across my cheek to catch the rest.

"Look," he lectures as he stalks back and forth in front of the closed door. "What the hell do you want me to do? I can't be in two places at once. I can either be downstairs with them trying to make sure your worst nightmare doesn't happen, or I can sit up here babysitting you. What's it going to be? You're really getting on my last nerve."

I look up just as he grabs the box of Kleenex and throws it at me harder than he needs to. I take one and press it against my cheek.

Kevin sits down on his bed and says, "Maybe you should come down and deal with him. Maybe that's just what both of you need."

"No way." My father's face isn't one I ever want to see again.

"So what do you want me to do?" Kevin asks, leaning toward me.

"Go," I say. "I'm fine." But the words hurt as they come out of my mouth, all spiky and pointy edges.

"Really?" he asks, like it couldn't possibly be true. With every step he takes toward the door I feel the room getting bigger and bigger, and emptier and emptier, and I can feel myself start to panic. But no, I know he needs to be down there even if it kills me.

I can't say that, so I nod. He comes back and squeezes my shoulder. His voice is softer now. "Just stay here and try to hold it together. I'll be back up as soon as he's gone, okay?"

I nod again.

He leaves and I toss the bloodied tissues into the garbage.

I pull out the first book I can find on the shelf, some old science fiction novel of Kevin's, and wrap myself in a blanket and try to read. The words swim upside down like dying fish in front of my eyes. I push on my temples. My head hurts and my stomach is starting to churn again. I can feel a spin coming on. It's so hard to stop the cycle once they start coming.

I'm really, really tired of the past. I just want it to leave me alone and stay where it belongs. But it's like that joke. You know, the one that says, "Don't think about elephants" and as soon as someone says that, all you think about is not thinking about elephants, which is really thinking about elephants?

———

Kevin is out playing, which means I get Mom to myself. She pulls out the book of poetry and gestures for me to sit next to her. I crawl up onto the chaise lounge, nestle my head under her arm and stick my thumb in my mouth. I'm five. Kevin would make fun of me if he was here, but Mom won't; this is our special time.

She reads my favorite poem in her soft voice, describing all the animals living under the water and how they're moving in the fading light.

I feel myself floating along with them. Bobbing in the warm water like I do in the tub. It's warm and safe, and I like that I can be weightless in my head.

Time jerks me forward, and I'm in the water looking for those twirling eels and minnows. I'm angry at Mom because she lied. They aren't here. All I see is garbage, and algae, and an old sneaker. The car sinks lower and lower and I have to get out.

There's no air. There's just... Wet. Cold. No...

I gasp, my heart pounding faster than I thought it possibly could, my hands clenched around the blanket as I lie on the bed. Everything looks like a ghost when I'm coming out of a spin. The past superimposed over the present like an old photo that's been messed up when they developed it.

Screw Mom for reading Sylvia Plath to a five-year-old.

"Breathe," Kevin says from his desk. The computer keyboard makes a sound like he's hitting the same single letter over and over.

It takes a minute for the spin to totally fade and for that minute all I feel is anger and a crushing loss. I miss my mom. I miss her poetry voice and her arm wrapped around me. I want this all to stop.

My eyes refocus on Kevin, sitting at his desk and attacking the keys like he wants to hurt them.

"Is he gone?"

"Yeah, he's gone," Kevin says, spinning around in his chair. My father being gone should make him happy, but he definitely doesn't look happy. It's also painfully obvious that he isn't saying anything else. In fact I start to make a list in my head of everything he isn't saying while he gets up and moves over to the bed.

He isn't saying, "Don't worry."

He isn't saying, "He's never coming back."

He isn't saying, "He'll never hurt us again."

When he does speak, it's to say, "Get up. Let's go for a walk."

I glance at the clock. It's six. I'm not sure how long I've been out of it, but there's something knocking at the back of my brain. Something I need to do, but don't remember. It isn't like I have to be anywhere. I don't have a game until next week.

The house is quiet as we head downstairs. It's Saturday night so Jim must have gone to play poker with his buddies. Kevin is as quiet as the house. It's never good when Kevin is quiet.

He ducks into the kitchen and takes something out of the freezer, and we stand there waiting like two gunfighters in an old western to see who makes the first move. Kevin pulls a chair out and sits in it, leaning his elbows on the table.

Then he says, straight-out, for the first time in five years, "Look, I get it about Mom ... I mean, what she did. And yeah, he used to use me as a punching bag. But—"

"Kev," I beg, shaking my head slowly. I lean against the counter for support.

He looks at me, tired and washed out against the fading and peeling wallpaper.

My legs start to shake. I'm praying that he's going to stop. I don't even want to hear the question he's about to ask, because I know what the general gist is.

"But he never hit you. So why are you so afraid of your dad?"

There are things I've never told Jim, or the counselors at school, or anyone. I've never told them how disappointed I was that life underwater wasn't what I'd been promised. And I've never really told them about the spins. I know it would get me put back on their drugs, or worse.

But most of all, I've never told them about The Night Before. I've never told anyone, not even Kevin. And there's no way in hell I'm going to start now.

I charge out the front door and focus on how the cool evening air feels on my face. A couple of deep breaths and all those bad thoughts go back where they belong.

Once Kevin catches up with me, I concentrate on how our steps are mostly synchronized and how good it feels to be outside with my brother when he isn't being a total dick. I'm glad he isn't ruining everything by pressing me for an answer.

I don't have to ask to know that we're walking to the monastery. It doesn't look like the ones in the movies. It isn't some huge gothic marvel. It's more of an old school that's been turned into a non-denominational meeting hall. Two levels, red brick. Nothing cool. There's a playground outside with all of the usual stuff you'd imagine. Swings, and a merry-go-round, and a wooden train you can climb on that looks like the engine from some oversized toy set.

Jim used to bring us here all the time. I guess he didn't really know what to do with kids in general and me in particular. I sometimes forget how hard it must have been for him to take us in.

Before That Day, Jim would only see Kevin a couple of times a month, and he always used to buy him stuff. Kevin always chose things he could share with me, like candy or comics. So Jim started buying me something too and getting Kevin the stuff he really wanted: CDs of loud angry bands I didn't like, or books on the lives of military guys who would find themselves in enemy territory and have to escape.

As always, I follow Kevin over to the swings and we each take one. Before we sit down, I stick my hand into my pocket. My fingers hit paper and I pull it out. Uncrumple it.

Seven numbers. Sarah's number. I never called her.

"Crap, I need a phone," I say, pressing on my temples to stop the sudden pounding in my head.

"Do you see a phone around here?" Kevin asks sarcastically.

I hate that neither of us has a cell. Kevin's allowance all goes to buy gas for the guzzling monstrosity he calls a car, and presumably toward saving for college, and Jim won't buy me one. Not like I usually have anyone to call anyhow.

"No, but..." I know he can't just wave a wand and make a phone appear, but I need to call her and I know that thought is going to hound me until I can't focus on anything else.

"You don't really *need* a phone," he says, in a tone that makes me want to rip his throat out. "Why, anyhow?"

I show him the paper but he doesn't get it.

"Seriously. Come on," I say, taking a few steps back toward the house. "I need to go back."

Kevin grabs my sleeve and pulls me down so I'm sitting on the next swing over from him. "Gordie, shut up for a minute. Just take a deep breath and stop talking."

He only calls me by name when he's pissed or trying to make a point. I wonder which it is this time. I slump down and swing gently forward and back while I bite at the inside of my cheek to keep my mouth shut.

"Okay," he says. "First off, whose number is that?"

I glare at him. "Sarah's."

"The Sarah from English?" A look of surprise dances across his face and then disappears. "She gave you her number?"

"For school." My right foot kicks off the ground and pushes

me higher. The swing set is creaking. It isn't made for kids my age, but I'm pretty skinny for fifteen so I'm not too worried.

Kevin looks at me with his mouth open. It's clear he doesn't believe what I'm saying. *Fine. Whatever.*

I do my best to ignore him and just enjoy the way it feels to close my eyes as the swing falls backward toward the Earth. Eventually the pressing urge to call Sarah fades and becomes just something I need to do later.

Next to me, Kevin clears his throat. "Thursday, Ice," he says, which puzzles me. I have no idea what he's talking about.

The swing propels me up and past him. The whole planet seems so far beneath my shoes, and even though I know it isn't true, it seems like if I just jump off I'll land on someone's roof or get stuck in the top of a tree.

"Hey," Kevin calls. His voice is no-nonsense enough to get me to drag my feet in the dirt and slowly bring myself to a stop. "Did you hear me?"

"You said something about Thursday." I do my best to think about the word and not what it might mean.

Kevin doesn't play along. Instead he kneels down in front of me, holding on to the chains of the swings, one in each hand.

"You have to go see your dad on Thursday. After school."

I breathe and relief floods through me. "Can't. I have practice." For an optimistic minute I expect him to shrug and accept it, but instead he shakes his head.

"I know. Jim is going to have to call your coach and tell him you won't be there."

It's true that bad things all happen at once. Just like

That Day happened, but The Night Before happened too. And neither could have happened without the other.

Up until this minute, I thought that having to spend time with my father was the very worst thing that could happen to me. But I was wrong. Missing practice on Thursday means being benched during our last game of the season on Friday. I need hockey. In spite of my recent actions, I need practice too—the speed, the chance to turn off my brain and let my muscles do the work. Going too long without skating makes it harder for me to concentrate and harder for me to bounce back after a spin.

"I have a game on Friday. If I miss, they won't let me play." My voice is a whisper eaten up by the wind. "Come on, please," I plead, but I know there's nothing he can do. I sometimes forget he's a kid just like me. Well, not just like me. But he doesn't get to call the shots either.

"I know." Kevin's voice is sad. He means it, but it doesn't change anything. "My dad is working, so I'll take you to DeSilva's office after school. They say it'll only be twenty minutes, and then it'll be over and hopefully he'll just crawl back into whatever hole he's been hiding in."

Twenty minutes is the length of a period of hockey without stoppages. Worlds could be created and destroyed in that amount of time.

Kevin pulls himself to his feet. Grabbing a handful of stones, he whips them, one by one, at the dead center of a tree. Each time one hits, my stomach twitches.

"What do you think I'm supposed to do there?" I ask.

Kevin rubs his temples and sighs loudly. "I don't know,

Ice. Just talk to him. Or let him talk. Maybe all he wants is for you to listen to him and then he'll go away."

My thumb starts twitching. There's nothing my father could say that I'd want to hear. I've heard his vulture voice enough to last a lifetime.

I push the swing off the ground, but every time I fly up, my stomach stays below. I pump my legs until I'm as high as the swing will let me go, and, just as it starts its descent, I jump. For a second, I'm free. For a second, it's just me and the air.

I hear Kevin yelling but I know how to land, bending my knees so I don't break anything. Once I'm on the ground, I walk over to the bushes and puke my guts out. It's probably the only thing that keeps my brother from kicking my ass.

———————

When we get home, Kevin's still muttering under his breath and I have to take a gulp of water to wash the taste of puke out of my mouth. It's eight o'clock. I wonder if that's too late to call someone on a Saturday night.

I expect him to yell at me some more, but instead Kevin says, "You might feel better if you talk about it," really softly. This is funny coming from him, because my brother never talks about anything that happened.

I shake my head. If I told him everything, he'd know it was all my fault. He'd hate me and even though it's probably what I deserve, I think that actually *would* kill me.

"You don't have to talk to me. You could try talking to someone else again," he suggests.

I stare at him. Given the number of hours he's had to spend with the school shrinks and the equal number of hours he's spent bitching about it, his suggestion is almost funny.

"No." I say. "I'll be okay."

I'm sure Kevin doesn't believe me. I don't even believe me.

"Fine. Here, Romeo," he says, tossing the phone to me, his version of a peace offering. I think about the chances of my pulling it together to call Sarah now, and about what I could say.

My heart is beating a little fast. I know I'm looking at the phone like it's some giant vat of ice cream that I want to eat and eat until I pass out.

"You really like her," Kevin says. I can tell he's relieved to be talking about something that makes sense to him. His little brother crushing on a girl.

"It's just school," I say, but we both know I'm lying, and that feels weird. I get up, so I don't have to see the look in his eyes, and find the paper with the phone number on it. Then I stare at each digit, waiting to see if they'll tell me what to do.

"Sure it is." Kevin says. "Go ahead and call her. Maybe it will help."

I nod, because doing what he says seems easier than trying to figure anything else out.

There's a dull buzz as I mechanically punch each number into the phone. A part of me hopes no one answers. A part of me is scared no one will. Somehow, where Sarah is concerned, I always seem to be feeling two opposite things at once.

"Hello?" I'm pretty sure it's her.

"Sarah?" My voice is all choked up like I've been smoking or something. I have to cough to clear it.

"Yeah?"

"It's Gordie."

I wait for her to say, "Gordie who?" or to ask why I'm calling or to tell me to go away.

"Hey, I was hoping you'd call," she says, and it makes my stomach flip.

I suddenly realize I have no idea what to say now that she's on the phone. The line is filled with silence. Too much. My hand starts to tighten and a shadow that may or may not be real moves across the room.

"Are you there?" she asks.

"Yeah. Yeah, just . . . sorry." I shake my head and the shadow disappears.

"Oh, okay," she says. "So, what do you think about going and taking photos tomorrow afternoon? Maybe somewhere around the monastery?"

She talks for a while about the things she can photograph. I'm not really paying much attention to what she's saying, just to the rhythm of her words. Eventually there's a pause and I know that I need to add something.

"Sure."

Kevin raises an eyebrow. I turn to face the other direction so that he doesn't see the small, embarrassed smile on my face.

"Does one o'clock tomorrow work?" she asks. "I can meet you there."

"One sounds perfect," I say, and I mean it.

NINE

Sarah is right where she says she'll be and already bustling around. I don't know exactly what she's taking photos of. And I don't know what types of "harbingers of doom" I'm going to photograph. It's snowing huge white flakes even though the sun is shining, and it looks like we're in the center of a snow globe. I know I need to care about the assignment, but I'm not sure I really do.

Sarah rushes around checking angles, shadows, and light while I climb up to the roof of the old wooden train and lie down, watching the snow fall around me like feathers. It's not cold out, for Michigan anyhow, and the snow melts as soon as it hits the ground, so I just look up at the blue, blue sky and watch the flakes and the clouds.

When we were little, Kevin and I would go into the yard with Mom and play the cloud game, trying to figure out what each cloud looked like to us. Mom would always see something funny: a rabbit with a top hat, or a flower being nibbled by an elephant. Kevin was always practical. To him the clouds were shaped like a truck. Or a cigar. Or a mailbox.

Sometimes I saw dragons, and castles, and elaborate scenes with moats and armies of knights. Sometimes all I saw were clouds. But it didn't matter. It wasn't the clouds that made the game fun.

A plane flies overhead somewhere in the distance. If I try really hard, I can hear Sarah's camera clicking away as she talks, to herself and to the things she's taking photos of. She even talks to the sun. I wonder if she really expects it to move just so that she can get a good picture.

I close my eyes and press on my eyelids, watching fireworks of color explode behind them.

I'm off, lost in the sounds and colors until Sarah's voice pulls me back as she climbs up to the top of the train.

"I wish it wasn't so bright out, but I think I got some good shots," she says, sitting down next to me.

I want her to keep talking, but she doesn't. So I sit up and watch her watching the sky.

It isn't just that I think she's pretty. It's that she seems more confident and sure of herself than anyone else I know. I can't even lie to myself about it anymore. I want her to like me, even though I've never cared what anyone thought about me before. Even though there's no reason she should.

"You could do something with that darker cloud over there," she suggests, pointing off in the distance. As she turns her head, a charm swings from a chain around her neck. Framed like a little painting is a bird with multicolored wings, wings that stretch out toward the side of her neck. It reminds me a little of the photo she put in my locker.

"Thanks," I say. "For the picture."

She breaks into a wide smile. "Glad you liked it. It won an award at my old school."

I feel a weird surge of pride swell through me, followed by something cold and empty. The more I learn about her, the less I understand why she'd want anything to do with me.

"Don't miss the cloud," she says.

I follow her finger and try to get my head back into our assignment. It's a good idea. People always used to try to get hints of their future by looking at the sky or following the weather.

I nod. She takes the camera from around her neck and hands it to me, but I'm not sure what to do with it. Mom had a camera when we were kids. I'm not sure what happened to it. We don't have many photos of anything since That Day, and the old ones are mostly packed away somewhere.

Plus, the camera Mom had was a little thing you could put in your pocket. This is different. This is more like what real photographers use, with lenses that come off and flashes that clip on.

"So how does this work?" I ask her.

She drapes the strap around my neck and moves behind me, up on her knees. I bring the camera up to my eye. When she leans over to show me how to adjust the lens, she rests her arms against my shoulders and my heart thumps double-time.

"Just look through the viewfinder and then use that little ring in front to zoom in and out."

It all seems pretty easy, but I'm so distracted by the weight of her arms on my shoulders that my hands are shaking. I freeze, with the camera pointed straight ahead. I'm afraid that if I move, I'm going to knock us both off the train's roof.

"Gordie, the cloud is up there," she says, laughing. I try to stay focused on the assignment, but it's hard. I could just watch the snowflakes for hours, but Sarah is distracting in a good way, too. I don't mind it so much. It just means I have to work really hard but not show it. I'd love to believe she thinks I'm normal, but I know that's impossible. Everyone in this stupid town knows everything about me.

I redirect the camera under her guidance and then she moves her hand on top of mine. "You just click this button when you're ready," she says. The wind moves her hair and I can smell some sort of flowers that must be her shampoo. It reminds me of my mom's lilacs and I inhale and hold it all in before I snap a few photos in the direction of the dark cloud.

She moves back and takes the camera from around my neck, playing with some buttons on the back of it.

"See." She flips through the images one by one. It's pretty cool, actually. I can see why she likes taking pictures. It freezes things in time. The cloud has already moved from where it was when I snapped it and it will never be back there again. I wonder if she could do that with me. Just freeze me in a moment when I'm not spinning off so I can stay here with her.

"What else do you want to shoot?" she asks.

I've thought about it, but really, I don't know. The only bad omens I can think of are really, really bad ones, ones I don't want to deal with. Ones that don't have anything to do with *Moby Dick*.

I shrug. "I don't know. Any ideas?"

"No, but we don't have to rush and do it all now, anyhow." She pulls her knees up and wraps her skirt over them. "It's so nice to be outside. I think I could live outside. Like when you're camping. You ever been?"

"Kevin and I used to camp in the backyard." I tell her about how I remember us sleeping out under the stars, eating chips right out of the bag and telling each other silly stories with just flashlights for light.

"That kind of counts," she says. "And it sounds like fun."

I don't know what it is, but it's both so easy and so difficult to talk to her. Being the town freak should get you over worrying about having to say the right thing all the time, but it doesn't work like that.

"Camping was always such a production when we were little," she says. "You know, it had to be the right tent and someone usually forgot the directions on how to put it up. And then there was the food and gas for the stove. Something was always left at home and we'd all blame each other."

She squints into the sunlight and tips her head back to look at the sky. I do too. Then she pauses and says, "We're going next Saturday night. Camping. Luke and Jessie and I are going to Ross Park. You could come if you wanted to. I hate when it's just them and me. You know what they're like."

Two things hit my brain at once, like trains colliding.

First, I realize that Sarah's brother is Luke Miller—the captain of our team.

Second, I realize she must be screwing with me. Why else would she invite me camping with them? Had the photography thing not been my idea, I'd be sure she was only here with me to win some sort of bet or something.

I feel myself inching away from her as my hand starts to twitch.

"Are you okay?" she asks. Before I can even think about answering, she puts a hand on my arm. "You don't have to come with us. You're allowed to say no."

I shove my hand under my leg and look at her. *Really* look at her. She doesn't seem like someone who is just trying to win a bet.

But if that's true, then she really wants me to come with them. And I'm not sure that makes a whole lot of sense either.

I want to say that I'll go, but can't imagine how much it would suck if I started to spin—not only in front of her but in front of Luke, too. I haven't even thought of sleeping over at anyone's house since That Day. But at the same time, I don't want to say no.

I swallow hard. "I need to ask Jim."

"Is that your dad?"

For a minute, I wonder if she's asking just to hear me say it. But maybe she really *doesn't* know, although I'm not sure how that could happen.

"No. Kevin's dad," I say, giving her the benefit of the doubt. In front of me is a pile of blue threads from the hem of my jeans, which I didn't notice I was pulling out. "But I live with him."

She looks confused but doesn't ask anything else. I'm sure Luke or any of the kids at school can fill her in on whatever she wants to know.

"Well, tell him that Luke invited you. I mean … he'd be

cool with that, right? Since you're on the team together and everything."

I shrug. I guess he'd be cool. I've never asked to do something like that before.

"Are you and Kevin close?" Sarah asks. "I've seen him at some of your games, but I've never really talked to him."

It's probably a normal question, just not one I've ever been asked. I tie some of the threads in knots and then toss them into the air. How the hell am I supposed to explain my relationship with my brother to anybody? There are times he makes me crazy and times when I'm sure I make *him* crazy. But I can't imagine what I'd do without him. I don't want to imagine it.

"He's my best friend," I say, because I don't know the words for the rest and that sums it up as well as anything.

Sarah smiles. "That's nice. I used to feel that way about Luke, but then we got to high school and he turned into a pain in the ass. All he thinks about is sports and girls, you know?"

I nod, because that pretty much describes almost every guy in our school.

"I think he and Jess are pretty serious, though. At least they think they are. My parents probably have their wedding all planned out already."

In truth, Luke and Jess scare me a little. I've seen them after games in the hallway outside the locker room. I've seen the way she looks at him, like he's her own sun, and how he touches her like she's the Holy Grail. It makes me jealous and uncomfortable, but I can't *not* watch them. When they kiss, they're like wax melting into each other.

Sarah opens her mouth and catches a snowflake on her tongue. She smiles like she's just eaten the best candy in the world, and I feel my whole body flush.

"I wonder what it's like," she says. "You know, to be with someone and think you'll be with them for the rest of your life. I mean, how do you know?"

I laugh. She could have asked the monks and gotten a better answer than I'm going to be able to give her.

"Maybe you just meet someone, and ... " I know I'm failing to get what's in my head out of my mouth, so I try again. "Maybe it's like a best friend. They just get you and you don't want to let that go. And if you're lucky, neither do they."

She tilts her head to the side, the snowflakes landing in her hair. "You make it sound a lot less scary," she says. And then she reaches over and puts her hand on my leg. It feels like all of my nerve endings come alive at once. "I hope you're right."

I nod because I don't trust my voice to work. I hope I'm right, too.

"Okay, so let's talk about the rest of your photos," she says.

I don't want to. I don't want to think about gloom and doom, or anything bad. Or even school. I just want to watch the snow; to watch her. I want her never to move her hand.

But she's waiting for me, so I don't have a choice.

In *Moby Dick*, there's all this superstitious stuff. All these dreams about hearses and things you supposedly need in order to have good luck. And there's a story about a hawk. We decide to go with the bird because it's the easiest. There are always hawks flying around here. Maybe because it's the only open space for miles and miles. Besides, the thought of going to a funeral home to take pictures of a hearse makes me physically sick.

In fifteen minutes, we're done and back on the ground. I only realize how quiet my head has been all this time when I start to feel an edgy buzzing. I wonder what happens next. It's been so long since I've talked to anyone besides Kevin, or about anything other than hockey, that I want it to keep on going. But I'm clueless about how to do that.

Sarah says she'll print my photos along with hers and bring them to school. She gives me a quick hug and then walks off.

Our goodbye is over so fast that I kind of miss it, and I stand there until she's just a tiny speck in the distance.

Nothing has changed. Everything has changed. *It's just school*, I tell myself. But this time, even I don't believe it.

TEN

It isn't until I get to the house that I realize I'll have a mountain to climb when trying to convince Jim to let me go camping. Actually, when trying to convince Kevin, because if I don't get through him, I won't even get to Jim.

And Kevin's reaction, not surprisingly, is to laugh at me.

Sometimes, regardless of how great they can be, brothers suck.

"Camping? Like setting up a tent? And pissing in the woods? And building a fire? That sort of camping?" He isn't bothering to hide his amusement.

"Give me a break," I mutter under my breath.

"Camping, like with bugs? And scary red food like hot dogs? And people you have to talk to?"

"Fine. Forget I mentioned it." I throw myself into my desk chair, which somehow ended up on his side of the room, and roll it back to mine. I grab a history book and do my best to ignore him, which turns out to be impossible because Kevin is cracking himself up.

He follows, sitting down on the edge of my bed and

struggling to stop laughing. "Okay, seriously, let's talk about this."

"No, let's not." I've already given up. It was stupid of me to think it was a good idea to begin with.

"Hey, Ice, I'm not necessarily saying you shouldn't go," he says while I lose myself in the politics of the Civil War. "I'm just surprised."

South Carolina is trying to secede when the book is pulled out of my hands.

"It was a stupid idea. Drop it." I'm pissed off and resigned to not going. The last thing I want is to talk about it. But I should know better. Kevin never ever gives up and never lets anything go.

"Look at me," he says, spinning my chair around and around. My eyes are clamped shut and I don't open them, so he spins harder. I give in only to keep from feeling like I'm going to throw up.

"If you really want to go, then you should. There's just one thing…"

There's always one thing with him, and I don't want to get my hopes up until I find out what hurdle he's going to say I need to jump. Sometimes, just sometimes, I wish Jim was really my dad so that Kevin could act like a normal brother and ignore me.

He leans over and grips the arm of my chair and stares into my eyes. "If you can hold it together on Thursday with your father, I'll talk to Jim," he says. Then he pushes me back so that my chair goes sailing across the room.

I close my eyes again and wait to see if I'm going to crash

against the wall. The floor is slightly sloped and all of our furniture is at the edges of the big room, so there's a lot of space to fly through.

"So, what do you think?" Kevin calls as I hit his bed with my outstretched feet.

I can't tie what's going to happen on Thursday to anything to do with Sarah. I know if I do, they're going to be knotted that way in my head forever and I won't be able to be her friend without thinking of him and The Night Before, and I can't do that.

So I shrug. And get up and grab my book from him.

"Thursday is going to happen whether you want it to or not," Kevin says. "Wouldn't it be better to have something to look forward to on the other side?"

This is how Kevin's mind works. There is now. And there is later. And then there is later still. One comes after the other after the other. He should hate my father more than anyone, but it's all divided up for him.

I never take anything for granted. Who knows what will happen on Thursday?

So I don't answer him. I go back to reading until he comes and rotates my chair around and around again and somewhere in the room I hear the air say, "You're a pain in the ass. You know that, right? Fine. No promises. But I'll see what I can do."

I don't know if Kevin talks to Jim, because every time he brings it up, I walk out of the room.

Sarah brings the photos to school and the four of us work on this cool *Moby Dick* storyboard that we'll present at the end of the week.

I keep waiting for Luke to say something to me about staying away from his sister. It seems so strange that I have all of this stuff going on with my father and Sarah, yet nothing else really seems like it's changed. Until Coach waves me over to the side of the rink on Wednesday.

I use the last of my practice energy to skate over to the boards.

He compliments me on a pretty awesome glove-save I made and then gets to his real point. "I heard you'll have to miss practice tomorrow. You know I'd love to break my own rule and let you play on Friday, but if I do that for you..."

"Yeah," I mumble. "I know. I get it."

Coach nods his head and pats me on the shoulder. "That's okay. There are plenty more games in your future, and this way we can give Walker a good send-off."

I've been doing a good job of pretending Thursday isn't going to come. But now that Coach knows about it, it seems real.

I move out of the way to let Walker onto the ice. I'm about to ask Coach if I can skip the game instead of sitting on the bench when I hear a string of swear words and a bunch of the guys cracking up.

I turn around. Walker is spilled on the ice, trying to pull

clear tape off his blades. "I'm going to kill you, Bowman, you freaking…"

Cody is in the stands, dressed in his street clothes because of his suspension. He's wearing the same fake-innocent expression I've seen on him before. "Wasn't me, loser. I'm up here, remember?"

Coach sighs. Someone always plays a prank on senior players at the end of the season. Only Cody is stupid enough to do something that could get his own goalie hurt.

"Both of you, over here. Now," Coach yells. I take the opportunity to slip into the locker room.

I hit the showers and try to wash all thoughts of Thursday out of my head, but no matter how far I turn the knob, the water isn't hot enough to do the job. By the time I give up and towel off, I'm as red as my jersey.

I can't believe this was my last practice of the season. I can't believe I'm missing hockey to see my fucking father.

I throw my clothes on and sit down to tie my shoes, but my hand is shaking and I keep dropping the lace. I'm sure I look like a total idiot who can't even handle something as stupid as shoelaces when Luke shows up at my locker.

Here we go. Get the freak away from your sister.

"Nice play out there." He shakes his wet hair into a towel. "I almost wish I was going to be here next year. You guys are going to be awesome."

"Thanks." I give up and shove the laces down the sides of my shoes. Even that's hard because I'm so freaked out by the thought of losing it in front of him.

Luke stands there looking like somebody who just stepped out of a magazine. All dark hair and pressed shirt.

"Look, Gordie," he says seriously. "I wanted to talk to you about this weekend."

Crap. I exhale breath and hope. *Of course.*

"I know Sarah didn't give you much notice. And you're probably busy, but it would be great if you could come with us." He shoves his practice stuff into his bag and sprays himself with expensive-smelling cologne.

"Why?" I ask before I can stop myself, then cover my mouth before I can say anything else embarrassing.

Thankfully, he laughs. "I think Sarah could use a friend here."

I want to ask him "Why?" again. I mean, Sarah is smart and talented, and so, so, so pretty. I'm sure she has a million friends. But before I can say anything, the door bursts open and Jessie comes in without knocking. I say a silent word of gratitude that she didn't come in while I was still half-naked.

Standing here in front of them makes me wonder if it really would be possible for me to go camping with them. I don't belong with them and their easy, normal lives.

"Gordie, right?" she asks. Her honey-blond hair drapes around Luke like a scarf.

I nod. "Hey," I think I say back, but I know I'm turning red just watching them, with their skin touching in so many places they might as well be melding into the same person. Her cheek fits perfectly into the crook of his neck and his hand is running absent-mindedly up and down her arm, which is wrapped around his chest.

I run my thumb over the strap of my equipment bag and try to concentrate on breathing.

I'm still watching them, but trying not to, when I hear a sound behind me. I turn to see Sarah's camera firing rapid photos of the three of us. I duck down to try to escape but she follows, leaning over and snapping photos inches away from my face until I tumble away, out of her reach.

Luke and Jessie seem oblivious to anything other than each other, so I get up and go over to where Sarah is leaning against one of the training tables, looking into her camera at the pictures she's taken.

I still want to leave, but I want to be close to her more. I crane my head over her shoulder. "Can I see?"

As she hugs the camera to her chest, a devilish smile spreads across her face. It gives her dimples that make me smile too. "Well ... how about this. Come camping with us, and I'll show you then."

I like her teasing. Aside from Kevin, everyone is always totally serious around me, as if laughing is going make me break into a hundred pieces.

Before I can say anything, Luke untangles himself from Jessie. "Come on, squirt, I need to drop you home. Jess and I have homework to do."

"Yeah, I'll bet." Sarah smirks at him and then winks at me. "But I need you to run me by the library first."

"Sarah ... " Luke folds his arms like he's going to put up a fight. "Gordie, you need a ride?" he asks in my direction.

I shake my head "no" before I realize what a mistake that

is. I watch as they all walk out, hearing their light-hearted fighting as they head out of the rink.

I'm filled with envy. I'm not sure if my conversations with Kevin are ever that simple.

I think about this as I walk home alone. And I'm still thinking about it when I get into the house and am assaulted by the nauseating smells of popcorn, cigarettes, and beer.

Kevin is laughing with his friends. It's obvious that Jim is out again and Kevin has claimed the den for a night of DVDs.

I make it upstairs without throwing up, talking to anyone, or, I hope, anyone seeing me. Something about being with Sarah and Luke, or Sarah really, has made me want to be by myself. Or with her.

But my plan is to not think about anything real. I figure if I plow through my math and history homework tonight, I'll have all of it done for class through Monday, even though it's only Wednesday night. I don't know what shape I'm going to be in tomorrow night, or what's going to happen after that, and it helps to be prepared.

I tackle geometry first. *Find X: m<AOB = 6x + 5, m<BOC = 4x - 2, m<AOC = 8x + 21.*

The bedroom door opens but I try to ignore it. Downstairs a plane drops bombs on an unsuspecting village. The sound of people screaming matches the ache in my stomach.

Kevin hangs over my shoulder; I fight to stay lost in numbers.

"Come downstairs," he says. "It's just Mark and Bryce."

<AOB and <BOC are adjacent angles, but something doesn't add up.

"Ice. Come on, take a break."

"Can't," I say. Xs flip over and over in my head.

Kevin spins my chair around to face him. I have to shake the numbers out of my brain.

"What's your GPA?" he asks.

"3.854," I answer without thinking.

"Really?" He's so shocked he actually takes a step back. Even my brother forgets that I'm smart. I nod.

"You're a freak. You know that, right?" But he's smiling. "I think you've earned time off for a movie."

"I can't. I have to get this all done tonight." I'm actually itching to get back to it. My thumb starts moving and my head is already halfway back into my homework.

"When's your … " He picks up my book and looks at the spine. "Geometry due?"

"Monday," I admit.

"So why do you need to do it all tonight?"

"Leave me alone," I yell, then cover my mouth with my hands. I never yell. I never yell at him. "Sorry," I say, making sure my voice is quiet. "Sorry."

He shakes his head and the smile disappears. I almost wish he'd scream back at me or something. It would be easier than this disappointed look.

"Fine. Have it your way," he says, but he just stands there like that's the last thing he wants. "You know, whatever he's done, you let him win when you do this," he says softly.

I think about that for a minute.

I turn back to my math. "He's already won."

ELEVEN

I have a plan. It may not be a good plan. It may be the stupidest plan ever. It might not even work. But at least it's mine.

My plan is that I'm going to sit there. I'm going to sit there, and stay quiet, and play a movie in my mind, and go somewhere else and let the vulture rant and rave on his own. My plan is that I'll be there, but I won't. My body might be in the room. I might be twitching like I've stuck my finger in an electric socket. But I won't be there. Not really.

I practice it all day. I'm in class, but I'm not. A few teachers look at me with that worried look I've seen too many times before, but I make sure I'm out of the room as soon as the bell rings.

I practice it in the car, when Kevin drives me to Ms. DeSilva's office. But that's a lot harder.

"You're in there, right?" he asks as I sit, statue still, in the passenger's seat.

"Yeah." I struggle to get the word out.

When we come to a stop sign, he takes a hand off the wheel and puts it on my arm and squeezes. I expect him to say, "It's okay," like he always does. But he doesn't, and I'm glad. There's no way I could take his word for it this time.

When the car starts moving again, he doesn't remove his hand, but I'm doing such a good job at being somewhere else that I don't fully feel its weight anymore.

Then we're in the building. I look around, amazed that nothing has changed in the last five years. The carpet is the same paisley pattern that looks like a rainbow vomited all over it. The closer we get to her office, the harder it is to believe any time has passed at all.

Kevin guides me through the halls with a hand on my shoulder until we get to Ms. DeSilva's office. Then he takes a deep breath and pushes me like a battering ram through the door.

I don't remember a ton about Amy DeSilva except that she was nice to me, she didn't say mean things about my mom, and she never told me things would be okay just to have something to say.

She looks exactly like she did five years ago. She still has that middle-aged-woman hairstyle you have to go to a salon to get—all puffy and curled. Only Kevin and I look different.

"Look at you," she says, holding my arms out. Kevin smirks, but I wish I could see what she's seeing. I can't imagine anything about me that would make her so happy.

I try to smile back, but I just end up biting on my lip as she leans over and gives Kevin a hug and gestures for us to sit down.

"So, I know this isn't how you boys want to spend this afternoon, but we all have to follow the law. The court has granted your father's petition for this supervised meeting, and I wanted to go over what will happen and make sure you don't have any questions."

A hundred million questions all rush to the front of my head, each of them yelling "Pick me! Pick me!" I'm determined not to let a single word escape my lips. If I start talking, I won't be able to stop. And if that happens, I'm afraid I'm going to start talking about what happened on The Night Before and there's no way I'm letting that happen.

I start snapping my bracelet and don't quit until Kevin leans over and knocks me on the leg. Then I sit on my hand, but I can still feel the muscles jerking.

Ms. DeSilva leans over her desk and clasps her hands together. Her nails are a deep shiny red that match the carpet. "Gordie, your father is going to be here in about fifteen minutes. I'm going to have my assistant take him straight into the conference room and let me know when he's there. Then I'll take you in. I'm afraid that Kevin is going to have to wait outside, but I'll be in there with you and I'll stay there for the whole visit. Okay?"

She looks at me, waiting for me to tell her it's okay, but nothing about this is okay. I manage a nod, but it's a struggle. I don't want to go in there looking like I really give a damn.

She obviously notices because she offers me something to drink. I can't imagine being able to hold anything down, so I shake my head again.

"I know you haven't seen your father in a long time, so this meeting will be short and we'll keep things casual, okay? We'll just see how it goes."

Then she looks at Kevin. "Are there any questions I can answer, or do the two of you need a few minutes?"

I have no intention of opening my mouth. Of course, Kevin can't keep quiet. "Thanks. I think some time might be good, Ms. DeSilva," he says.

She gets up and gathers her papers. "You know, I think it would be all right if you called me Amy. You aren't little boys anymore."

Kevin nods. Aside from Jim, I've never called adults by their first names. Even with Jim, it's easier not to call him anything at all.

The door lock clicks as she closes it.

Kevin turns his chair to face mine. "You can do this, Gordie. It's just twenty minutes."

I nod, even though "twenty minutes" with my father sounds like a lifetime.

"Give me your watch." He holds his hand out and I undo the strap and hand it to him. He fiddles around with it and gives it back. I don't look at it when I put it back on.

"Are you going to talk to him at all?" Kevin asks. He sounds calm, but he's running his hand through his hair like it's an animal he's trying to tame.

I try really hard to wrap my lips around one word, to say "No," but my plan has taken over my brain. I shake my head.

He closes his eyes and swears under his breath.

"You realize that all you're going to do is to piss him off, right?"

I shrug. I don't care.

"I don't suppose you want to let me know what the hell you're thinking?"

I don't shake my head this time. He knows better.

"Ice ... " he starts, but leaves the rest of the question in the air and sighs. "Just sit tight for a couple of minutes."

I close my eyes to the sound of the door shutting. I let myself go, but it isn't really a spin. It isn't some memory from when I was a kid. Instead, I'm on top of the train with Sarah. I can feel the soft snow landing on my hand. I can feel the weight of her arms on my shoulders as she showed me how to use her camera.

It's nice. It's strange. It probably means I'm crazy, but right now, I don't care. I focus on how she smells like the lilacs we used to have in the backyard of our old house.

There's music in the way she says my name. I feel like I could fly on the sound her words make. My breathing slows and my hand relaxes.

Then the door opens and it isn't Kevin. Ms. DeSilva pulls one of the chairs over to the couch where I'm sitting.

"Your brother says you're scared to see your father."

My hand clenches again and I knock it into the arm of the couch. My brother has a big mouth.

"He's worried about you. I know it's been a long time since you've seen your dad. The last time was at the funeral, right?"

I nod.

"Can you tell me if there are any other concerns you have?"

Other concerns? My mind races with them, each worse than the one before. I imagine telling her everything about what my father used to do to Kevin and about The Night Before. I imagine how pissed my brother would be at me for blabbing his secrets, and what he'd think of me once he finds out what a coward I am.

I jam my hand under my leg and shake my head. I know she gets that there's stuff I'm keeping to myself. But she's a lawyer or something, not a shrink. I don't think I have to talk to her even though she's nice and if I was going to talk to someone, I know she wouldn't be a bad choice.

"Gordie, is there anything I can do to help you?"

I can tell she means it, and for a minute I feel bad for not confessing my secrets to her. I force myself to swallow and to say softly, "No. Thank you."

Her face falls, but she nods at me anyhow. "Okay. But you know that you can talk to me if you need to."

She stands up, straightens her skirt, and opens the door. "Come on. He's waiting for you."

I follow her out of her office. She's walking slowly, and it's like being in one of those old pirate movies where the guy is walking the plank. I want to stop and say that I've done nothing wrong and don't deserve this, but I know that isn't true so I keep my mouth shut.

When we get to the end of the hall, she pauses outside the door and Kevin pulls me aside. He looks almost as jumbled up as I feel.

He grabs my arm and pushes a button on my watch, then whispers in my ear: "Twenty minutes and it will be over."

I look down and see the stopwatch on my wrist counting down the seconds.

Ms. DeSilva opens the door and leads me in. I look at the floor, following the trail of paisleys in. I don't want to look up. I don't want to see his eyes, but I can feel them on me. Stripping me. Cutting into me.

I can see the legs of a chair so I push myself into it. I grip the arms, and I look up.

TWELVE

Five years. I've grown a foot and gained forty pounds in the past five years. Our country has elected new presidents. The National Hockey League has added a few teams and restructured the divisions. But my father has stayed the same.

It's weird because I expected him to have changed. Instead, he just looks grayer. I can see the muscles bulging on his neck, and it makes me a little sick to think that he works out and could probably squeeze himself into his old hockey gear.

That thought makes the back of my neck start to tingle. I pull my shoulders up and rub my temples, which doesn't keep my head from feeling like it's going to split apart.

His mouth opens and I push myself back into the chair, waiting to hear the vulture sounds, but I don't. All I hear is blood rushing through my head.

Ms. DeSilva is staring at me the same way that Jim stares at Kevin's meals; like I'm a science experiment she's waiting to turn color or boil over.

His lips are moving, but I don't hear anything. Just *whoosh, whoosh, whoosh.*

I look down at my watch: 18 minutes, 3 seconds, 1 tenth. Tick. Tick. Tick. Tick.

I get up and walk over to the glass wall. It's cool under my hands and I can see myself reflected, along with him. I wonder if this is like the interrogation rooms on cop shows on TV. The ones where they can see in but we can't see out. I wonder if Kevin is on the other side watching me. I wonder if he's going to be angry that my blood is so loud I can't hear anything else.

I feel Ms. DeSilva's arm, gentle around my shoulders. She's turning me so that I'm facing him. He puts his hand out. I look at it. It's calloused like I remember. And large. I used to think I only remembered his hands being so big because I was a kid, but no, they're still really big. Even now.

In my head I can see those hands punching Kevin over and over. My whole body shudders until I look away.

Tick. Tick. Tick. Tick. 13 minutes. 42 seconds. 3 tenths.

I sit back down, wishing I could think about Sarah, but I don't want to think about her here. I want to think about Mom, but something about that seems wrong too. I don't want to betray her by doing that with him right in front of me.

Instead, I think about hockey. I think about skating really, really fast around the rink. It's the closest I can get to flying. It feels free, and light, and cold, and everything is clean, and pure, and white. If I was asked to build a rink, I'd build one shaped like an Olympic swimming pool, long and thin. I want to skate for an hour in a single straight line, gaining speed all the time like I'm doing in my head now.

I can feel the wind in my face and over the whooshing sound I can hear blades cutting into ice. It's one of my favorite sounds in the world; the call of some metallic bird flying through a frozen sky.

My breath speeds up as I zip across the surface of the ice. I want to keep skating until I'm a million miles away from here.

Something clamps down on my shoulder and I struggle, but it's stronger than I am. My eyelids flutter as I'm pulled from the rink in my mind.

When I open my eyes Kevin is there, but he isn't supposed to be. I wonder if he's going to get into trouble. I look at my watch.

8 minutes. 12 seconds. 4 tenths. Tick. Tick.

Everyone is buzzing around and making me dizzy. I wonder if this is what it feels like to pass out.

Kevin leans down and puts an arm around my neck. "This is over." His voice is loud and sharp and sounds like someone else.

"Yes," says Ms. DeSilva. "I agree. I think we need to stop for now."

"What the hell have you done to him?" I hear, in vulture rasps.

"Get the fuck out of here," Kevin says, in a tone I haven't heard him use in years. I get a whiff of Ms. DeSilva's perfume as she crosses in front of me, and suddenly we're alone. Just me and Kevin. I breathe a sigh of relief.

"Are you okay?" he asks. His voice is still weird, like he'd punch something with it if he could. His hands are clenched so tight his knuckles are white.

I nod. "Yeah. I was ... I was skating," I know it sounds weird, but I expect my words to reassure him even though they don't. "What's wrong?"

"You can't … " He turns his back to me and I think for a second that he's going to lose it and hit something. I pull back hard in my chair. "Damn it, Ice, don't … "

He takes a deep breath and then lets it out. Ms. DeSilva comes back in and shuts the door. "Is he okay?" she asks Kevin.

People do that sometimes—talk as if I'm not there. Sometimes it's fine, because it means I don't have to answer, but usually it's just really annoying. I'm not sure which it is now.

"As okay as he ever is," Kevin hisses, spinning away from me.

"Does this happen often?" She looks from him to me. I'm not sure if I'm meant to answer or if she's still talking to Kevin.

"Yeah, my brother does stupid shit all the time," Kevin says as he paces in front of the conference table.

When I stand up, my head swims a little and I have to grab onto the table to steady myself. "What are you so pissed about?" I ask.

"You really don't get it, do you?" He scowls.

Ms. DeSilva sighs and sits down. "Gordie, I think you and I need to talk."

"Sure." I pull out a chair and sit down. Now that my father is gone, all of this is much, much easier. I just wish Kevin would calm down before he gets into trouble.

"Do you have these … episodes … often?" she asks.

I exhale. I don't talk about spinning. Ever. And this wasn't really a spin, it was … I don't know what it was. Escape, maybe.

"I … it depends … some lately, but … " I fold my arms tight over my chest. *I'm okay. He's gone and I'm okay.*

"Have you told anyone? Jim? Or the counselors at school?"

"Jim ... I guess he knows, but ... why does it matter?"

"It matters, you idiot, because your psycho father is going to dump you in some hospital and throw away the key after that performance." Kevin is raging now. He's charging up and down the room, looking like he wants to beat the hell out of me.

"You said that I should just listen to him," I whisper.

Kevin gets right in my face. "Did you hear one word he said? Did you?"

"No," I admit. "But ... "

He slaps the table and all of Ms. DeSilva's papers jump. I do too.

"Okay, let's all take a deep breath," Ms. DeSilva says. But she doesn't get that I'm not breathing. I'm trying, but it's like something is sitting on my chest and pushing the air out of me. My hand is going nuts and I let it. I don't care anymore if she knows. I'm not sure what I've done wrong. And if it's what made my father leave, I'm not even sure I care.

"Kevin, do you mind giving us a few minutes?" Ms. DeSilva exchanges a look with him. My brother glares at me like he wants to break me in two and storms out.

The air in the room settles once he's gone and Ms. DeSilva takes a deep breath, sounding like she's trying to suck it all up.

"Okay, Gordie, can we start from the beginning?" she asks, only I'm not sure which beginning she means. Does she mean today? Or with the first awful thing I can remember my father doing? Or with The Night Before?

"The beginning?"

She nods. "I need you to help me. You need to tell me what's going on so that we can figure out where to go from here."

I don't want to talk about anything, not even with her, but it feels like the words are pushing against my lips; if I start talking, I might not be able to stop and that scares me so much I think I might be shaking, but I'm not sure.

I push my sleeve against my mouth, but that doesn't help and the words pour out of me like rapids around the soft cloth.

I explain to her about the spins. I tell her about the memories. I tell her everything I can think of, except for The Night Before. She nods and takes notes.

I try to not think about how everything I'm telling her is being committed to paper.

"You talked to some counselors, right? I have notes here that the school arranged sessions for you?"

I try to nod and shrug at the same time. "They didn't get it," I say, feeling like a total loser. "I tried."

I must look like crap, because she moves over and puts her hand on my arm.

"No one is saying you didn't try. It's okay. Just tell me what happened."

"They..." I think back and try to let some of the memories in without letting the rest overwhelm me. "They gave me a bunch of drugs and... I couldn't study or play hockey. And then Jim talked to them, or Mr. Brooks, or someone, I guess, because they stopped. I...I got used to it, I think."

I glance down. My watch is stalled. Flashing 0:00:00 over and over and over again.

"Am I in trouble?" I ask her.

She squeezes my arm and shares a grim smile. "No. You aren't. I promise. Why didn't you tell me before?"

I think back. "I didn't want you to be mad at me," I say, feeling like I'm ten again. "I knew you wanted me to talk to them."

She lets out a huff of air. "It was never that I wanted you to talk to them. It's that I wanted you to talk to someone who could help you deal with everything that was going on. I still want that."

My muscles tighten and I know I'm on the edge of going into full panic mode. She puts her hand on the back of my neck and says, "Hey, it's okay. I'm not going to force you into anything. Just understand that there are other doctors and other methods and if you ever change your mind, you just need to let me know. Okay?"

My teeth are clenched even though her words should make me relax.

Breathe. Breathe. Breathe.

She stares at me and waits for me to calm down. She doesn't realize she could be waiting for years.

"How often do these spins happen?"

It's kind of like asking someone how often they blink or how often they're hungry. The spins are just there. They're just me.

"Sometimes." It's only been for a couple of weeks this time, but it's hard to think back to when I didn't seem to either be spinning or coming out of a spin, so I grab at the only thing I can.

"When I found the letter, it got worse." My hand shakes hard. I close my eyes. There's silence and then I hear her gathering her notes together.

"Okay," she says softly. "Are you ready to go get your brother and head home?"

I nod. I wish we could teleport there and I didn't have to deal with Kevin until he calmed down. But one question is beating itself against the walls of my head and as we get to the doorway, I have to stop to let it out.

"Can I ask you something?"

"Of course," she says as she turns back around.

"Why?"

She looks puzzled, so I give it another go. "I mean, why did he . . ."

"People have different ways of dealing with grief," she says before I finish. "I guess he couldn't handle losing your mother and your sisters and brother."

At first I'm confused, because I don't think that has anything to do with the question in my head. Then I realize that she only sees the outside of my father—smiling with those sharp teeth. She doesn't know what he's really like, so, of course, the question she's answering is "Why did he leave?" not "What reason could he possibly have to come back?"

I can't take talking about this anymore, so I shut up and follow her out the door with my stomach tying itself in knots.

It doesn't take long to find Kevin pacing in front of Ms. DeSilva's office, his hands still clenched like a boxer's.

I nudge by him and go into her office to grab my backpack as they exchange a few words I don't catch.

Kevin and I don't talk until we're halfway home. I don't need to hear his words to know he's still pissed at me. The air in the car shimmers with his anger.

"Kev…" I start, but really I don't know what to say.

It doesn't matter, because his hands tighten on the steering wheel and he cuts me off. "Not now. Okay, Gordie? Not now."

I lean my head against the window. Someday he's going to get mad at me and leave and I'm going to be completely alone, just a freak who was meant to die but didn't.

Kevin doesn't say a word until we're out of the car. He comes around to where I'm standing, leaning against the door and massaging my hand. He looks at the ground, not at me. "Sorry I got so mad back there."

His apology hangs in the air between us. I can see its furling edges as it spins over and over. I want to reach out and touch it. I want to hold it in my hand. Put it in my pocket. Keep it.

He still looks angry, though. He looks right into my eyes, right through me, and crosses his arms and swallows so loud I can hear it. "It's silly, but… I'm scared too," he says. "Of him, I mean."

When I was really little, I was afraid of lightning. Instead of going to Mom's room—we never knew what shape she'd be in—I'd go to Kevin's and climb onto the foot of his bed. At some point he'd wake up and know I was there. We'd pull ourselves up to the windows and watch the storm together.

Kevin isn't scared of anything. Never was. When I was little, and with him, I never was either.

All I can do is stare back.

His words circle around and make me dizzy.

When I'm freaking out, Kevin always knows what to do to help, but this is the first time that I'm the one trying to help. I don't know if I know how.

I rest my hands on his arms, which are still crossed tight. I will him to be okay. I make silent promises to be nicer to Jim, to eat whatever Kevin cooks, to ace my next test. But it doesn't matter. His eyes look shiny, which makes my stomach feel like it's cracking in two.

Something wet hits my hand. I think I'm bleeding until I reach up to my eyes and find that, for the first time in five years, I'm crying.

THIRTEEN

I stumble backward and lower myself down to the concrete step. The air feels thin in my lungs. I don't want Kevin to hate me, but I can't stand the thought of him being scared. There's so little I have to give him, but I have this: the truth. Maybe that's enough to make him realize that there's nothing silly about being afraid of my father. Nothing at all.

I take a deep breath, clench my hands tight and look my brother in the eye. "He had a knife," I say. And then I swear him to silence and tell him everything.

———

I'm ten, and I'm walking home from hockey practice without Kevin because Jim picked him up from school. I'm not really alone, though, because there are two other guys on my block who are on my team so we walk together, swinging our backpacks, joking around, pretending we're still at the rink.

We get to my house first. My father's car is in the driveway. I'm not sure when he was home last, but it's been a while. I wave to the guys and slowly walk up the steps, afraid of what I might find. Before I even open the front door I can hear the twins crying. Sophie and Jason are a pain because they always set each other off. They should both be sleeping by now. I wonder if Mom remembered to feed them.

I try the door but it's locked, so I pull the key out of my backpack. Just as I'm about to unlock the door, I hear a loud crash. Crashing isn't unusual at our house. Sometimes it's the kids just being kids. Sometimes it's Mom and Dad just being Mom and Dad.

I push open the door. I can't tell what's crashed, but it doesn't matter because what I see is Dad waving a knife around. Kayla is huddled in a corner and Mom is on the couch crying. The twins are in their playpen screaming their heads off.

I freeze in the doorway. I want to run to Mom. I'm not close to the kids, but I want to pull Kayla farther away from Dad. He's tall and the knife is the biggest one we have; the one we use to cut through chicken bones and stuff.

When he sees me, he doesn't put the knife down. He looks at me like everything is normal and says my name.

I move over to Mom and she wraps her arms around me. She's shaking and crying. Her tears wash over me like a stream.

"Dad?" I think that maybe this is a joke or some grown-up game I don't know how to play.

"I'm moving to California," he says with a puff of air that smells like smoke and beer. "You want to come with me, right? You and maybe your sister here?" He thrusts the knife toward the corner where Kayla is looking up at me, terrified.

I know where California is because we had to memorize the map in geography class. It's about a million miles away from here. And I'm not sure what he means about "you and maybe your sister."

"Mom?" I'm hoping she's going to explain things. "Are we moving?"

Dad laughs and says, "No, not her. Just you and me. And maybe Kayla. What do you think, Gordie? Do you think she's going to grow up to be something or just end up like your mother?"

"I don't want to move," I whisper. I know it isn't what he wants me to say, but I can't help it. I start crying too. I can't imagine moving away from Mom and Kevin and even the twins. I'm just getting good at hockey and our team really has a chance this year. I don't know if they even play hockey in California.

"See?" he says, his words slurring as he stabs the knife over and over into the soft rail of the playpen. "See, son, this is why I need to get you out of here. You're worse than a little girl. We need to toughen you up or you're never going to make it in the NHL."

Hockey? This is about hockey? I'd gladly give up hockey if it means he would go away and leave us alone.

"No," I say, stamping my foot. "I'm not going. I'm not leaving Mom and Kevin."

Lightning fast, he puts the knife down, walks over, and backhands me across the face. My head hits the back of the couch. It stings even worse than when I've been checked really hard during a game. I start crying harder, not only from the pain but because, even though I don't like him much, he's my dad and I don't want him to want to hit me.

For all the times I've seen him wale on Kevin, he's never touched me. He's yelled and threatened, but he's saved his slaps and punches for my brother. I've spent a lot of time almost wishing he'd hit me instead. Kevin is my best friend and he protects me from the bigger kids at school. As much as I hate the pain, it's even harder to watch Kevin struggle to be strong.

"Oh, Kevin," he says in a mocking voice. "Your bastard brother has nothing to do with this."

I wipe my tears away on my shirt sleeve and wrap my arms around myself to keep from running up and hitting him. I hate him so much. Why couldn't he just leave and stay away? Why does he have to keep coming back and making Mom cry?

I've seen my parents fight before. Big, scary, loud fights with things getting smashed and broken. But never like this. Never with knives. And no one has ever talked about splitting us up.

Mom pulls me back up and hugs me. I can smell her fear, a mingling of perfume, smoke from his cigarette, and some sort of alcohol. She whispers into my hair, "Honey, take Kayla and go up to your room."

I look at her to make sure she's serious. Part of me thinks I should stay down here to try to protect her, but the rest of me wants to run like hell. She's pointing upstairs, saying, "Go on now," so I grab Kayla's hand and drag her up.

I walk backward up the stairs to make sure he doesn't move. All the time, his eyes cut through me like that knife would have.

I sit down on the floor and hold Kayla in my lap. I slap my headphones on and play the loudest music I can find. It's something of Kevin's—I don't even know what it is, but it's angry with lots of drums and bass, not like what I usually listen to.

I can feel my parents' fight rumbling through the floor.

Kayla falls asleep. I sit there for the rest of the night until I crash too, playing the angry music over and over and over on *repeat until it's burnt into my brain, blocking out whatever is happening downstairs.*

Here's what I don't do:

I don't call Kevin.

I don't call the police.

I don't climb out the window and go for help.

I sit there and listen to music while they terrorize and threaten each other.

I fall asleep while Mom decides that killing us and herself is a better idea than letting him have us. Have me. Because I was the one he wanted the whole the time.

They all died to save me from him. And all I did was listen to music.

FOURTEEN

I can't figure out if our room is too hot or too cold, too quiet or too loud. All I know is I'm still awake, and restless, and it looks like I'm going to stay that way.

I don't want to wake Kevin, so I wander down to the kitchen. I also don't want food, but I don't know where else to go. I just sit at the table and stare at the wall. It feels strange for Kevin to know about The Night Before—to have him know what I did and to know he doesn't hate me for it. It feels strange not to be afraid of that anymore.

When I told him, all he did was put his arm around my neck and pull me toward him. Then he smacked my head and told me I was an idiot for thinking he'd be upset with me for hiding upstairs while it was all going on. He reminded me that I'm supposed to trust him—I'd broken our pact. *Again.* And as punishment, I needed to wash his car. I think about going out to do that now, but it seems like a silly thing to do in the middle of the night.

I sit in the kitchen so long I lose track of time.

The light snaps on.

"Hey, kid." Jim opens the fridge and pours himself a glass of milk. He gestures with the carton, but I shake my head.

As he puts it back in the fridge, he says, "Heard you'd like to go camping on Saturday?"

I shrug. With everything else going on, I'd almost forgotten about it.

"With that boy on your hockey team, right?" Jim is smiling, but all of the blood in my body rushes to my cheeks. I think about telling him that Sarah is the real reason I want to go, and that I'm not really friends with Luke, and that I know we're both thinking it's the first time in five years I've considered doing something with a kid from school, but all I do is nod.

"It sounds like fun."

I never seriously thought I'd be going, so I didn't prepare myself for thinking about things like what I need to bring, how it all works, and how I'm going to hold it together around Sarah for two whole days without her thinking I'm some sort of loser.

"Sorry I wasn't there today," Jim says as he sits down across from me. "Sorry it had to happen this way at all."

"Yeah," is all I can say. Nothing would have been different if he'd been there. But it's kind of cool that he thinks he should have been.

He puts his milk down and opens a pack of Oreos. He twists the top off a cookie and eats the cream out. I thought only kids ate them that way. Funny how you can live with someone for five years and they can still do things that surprise you.

He dips the rest of his cookie in his milk and stares at me

for the longest time. "It's amazing, isn't it? The stupid things adults do to screw their kids up?"

His words surprise me even more than his cookie-eating. One, he usually doesn't talk to me much. And two, when he does, he always seems a little nervous, like I'm going to flip out or something. I don't remember a time when he's talked to me like he talks to Kevin.

I guess he doesn't expect a response, because he keeps talking. "Your mom..." He smiles like he's picturing her in his head. "Your mom was so pretty when I met her. She had eyes the same color as yours. That same green. She was sitting in the park with a book on her lap and this big old Labrador she had before you were born. I couldn't take my eyes off her."

This is uncharted territory, the equivalent of those parts of old maps that say "Here there be dragons." Jim has never talked to me about my mom like she was a person, or anything other than just my mom. Like Kevin, he never mentions her much at all.

I don't move. I don't even breathe. I'm afraid if I say anything or distract him he'll stop, and I want to hear this so, so, so badly.

"She always wanted to be a mother," he continues. "That was what she wanted more than anything. No one was happier when your brother was born. But for me—nothing against Kevin, I adore that kid—I just had other plans." He looks embarrassed, like he's suddenly remembering who he's talking to. "I'm sorry. Do you even want to hear this?"

I nod hard. I don't think I've ever wanted to hear anything as much as this.

"Anyhow, I wanted to travel, see the world. I was thinking about joining the Peace Corps or teaching in Japan. I already had plans to go backpacking through the Smokies when I found out Ava was pregnant. She said I should go, that she didn't want to hold me back. So I took off and left her to it, and she met your father. And then they had you."

Jim runs his finger around on the edge of his glass. I wait for the sound glass makes when you do that, but there's only silence. "He's a hard man, your father. I don't really understand him. At one point I tried…" He stops himself. "Never mind, that isn't your problem. But in the eyes of the law, he's still your dad, and maybe you should give him a chance."

I wrap my arms around myself, suddenly cold. I open my mouth, wondering if I can tell Jim about The Night Before, hoping that maybe he'll get it just like Kevin did. But I can't get a sound out. What chance would I ever have of staying with him if he knew what I was really like?

"Anyhow," he continues, "I'd taken this job to save up for a trip, but after everything that happened, well…" He crumbles a cookie in his hands. "You're a good kid, Gordie. A real good kid. Don't let anyone ever tell you differently."

My eyes well up. He wouldn't be saying that if he knew. Kevin promised he wouldn't tell, but what if he does? Would I get shipped off somewhere?

"I didn't do so well at keeping your mom safe from him. But I'm going to try to do better with you. I want you to know that."

It takes a minute for his words to hit. For them to really fight their way through the cobwebs of my brain and get to a place where they make sense. Once they're there, they do something to me, inside, that I don't understand.

Before I know it, I'm on the other side of the table with my arms around Jim, hugging him, and he's hugging me back.

It's so odd. It's like a dream I'm sure I'm going to wake up from. All this time, I thought Kevin would hate me if he ever knew what I'd done. I was wrong. All this time, I thought Jim didn't give a shit about me. Maybe I was wrong about that, too.

I guess everyone felt like they'd failed to keep Mom safe. You'd have thought that between Jim, and Kevin, and me, one of us would have gotten it right.

I manage to get "thanks" out of my throat, which feels sore from all the talking I've done today. I pull away just as Kevin comes down the stairs. His hair is standing straight up and he looks like he's only half awake.

"Did someone decide to have a party and not invite me?" he asks, yawning.

"Nope." Jim gets up with a sad smile on his face. "Just having a glass of milk and a chat with your brother here." He winks at me and heads up the stairs.

"What was that about?" Kevin asks, his voice still filled with sleep.

"Just … stuff." I push past him and head toward the stairs.

"Stuff? What stuff?" Kevin asks. He isn't used to being the one left out of things.

I don't answer. I've done enough talking for one day.

Besides, it feels kind of good to be the one who knows stuff for a change.

FIFTEEN

"You're going to wear a hole in the carpet," Kevin says. "Sit down. You've got ten minutes to go, anyhow."

He's right, but waiting for Luke to pick me up is making me edgy. I've packed and unpacked so many times, I don't even know what's in my bag. I wish Kevin could drive me to the campsite, but the idea of needing my brother to drop me off makes me feel like a little kid.

I look out the window. "What're you doing tonight?"

"Enjoying having the house to myself for a change," he answers as he flips channels on the TV. He only stops when he lands on a show where some chef is setting something covered in sugar on fire.

"Maybe I should stay here," I mumble. I can already picture the house going up in flames with the smoldering remains of some burnt dessert fossilized in the oven.

"I'll be here if you need to call or anything," Kevin says, completely missing my meaning.

"Call? On what?" Not like I have a cell phone or anything. I pull the dusty green curtains apart and check the driveway again. "Besides, what could possibly go wrong?"

Kevin opens his mouth but then closes it without saying anything, smiling like a cat gorging on a mouse.

"Yeah, fine." I glare at him.

"It'll be good. Really. Just ... don't feel pressured about anything."

"Pressured about what? What are you talking about?"

He puts the remote down and gives me a look like he wishes he hadn't said anything. "I mean, just don't feel like you have to do anything you don't want to."

His words stop me. For a minute I think he means fishing or something, but then I recognize the expression on his face and feel a wave of heat rise all the way through my body.

"Don't be a dick. Sarah and I are just friends. She's just being nice."

He laughs as I hear Luke's muscle car pull up. The bass from the car's stereo is cranked so high, it's beating through the floor.

I look back at Kevin. Suddenly, I feel like I'm being thrown into the deep end of a pool while my life ring is on dry land making incendiary desserts. Sweaty and shaky, I wish I could go back upstairs and hide under the covers.

"Seriously, I mean ... " My stomach feels like it's in my throat.

"Just go," he says, throwing my backpack at me. He puts his hand on my neck and pushes me toward the door, and not gently either.

So here's the thing. It isn't that I don't want a girlfriend, whatever "girlfriend" really means. It's more that Kevin is right. I'm not sure either of us really knows how to do it. And at the same time, I mean, come on. What girl is ever going to like me that way? Sarah probably just feels sorry for me, or, like Luke says, she's bored when she goes camping just with them.

I squeeze my eyes shut and try to block out all my questions. I'm pretty sure Luke must have filled her in about me by now and she's regretting ever asking me.

With a quick push from Kevin, I'm out the door. I steal a quick glance back at the house and propel myself toward the car. Luke has, thankfully, turned the music down. Not enough to have a conversation, but at least enough that it isn't making my teeth shake. Sarah leans over and opens one of the back doors for me, a look of anticipation on her face.

It was one thing to think about going camping with this strange girl and her perfect brother and his equally perfect girlfriend. It's another to be standing here, faced with the reality of actually doing it.

The way she's leaning, half out the door, Sarah's dark hair makes her look elfin, like something from a storybook. The bright blue of her top sparkles against her skin. For a minute I'm blinded by the color and the strange possibilities that seem to stretch in front of me where before there was just empty road.

Part of me wants to run back into the house and forget about this whole thing. But the other part of me, the part that's stupid enough to want to step off the widow's walk and fly, makes me slide in next to her. I feel like Alice down the rabbit hole, like I've stepped into someone else's life.

She's wearing her bird necklace again. And even though we did our presentation in class yesterday, me standing next to her while she explained my photos, that was just school. Sitting next to her now, pretending I belong here, is a different thing.

The campsite isn't that far away, only fifteen miles or so. But suddenly I'm glad for the loud music, because it means I can stay quiet and watch the unfamiliar scenery go by. I look out the window and listen to Luke and Jessie talking in the front seat. Luke is used to me being quiet, I guess. I'm not sure Jessie really cares whether I'm here or not.

A few times, I screw up my courage and catch Sarah's eye. Each time I do, she's watching me, smiling.

When we get to the site, Luke goes to the trunk and starts pulling stuff out. Poles. Tents. A gas stove. As I watch him, Sarah comes over and loops her arm through mine.

"I've learned the hard way to wait until he screws it up and asks me to help. Otherwise he just gets all upset and tells me I'm doing it wrong," she says.

The complicated pile of pieces that Luke and Jessie are standing over look like big metal pick-up sticks. I can't imagine how they'd fit together. "I'm not sure how much help I'd be anyhow," I admit.

"How are you at collecting firewood?" she asks, pointing toward a dense group of trees. She has a way of asking things that makes it sound like there are other questions beneath the surface. This time, it sounds like she's asking something about me letting her lead me into the woods, about her teaching me another new thing.

I nod. "Okay, I guess." My voice breaks as I answer the

question I think she's asking as well as the one she actually said out loud.

She calls out to Luke that we're going to gather wood. He waves us off and turns back to the puzzle pieces of the tents while Jessie reads him directions.

We're both quiet as we pick up branches and twigs. Sarah shows me how the bark of a white birch can be pulled off in strips to use as kindling.

I should be telling her a story or something. She invited me here, and now I should be entertaining her. But I'm not good at stories, and the ones that fill my head don't make for easy conversation, so I stay quiet.

When we get back, Luke and Jessie are finishing off the second tent and I get a little sick thinking about how this is all going to work. I mean, Luke is cool and all, but the thought of sharing a tent with him and having to talk about whatever normal guys talk about when they're holed up in a tent together is intimidating as hell.

Better—or worse, I'm not sure which—is when watching Luke and Jessie together makes me realize that I have to at least consider that the person I'll be sharing a tent with won't be Luke. But I try to force the thought out of my head the minute it announces itself, because I can feel the muscles in my hand tighten. I so badly don't want to lose it here.

After a round of hot dogs that I manage to swallow without choking, we spend a little time sitting around the fire. Luke catches me up on how we won our final game and the three of them talk about school. Then it starts to drizzle. Luke and Jessie huddle under a tarp in a way that makes it clear that their only plans for tent-sharing are with each other. Leaving Sarah and me together.

If it's possible to be excited and petrified at the same time, that's me. Luke and Jessie are already off together, and Sarah is waiting inside her tent. All I can do is stand in the cold rain and stare at the door.

For a strange moment I wonder if Mom had the same feeling I'm having before she drove her car into the water; like she was putting something into motion that couldn't be taken back. I know that once I go in there, everything is going to change and there won't be anything I can do about it.

My stomach is so tied up in knots that I think I'm going to be sick. I stand there weighing my options. Puking doesn't sound like much fun. I could tell her Kevin needs me to come home, but of course I don't have a phone so that would be stupid. Maybe I can make up some weird allergic reaction to birch trees.

Sarah's head pops out of the tent. "Why are you standing out there in the rain?"

"I'm…" I look up at the sky and a raindrop lands right in my eye. No matter how scared I am, even I know that being in a tent with a beautiful girl is better than standing outside getting soaked. So I take a deep breath and head in.

———

Rain is bouncing off the outside of the tent. It sounds like Ping-Pong balls. I guess you aren't supposed to want rain when you're camping, but the sound is relaxing and once I get inside, I realize it's nice to sit next to Sarah in the tent.

We crank up the heater, spread out our sleeping bags, open a bag of chips and some cans of pop, and play Scrabble. She's good, but I'm better, which seems to surprise her and make her happy at the same time.

I'm not spinning, but I'm not sure where the time goes, either. Again, I notice that being with her is easy in a way I haven't felt before. Kevin knows almost everything there is to know about me, which is great and all, but I'm kind of a clean slate with Sarah. I guess she didn't ask Luke about me after all. She doesn't seem to expect me to screw up, and so I haven't. Not yet anyway.

After the games, I lie back on the crinkly fabric of the sleeping bag and watch the shadows of the trees outside play on the sides of the tent. Far off, I can hear Luke and Jessie laughing. I listen to the crickets and birds and sounds from animals I can't recognize. It would be nice to capture the noises of the campground and the smell of wood smoke, and the lilac scent that seems to follow Sarah like it wants to be as close to her as possible.

She stretches out on her own bag, next to mine. Like most of the clothes I've seen her in, her bag is black; it sits on top of the tent floor looking like a giant hole. She's lying stomach-down on it, propped up on her arms, which are freckled like some connect-the-dots game, and I have to link my fingers together to keep from reaching out and doing just that.

"I'm glad you were able to come," she says.

"Me too." Then I ask something I've wondered about, because it isn't like I have any real experience with things like a normal family or rules. "Do your parents always let you do stuff like this without them?"

She looks toward the door of the tent and everything in her seems to stiffen. "Yeah. Well." Then she flips over and sits up, her legs crossed in front of her. "It's all about Luke." She looks down and plays with the hem of her jeans.

"Luke?" Now I sit up too.

"They never say no to him. Haven't you noticed that my perfect brother pretty much gets to do whatever he wants?"

I think about Luke and his movie star looks, and his trophies, and Jessie on his arm. He's like the star other planets rotate around. I guess it would be different to be his brother than to be Kevin's, since Kevin is always looking out for me and giving stuff up to make sure he's around.

"I hadn't thought about it," I admit.

"There's no reason you should. But it gets old. It's like I'm lost in the shadows when Luke's around. On the other hand..." She shrugs. "Sometimes it's good not to be noticed."

"Sorry," I say, and I am. I get what she's saying. I spend so much time trying to fade into the woodwork and not be noticed, but everyone is always watching me, waiting for me to fall apart. It's strange to hear someone talk about things being reversed for them.

"It's fine," she says. "I mean, really, there are a million ways it could be worse. It's not like I'm immune to him either. I'd like him even if he weren't my brother. And I get to tag along when he gets it into his head to do something like this."

She pauses. One of those big pauses that lets you know that whatever comes next is important.

"I ran away from boarding school," she says in a voice that's trying to be casual. But the way she looks at the tent door gives her away.

"Boarding school?" The words come out of my mouth as a hundred other things fall into place in my brain.

She smiles and kicks my foot. "Yeah. You mean, you didn't wonder why I was never around before this semester?"

"Yeah, but..." I can tell I'm blushing again by the fact that my cheeks feel like they're on fire. I lean my chin into my hands, hoping to hide most of it. "I thought I just missed seeing you or something."

Sarah bursts out laughing and shakes her head. "Right. No, I used to go to Fairlane."

Oh.

"Don't look at me like that," she says, but she's still smiling so I know she isn't really upset with me. At least I hope she isn't. Fairlane is a school for smart kids who get into trouble a lot. Kevin and I could have ended up there if not for the really expensive tuition, but I can't imagine what would have landed Sarah there.

"So, aren't you going to ask?" She tilts her head to the side like a bird, or like a dog who knows you're talking to it.

"No." I would never ask someone to share their secrets. "You can tell me if you want, though."

She laughs again, then leans over and takes the frayed cuff of my shirt in her hand, running her thumb over the loose blue threads. I don't get how her touching my shirt could make me feel like she's really touching me, but it does. I should have worn something that wasn't messed up from a spin, I should have thought—

"I'm the bad seed," she says. I can't tell if she's kidding or not, but then she continues. "Okay, not totally. But my mom doesn't get me. I used to take all these cool pictures of things I guess I wasn't supposed to. You know, like funerals and stuff. And then I took a photo of my mom with this guy and sent it to my dad."

I can feel my eyes open so wide, I wonder if my eyeballs are going to fall out.

"Anyhow..." She moves her hand down to enclose mine. I manage to stop myself from gasping by holding my breath, but something inside me is twisting around like a pinwheel. As much as I want to know what she's about to say, it's a struggle to keep myself focused on her words while her hand is so hot on my skin. "I guess things weren't what they looked like. But basically, I just got sick of being ignored all the time, so I used to do a lot of stupid stuff."

I want so badly to ask what kind of stupid stuff. I mean, stupid like setting fires, or shoplifting, or stupid like...? I don't know. I always try to follow all the rules, try not to get noticed unless it's on the ice.

"So, I decided that instead of being locked up in Fairlane or being ignored at home, I was going to get out. When I was home for winter break, I took my mom's debit card. I got enough money out of the bank to buy a train ticket to Boston."

There's an ominous crack of thunder from outside that stops her before she continues. I don't say anything. I don't want her to stop talking, but I'm in awe. I can't imagine really leaving and being on my own. I can't believe she'd seriously try it.

"My aunt lives in Boston. She never had kids and I've always been close to her. I thought maybe I'd be better off there."

"What happened?" I ask, trying to find my voice.

"My aunt was majorly upset with me when I called her from the station. But she calmed down pretty quick once she called my mom and found out that my parents hadn't even noticed I was gone. They figured I was with my friend Laura or something and never bothered to check. So, when my aunt stopped yelling at my mom, she drove me back to the train and I came home. They pulled me out of school for a couple months to keep an eye on me, which is a major joke because they don't. I was grounded for forever and had to see a shrink. Things were better for a couple of weeks, but..." She shrugs. "Business as usual."

She looks kind of sad as she takes her hand away from me and plays with her necklace. I try to think of something to say to make her feel better, but I don't know what that would be. And then she asks her own question. "So how come you live with Kevin's dad?"

My stomach sinks a little. It's a minute before I can answer her and when I do, my voice quivers. "Do you really not know about me?"

She looks genuinely puzzled. I'm relieved that she really doesn't know, that she isn't just screwing with me. The problem is, I don't know if I want her to know. The only options I have are to spill it all or lie, and I'm a horrible liar.

I twist the leather band on my wrist and close my eyes, hoping she'll still be my friend afterward. As I try to figure out where to start, I realize I've never had to tell anyone. Not one single person. Everyone knew about That Day. The teachers and counselors all knew what happened, from the cops. The kids at school all knew, from their parents or older brothers and sisters or the Internet.

Maybe now there are some kids at school who don't know. Maybe some think I was born this way, or that I'm just a kid who's smart in class and good at hockey and screwed up in every other way imaginable for no good reason.

But not once, in five years, have I met someone who I was *sure* didn't know my past. Not once have I met someone who I almost wanted to tell.

I open my eyes and focus on a spot just behind her, over her shoulder. I start slowly. "Our mom is dead," I say.

It's the tip of the iceberg. It answers her question. Maybe she won't even want to know more.

Her face crunches up in the way that people's do when they find out you're a kid with a dead parent. Her mouth forms an O and then she asks, "What about your dad?"

I feel my lungs seize up, suddenly empty of air. "He's…"

I have no idea what to say. I blink my eyes, trying not to spin off. I don't want to talk about him. I just need to get a word out so that the conversation goes somewhere else, but I can't.

I must spin a little, though, because she looks at me like she's been waiting a while. She puts her hand on my arm and says, "It's okay. You don't have to talk about it."

Somehow, her saying that makes me *want* to tell her. I look into her dark, patient eyes and feel my body remembering how to breathe. I twist the band again. It forms a figure eight and I let it snap back hard against my skin. I lie down and look at the top of the tent, at the way that it buckles slightly when the water hits it.

"I don't think my parents liked each other much," I start. "And my dad...I don't think he liked anybody. My mom was kind of sick sometimes, and he was really mean to her." I don't talk about what he used to do to Kevin, and I'm not really sure that anything I'm saying makes any sense to her, but I just keep going because I'm afraid if I stop, I won't be able to start again.

I close my eyes and tell her about the kids. I tell her about That Day.

I don't tell her about The Night Before, because even though Kevin isn't upset, I don't really believe anyone else would get it.

She doesn't say a word. Not even when I pause and get stuck. She just waits. Not in a bad, pressing way. Just like she's willing to wait for however long I need her to.

And when I'm done, I feel a little lighter. I don't feel like I'm spinning off anywhere, I feel good. Almost...normal.

When I open my eyes, instead of talking about it, instead of asking more questions, she lies back down, reaching over and brushing my bangs out of my eyes. "I like your hair," she says. "It's really soft."

She leaves her cool fingers on my forehead. Without thinking, I roll my head so that more of her hand is on me. It's like she's a magnet or something. I'm not sure I can move, or that I want to. I just want her to keep her hand there so badly that I'd cry if I didn't mind her knowing how messed up I am.

She moves her arm down and puts it around my waist,

which is even nicer. Then she puts her head on my shoulder. Its weight is a comfortable pressure pinning me here. I can feel her breath on the side of my neck. "I'm sorry, Gordie. I didn't know."

I don't know what to do with my hands. She's lying against my left arm and I'm afraid to move it because I don't want to hit her breast or anything. My right thumb is twitching like crazy and I just try to take long, deep breaths, but my heart is racing like I'm in goal and I've got pucks coming at me from all directions.

I feel a little guilty for not telling her about the spins, or about what's going on now with my father. It all threatens to spill out of me in one compulsive burst, but I bite the inside of my cheek and try to focus on her weight on me. I'm not keeping anything from her, I tell myself; I just don't want to talk about it now.

I don't know how to respond to her comment, either. I mean, I can say, "It's okay," but that's a blatant lie. I could say nothing, but that's a lie in its own way too. So instead of talking, I reach my hand up and take hers. Her skin is so soft. Touching her feels so good I'm sure it's something I'm going to get in trouble for.

"I'm sorry for before. For whining about my stupid problems with my parents," she says.

"Why?" I ask. Then it hits me. "No, it's fine. I just ... "

"You must think I'm a total spoiled brat."

"No way." I mean it. I know that what happened to me isn't normal. Most parents don't try to kill their kids.

We stay like that for a while before she asks if I want to go for a walk.

I listen to the rain, which is falling even heavier now. "You know it's rainy, right?"

"Yeah," she says. "I love the rain."

I love the rain too, when I'm inside and watching it fall or listening to it. I'm not much for being out in it. I've had enough wet to last a lifetime.

But I let her pull me up and lead me outside.

Water is pooling in the dirt, reflecting the dusky campground light. Drops are falling into Sarah's straight dark hair and getting stuck there like tiny crystal balls.

She giggles as she leads us away from Luke and Jessie's tent, toward a canopy of trees. We walk for a few minutes and I try to ignore how wet I'm getting. I think of sunny days, and warm blankets, and her hand in mine.

We reach a path and have to walk single file. Ahead of me, Sarah's too-light-for-March jacket is heavy with rain. I try not to stare at her shape, but have to look away and think about hockey, and school, and Kevin's cooking. Anything other than how the wet fabric is clinging to her and how badly I want to be where it is.

She leads us to a huge willow tree. Its branches are knit together like a giant umbrella that's keeping the rain out.

"Wow." I stare up through the branches and try to wipe my wet face with my equally wet sleeve.

"I know, right?" Her face is tilted up, looking at the top of the tree and she's smiling like it's the most beautiful thing she's ever seen.

I'm glad it's a warmish night, but I'm shivering. I don't know if it's from the water or her. I try to stop myself, but she notices and rubs my wet arms with her hands.

"You're shaking. We should have grabbed towels."

I'm trembling so hard I don't know if I can stop, but I'm not sure I really care.

"We should go back before you freeze." She starts to take my hand again, but I stop her.

"No, Sarah, wait." I plant my feet and stand my ground, clenching my teeth to stop them from chattering. "I don't want to go back."

She moves so close to me I can feel the heat coming off her body. One side of her mouth lifts in a smile. It's the kind of smile I've seen on other girls before. I've seen Jessie look at Luke with a smile like that.

"So what *do* you want?" she teases.

What do I want? I want to wrap myself up in her arms until I stop shaking. I want to stay in this moment and not spin off somewhere. I want to say something clever like they'd say in a movie, but I'm too aware that I'm just an inexperienced screwed-up kid standing here, dripping with rain and shaking under an old willow tree. I look away, hoping she doesn't see how embarrassed I am.

"Don't be scared," she says, so quietly I'm not really sure she's said it out loud.

I think about protesting and telling tell her I'm not scared, but that's a lie. I'm terrified. But it's a different kind of fear from seeing my father or when I think of Kevin leaving. I'm scared because I don't know what I'm doing, or even what I'm supposed to do. I don't know what she wants or how I'd give it to her even if I did know. I don't know how to flirt back and be confident and casual.

I force myself to let go of her hand and walk over to the trunk of the tree and then to the other side of it, trying to get just a minute's worth of space. I lean back and feel my chest tighten. I don't want to lose it here. Not in front of her. Not now.

I sink down onto my heels and bend my head forward, trying to slow my breathing while I snap that damned band so hard I'm sure I'm going to have a welt.

And then I feel her hand on my head and everything in me stops. She leans down so that she's next to me, our shoes lined up next to each other.

"It's okay, Gordie. I'm just playing."

"It isn't..." I manage to squeak out before her hand works its way through my hair. It feels so good it makes me dizzy. I close my eyes and know that if I let go, even a little, I'll lose myself to the rhythm of her fingers.

"Then what is it?" she asks. Her voice sounds really far away, like a part of me has already floated off and landed somewhere else.

I don't know the right words to try to explain what I'm feeling; this weird mix of fear and longing. I can't imagine a scenario where she'd want anything to do with me, much less... I swallow all the words I don't know how to say and watch the rain hitting the trees and the ground, and everything that isn't us here under this safe and protected tree.

Sarah smiles and stands, pulling me up with her. Before I

know it, she's in front of me, leaning in, and her lips are pressing against mine. Everything seems to slow down like it does during a spin. I don't know how long we kiss for. Only that it could never last long enough.

"There. That wasn't so scary, was it?" she asks.

I don't say it, but right now, it's hard to believe that anything could ever scare me again.

SIXTEEN

We're both quiet as we head back to the tent, but it's a good kind of quiet. A comfortable kind of quiet.

It's still raining, but I don't care anymore. I don't feel cold and I don't feel wet; all I feel is her hand in mine. It's like the only part of me that has any feeling is the part that's touching her.

When we're back in the tent, she reaches over to turn on the space heater again and gestures at my pack. "I hope you have something warm and dry in there."

Do I? There must be other clothes in there, but I don't know how I'd get into them with her right there. I change clothes in front of guys in the locker room all the time, but this is different. So different.

Still, I unzip the pack and pull out a pair of sweats and a hoodie. I congratulate myself on achieving this little bit of practicality, but it's equally possible that Kevin threw them in.

Rather than wrestle with the logistics of getting out of clothes and into others, I start to put the hoodie over my damp shirt.

"Are you trying to give yourself pneumonia? Take your wet clothes off and change."

Sarah is standing directly in front of me, so that's not going to happen. "You don't actually get sick from wearing wet clothes, you know," I say through my chattering teeth, stalling for time.

She laughs and then says, "Well, even if it doesn't make you sick, it won't make you comfortable. But if you're going to insist on being shy, I'll turn my back and change over here."

I watch as she pulls a set of hot-pink flannel pajamas with little Scottie dogs out of her bag. I've never seen her wear anything with so much color, and it makes me smile.

When she turns her back to me, her bird necklace swings around and catches my eyes, not letting go. I'm still staring at it as I slowly pull my shirt off. The fabric sticks to my skin like my eyes are stuck on her. Like a magician, she wraps a huge towel around herself and then I see her shirt drop, followed by her jeans and a bra.

Still somehow wrapped in the towel, she slides into the dry flannel.

I haven't moved. I'm still standing there, shirtless, when she turns back around. For a minute I'm embarrassed that she caught me watching her and I expect her to get mad, but she doesn't. Instead she picks up the other towel and starts drying my chest off. It's a crazy feeling, almost like flying. I stay there like an idiot, shivering and knowing for sure it isn't from the cold this time.

When she looks down at my wet jeans, it takes every single bit of control I have to force my hand up to take the towel from her and form the words, "I got it."

She laughs and turns away again, pretending to sort through her backpack. "Well, if you're sure."

I scramble out of my jeans and into my sweats. My whole body feels like it's about to explode. I go over to the space heater and sit down, holding my shaking hands up to the hot air.

"What do you think Luke and Jessie are doing?" she asks as she sits next to me.

I look at her and raise an eyebrow. I have a good idea of what they're doing, but I'm not going to talk about it. I can't even think about it without turning red, which I'm sure I'm already doing. I just focus on rubbing my hands together.

"I'm glad you're here," she says.

I stop rubbing and drop my hands to my lap and look at her. "Me too," I say, but I know there's no way I can capture what I'm feeling in words. "I wish we could stay up all night." In my head, another list forms, a list of other things I wish but don't have the courage to say, much less do.

"We could try."

"I want to," I say. I think about spending all night next to her. Talking or not. Kissing like we did under the tree. But I'm so tired and more than a little freaked out about what will happen in the dark hours that stretch ahead. "I haven't been sleeping well," I add.

She takes my hand and links my fingers with hers. It does a better job of warming me than the heater.

"Why?" she asks.

I know I could say I'm worried about school or something, but I don't want to lie to her and I rarely worry about school. I don't want to tell her the truth either, but I give her a little of it. "I have...kind of nightmares...about..."

I don't finish, and I see in her eyes that I don't have to. "I know it's stupid," I add. "I just wanted to warn you." I'm pretty sure I've said too much and she's going to decide that I'm some stupid broken kid who isn't worth her time.

She squeezes my hand. "It isn't stupid at all."

I follow her lead as she straightens out her sleeping bag, and then we each climb into our own.

"Sarah..." I know I have to ask the question, but I don't want to sound like an idiot.

She rolls on her side, putting her arm around me and her head on my shoulder. "Hmmm..." she murmurs into my neck.

"There are a million people you could have invited. Why me?" I blurt out.

She looks at me with the same expression Kevin gives me when I've said something he thinks is crazy.

"I've invited Laura a few times, but camping isn't her thing, and, honestly, I don't know. You're just unlike anyone I've ever met. I mean, you're so good at hockey and really smart in class, but..."

The sleeping bag bunches in my hand as it contracts, and I finish her sentence for her. "But I'm a freak?"

She picks up her pillow and hits me with it.

"No. It's just..."

"Why?" I close my eyes and try not to pay attention to the list that's running through my head. The one that says I'm just some charity case, or that Luke is forcing her, or...

She squeezes my arm. "Gordie."

I wait for her to go on, but she doesn't. So I open my eyes.

"You're different. You're interesting. You're so quiet, it's like you've got a whole other life going on in your head. All last summer, I wanted to talk to you." Even in the darkness, I swear I see her cheeks flush. "And you're cute."

"I am?"

She nods. "Yeah. And you pay attention to me. I mean, you really listen to me like what I'm saying matters."

"It does," I say, and she smiles. I can see her eyes sparkle. "It really does." I want her to believe me so, so, so badly, and my heart is beating even more unevenly than it did when we were kissing earlier. "It does."

She laughs and then I do too, even as I realize that it works both ways. She pays attention to me, too, and not just because she's waiting for me to fall apart.

"I like that you make me laugh," I say.

She leans back down and takes up her position against me again. "I like that I make you laugh, too."

As amazing as it was to kiss her, there's something strange, and safe, and totally wonderful about lying next to her with the weight of her arm across me. It's like she's holding me down, keeping me here. Keeping me from flying off someplace else.

At the same time, I can feel her heart beating against my side and it's both the most dizzying and the most comforting thing I can imagine. I don't remember the last time anyone held me close like this, and I don't want to waste a minute of it.

I try to stay awake. I do math in my head. I count the raindrops as they fall. I run my hand in ever more complicated patterns along Sarah's arm, recreating hockey plays, spelling out bits of remembered poetry.

I think this feeling might be something that other people get all the time. But then I'm sure I'm wrong. How could anyone function if they felt like this? How do they get up and go to school and to work? How do they walk away?

I watch the designs that the blowing branches make against the side of the tent. Sarah's breath is warm and even on my neck, making the hair on my arms stand straight up, running shiver after shiver through me until I think I might burst from sheer happiness.

I realize I have no words for what I'm feeling. *Pain, loneliness, fear*; those I know. Those I can name from miles away. I can see them coming like long-lost friends in the dark. But not this. I grasp at the words parading through my head. *Safety. Warmth. Protection. Want. Need.* None of them even come close.

I take a deep breath, inhaling that lilac smell that's no longer the scent of a flower but the scent of a girl. I hold my breath until I think my lungs will explode with it. Until Sarah props herself up on her arms, laughing.

"I thought you were so tired." Her eyes are bright despite their obvious sleepiness.

"I am," I say. "I just..." I turn my head so she can't see me blushing even though the darkness of the tent is darker than anyplace I've ever been, even darker than the river, where daylight danced across the top of the water, drawing me toward it.

She props herself up on my chest and even in this nonlight I can see the flirtatious glint back in her eyes.

"You just what?" she asks expectantly.

I want to know how to do this. How to flirt back. But it isn't something I can ask her to teach me so I bite the inside of my cheek and stay silent, my mind a snarl of thoughts and emotions I don't know what to do with.

She reaches up and brushes my hair back off my forehead. I'm glad I'm lying down, because I'm pretty sure I wouldn't be able to stay upright with her touching me like that.

"Talk to me," she whispers. "Talking is always less scary in the dark."

She's right; everything feels safe here, but that doesn't mean that I want to spend our time talking. I swallow down the lump in my throat and try to figure out what's most pressing: my hungry need to kiss her again, or all those things that remain hidden that I don't want to—but think I should— share.

"I love watching you in goal," she says. "I've never seen anyone so focused."

"Yeah," I try to joke. "I'm good at focus."

She rewards me with a giggle. "Is that what you want to do for real? Play hockey?"

"No, I don't think so," I admit, but it's the first time I've ever said that out loud. "He did, though. My father. Until he got kicked off his college team for hurting someone."

I haven't thought about that in a long time. All the stories I heard about him checking one of his own players during practice. About the other kid ending up paralyzed.

I try really hard to stop thinking about it and to think

about nothing but her hand running through my hair, over and over and over until I can't take it anymore.

"Sarah." Her name escapes my lips with a breath, but without any plan on my part. I think she knows that, because before I have to think about saying anything she's leaning down and we're kissing again.

My hands reach up, clenching gently around the fabric of her top, pulling her to me with an urgency like wings battling against a breeze, pushing forward, afraid to stop, afraid to fall.

For the first time I can remember, I feel solid and so tethered to *now* that I almost believe the last five years were nothing more than a bad dream.

SEVENTEEN

"Morning, sunshine," Sarah whispers, kissing me quickly. I reach up and touch my tingling lips. I don't even think about the fact that she's watching me, and for some reason it makes her laugh. "Sleep well?"

"Yeah, really well," I say, realizing that for once it's completely true. We both pull ourselves up so that we're sitting in our bags.

"Good. I wish we could stay out here for the day, but Jessie has some cheerleading thing." She says "cheerleading" like some people might say "leper." "Man, I can't wait until I can drive."

My stomach twists when she talks about leaving. I feel like all the good stuff is going to stay in the woods without us. I'm worried she'll think back and realize I really am a nutcase and won't want anything to do with me tomorrow in school. I mean, the *Moby Dick* project is done, so we don't have to work together in class. And now camping is over and she kind of had to let me come after she'd already invited me, so...

My hand starts spasming at my side and my thoughts race until I'm convinced that this is the last good minute I'll ever have.

"Gordie." Sarah squeezes my arm. "Are you okay?"

"Yeah, I'm fine," I lie. I jam my hand under my leg.

"Bull." She tugs on my arm and pulls my hand out from underneath me. She wraps her own hand around it, but it flops like a dying fish. I wish I could control it.

"Is this from what happened?" she asks.

It's funny—most people don't. They might look at me like I'm nuts or like I have something they can catch, but they don't ask. Adults never ask. Only little kids usually have the guts to try to find out the answers to things that puzzle them.

I pull my hand back and rub it self-consciously. Even though I can feel the jolts and see it jumping, my hand doesn't really feel like a part of me. "Yeah, I guess," I say. "That's when it started, anyhow."

My hand slides automatically back under my leg, but she shakes her head. "Stop. You don't need to hide it."

I let her words straighten themselves out in my head. I want to ask her if she means it, and if she can teach me how not to hide. Everything I've done over the past five years has been about trying to bury all the bruised things that make me different.

She holds my eyes with such intensity that I have to fight not to look away. I take a deep breath. When I pull my hand back out and cradle it in my lap, we both sit watching it until the spasms ease.

Then she puts something into my hand. Her necklace.

"I've seen you looking at this. It's a picture I took last year. I had it developed in black-and-white and then I colored it with pencils."

My hand clenches around it. "It's beautiful," I tell her, then move to give it back.

"You can keep it."

"What?" I don't think anyone has ever given me a gift like this. Something they made. Something that wasn't for my birthday or Christmas. Only Sarah.

She takes it from me and slips the long chain over my head. I smile at her.

The smile she gives me back, the one I want to fall into and imprint onto my screwed-up brain, is like sunlight glistening on water.

———————

I feel like I've landed on an alien planet when I open the front door to the house. Everything's the same as it was yesterday morning when I left, but it's like I'm looking at it through those glasses that make things stretched or kaleidoscopic.

Jim must be out, and Kevin is probably upstairs, and the inside of my head is uncomfortably quiet. I stand and stare at the phone, wishing I could pick it up and have Sarah's voice fill all the empty spaces.

I know she isn't home yet because they've just pulled out of the driveway, but I already miss her so much I can feel it inside, in some organ I didn't know I had.

I wrap my hand around the bird charm.

I'm still standing like that when Kevin comes downstairs. "You didn't get eaten by a bear?"

I hear his words but don't really make any sense of them. "What?"

Kevin smirks. "Never mind. So how was it?" He throws

himself on the couch, taking up all the room so I have to go and sit in Jim's lounge chair.

"Good," I say. "It was good."

Kevin stares at me. I know he's expecting more. I always tell him everything, but I don't know how to put any of the last twenty-four hours into words. How do I tell my brother how safe it felt to sleep with Sarah's arm across me and how my lips are still buzzing from her kiss? How do I tell him how empty my hand feels without her squeezing it, like she did the whole way home in the car?

I can't explain to him why I feel like I can trust her, and how each kiss felt like a bandage to a wound somewhere deep inside me.

Kevin sits up and wraps his arms around his legs and doesn't even blink. I end up having to look away because it feels like his eyes are stapling me to the back of the chair.

"And?" he asks sharply.

I get up and start rifling through my bag. "It rained," I say as I pull out my damp shirt and jeans, followed by underwear and socks and a certain amount of grass and clumped-up mud.

"Yeah," he says. "It did here too."

I ignore the suspicion in his voice and walk through the kitchen to stuff my clothes in the washer. Just seeing them makes me think of the towel in Sarah's hand, the cloth running over my chest. I shiver. It feels really strange not to be with her. I don't understand that. I've only really been aware of her for two weeks, but I'm not sure I remember how it felt to not know her.

When I turn back around, Kevin is standing there watching me, looking concerned.

"Ice? Talk to me."

I turn one of the chairs and lean a leg on it. I don't know what to say. I've never wanted to avoid talking to him before. But I feel like if I tell him everything that happened it won't be ours anymore. Sarah's and mine. My chest feel like it's going to burst open, full of the concept of "ours."

"What did you do when it was raining?" he asks.

"We played Scrabble," I say honestly. "And we took a walk."

"In the rain?" he asks, shaking his head. He knows how unlikely it would be for me to do that normally.

"Yeah. We ended up under this huge tree. It had branches like an umbrella," I tell him, but it only brings words into my mouth that I can't let escape my lips, so I force them together to keep everything private inside.

As I turn, I feel the bird charm swipe across my chest. He leans over and inspects it, then lets it fall back hard.

"What's that?"

I shrug out of his grip and shove the charm into my shirt. "It was a present, and I'm fine. Really. I went camping. I didn't jump off the Empire State Building." Kevin's face goes pale. "I didn't jump off of anything," I say, hoping it will put his mind at rest. But I know Kevin better than that, so it's no surprise when he doesn't stop.

"So, you and Sarah?"

"I don't have to tell you everything," I snap. And then, because the words sound so strange coming out of my mouth and because Kevin's face falls in a way I've never caused it to fall before, I apologize. "Sorry, I didn't mean . . ."

"No, that's fine." Kevin's voice teeters between hurt and

anger, like it did when we were kids and my father would make some unreasonable demand or insist he give up something that really mattered to him. "You're right. You don't have to tell me anything at all."

His words are razor-sharp and I can feel each one stab into my skin. I'm overcome with waves of guilt and I know I need to catch him before he's out the door.

"Wait."

He turns around and his expression is hard and defensive. "It's fine. Really. I'm glad you had a good time."

I need to toss him something to keep him from walking out. I need to give up something of value, because he'll see through my words and know if what I'm telling him is just something to try to make him stay.

"She kissed me," I force out. "I mean … we kissed."

His harsh expression cracks slowly into a smile and he nods his head slightly. "Is that all?"

I can feel the blood rushing to my face. "Yes. God … "

Kevin's shoulders fall and he starts laughing. I look away in embarrassment and because guilt is still sitting like a rock in my stomach.

"Did you like it?"

Before I can think about it, I get caught up in the way we usually are, Kevin and me. And I tell him everything. When I'm done I feel a little empty, like the words took something with them when they left my mouth. But it's okay. Kevin and I are okay. And that's all I've ever needed.

EIGHTEEN

Monday morning hits me like a train. My muscles ache, and I have months before summer hockey camp starts and I can really work them out. I decide to hit the public rink after school, and that's all I can think about until I get to English and Sarah drops a little paper swan onto my desk.

I twist to look back at her. She smiles and makes a motion like she wants me to unfold the swan. I don't really want to. It's pretty intricate and very cool, made of paper the blue-green of the ocean with little flecks of silver running through it.

I look back at her again to make sure she really wants me to ruin her work.

But when she nods again, I do it.

Inside the swan, looking like it was swallowed, is a note: *Meet me at my locker after last period. I have to talk to you.*

I rationally know that most people wouldn't deliver bad news in a paper swan. At the same time, in my experience, no one ever says they need to see you in advance unless it's about something that's going to suck.

I look back at her again, and I'm pretty sure she can see my fear because she gives me a big smile and rolls her eyes.

Her smile should put me at ease, but it doesn't. I'm not even sure what I'm afraid of, but I can't concentrate on Mr. Brook's pop quiz even though I know all the answers. When I try to write them down, the letters come out all wrong and I have to keep scratching things out.

Mr. Brooks stops next to my desk before sitting on the edge and putting his hand over mine.

I look down. I hadn't noticed that I was clicking my pen.

"Do you need to take a break?" he asks.

I look back at Sarah, who's busy writing down her answers.

"I . . ." I start, and then my voice breaks in two and I clamp my mouth shut to avoid embarrassing myself.

"It's okay, you can make the test up tomorrow," Mr. Brooks whispers.

I wish I could crawl under my desk. I want to say "no" and stay sitting here, but if I can't control it, everyone is just going to be watching me, waiting for me to lose it in class. It's better, I've learned, to just get up and hope they go back to their own papers.

I feel like I'm sleepwalking as I pick up my books and cram them into my bag.

Mr. Brooks motions me to follow him to the back of the room, which is like a million miles from everyone else. This room is actually three classrooms in one separated by dividers that can be opened or closed. I know whatever we say back here won't be overheard by anyone else and Mr. Brooks is awesome. But I'd rather not have the conversation I know is coming.

He sits on the corner of another desk, his leg waving back and forth like a pendulum and his arms crossed.

"So, what's going on?" he asks.

"Nothing," I say, slumping down in a chair across from him.

He makes a harrumph sound and clears his throat. "Let's try this again. What's really going on, Gordie?"

So here's the thing. I used to have this fantasy that Mr. Brooks might adopt me. I know it's crazy. I mean, why would he ever want me for a son? But he's like this guy who seems to have all the answers to everything and he never seems to get pissed off, either.

So, for a second, I think about how cool he is in his Club Metro T-shirt and his purple sneakers. And how maybe, just maybe, if I told him about going camping with Sarah, and her paper-swan note, he might be able to make sense of it all for me. He might be able to tell me if I've done something wrong.

Then I glance back at the rest of the class. I'm sure that none of them are so lame they have to ask a teacher what to do when a girl says she wants to see them after school.

I sigh and pull at the loose fringes of my sleeve. "There's just some stuff…" I hope if I'm vague enough I can draw things out until the bell rings.

"Stuff?" he prods.

I look out the window and imagine something flying in and whisking me away to a place where everyone will stop asking me questions. I reach up to touch the bird charm under my shirt, but then drop my hand. I don't want to have to explain that to him, too.

But he's waiting, and it's Mr. Brooks. I don't want to be a

dick so I sort through all the issues in my brain to see what I can tell him that doesn't involve Sarah.

"My father," I say. I didn't even know that's what was on my mind until the words came out.

"Jim Allen?" His brow scrunches up and I shake my head. Mr. Brooks knows the whole crappy story and I have to be careful or he's going to feel like he has to *do* something, and too many things are already changing.

"Your real father?"

I hate that Jim, who's given me a home for the last five years, who's Kevin's "real" father just because he slept with Mom first, is considered my fake dad or something. While the person I hate most in the world is given credit when he's really to blame for everything.

Now that I've said the words, though, I feel all clenched up and shaky.

"He wants…" I twist and twist the band on my wrist, trying to force myself to push a whole damned sentence out of my mouth. "I can't…"

Mr. Brooks puts a hand on my shoulder and squeezes. "It's okay. Do you want me to get you an appointment with Mr. Williams? Just to have a chat?"

"No," I blurt out, loudly enough that a third of the class turns around to stare. I push my lips together and turn away because I don't want to know if Sarah is one of them.

Mr. Williams is the same stupid school counselor I saw before. He's just going to thrust his referral pad at me to go see someone who can give me a prescription. Besides, I hate, hate, hate that everyone thinks I need to see a shrink.

"Sorry." I try to keep my voice steady and quiet. "I'll be fine. Really."

It's clear that Mr. Brooks doesn't believe me, which kind of bugs me even though I don't blame him.

"Or you could talk to me," he offers.

I used to talk to him all the time, but I was just a kid then. Everything is so different now. Besides, I don't really know what to say and I've learned that saying nothing is way better than sounding like an idiot.

There's five minutes left of class. That's five minutes before I can see Sarah and find out if I did something stupid yesterday or if maybe she regrets kissing me.

"Thanks. Maybe," I say, even though he knows it means I won't. I just shuffle around and wait for the bell, which feels like it's never going to ring.

"Well, you know where to find me."

"Yeah."

"Okay, just..." He pauses. "Come ready to take your quiz tomorrow."

It's clear he wants to say something different, but the bell goes off and I fly out the door into the hall and stand, bouncing up and down on the balls of my feet, trying to keep myself from pacing while I wait for Sarah.

She comes out, already looking for me. "Hey, are you okay?"

She looks worried. I want, more than anything, to lean over and kiss her. But we aren't camping anymore. We're in school, and I'm not completely sure what the rules are here. Maybe I imagined what happened. Maybe it was something that just belonged to that moment in the woods and will never happen again.

"The swan…"

"You didn't like it?" She sounds disappointed, and I hate being the cause of that.

"No, I did. Really, it's just—"

"Relax," she says as she reaches up and tousles my hair.

Her touch makes me feel lighter and less worried, but her message still plays in front of my eyes like a scrolling marquee. I try to give her a real smile.

"That's better." She leans in and gives me a feathery kiss on the cheek that banishes most of my fear. "Gordie?"

"Yeah?"

She smiles. "Not all surprises are bad."

Her words seem like something I need to consider, but before I can, the bells rings.

"Come on," she says, pulling my sleeve. "We're going to be late."

It's good that we have our next classes near each other, because she makes me feel like a ship being drawn in by the safe beacon of a lighthouse. I want to go wherever she's going; I don't even care where that is.

———

I've never met anyone who was so good at so many different things. In addition to her other hobbies, Sarah plays the flute. Not classical flute. Rock flute. I didn't even know that existed.

She talks about it like it's no big deal, but now I'm standing in front of her locker after school and she's holding out her old MP3 player, the one she doesn't use anymore, the one she's loaded up for me.

She's smiling. She looks proud of herself. She thinks she's giving me something great and special. I look down at the small blue square in her hand. I want to want to take it, but that isn't the same thing as wanting it.

Music is great and all, but it's tied up with The Night Before for me and I know if I take the player, she'll expect me to listen to whatever she's put on it. I don't think I can just pretend to do that.

"What's wrong?" Her smile has wilted a little.

I'm glued to the floor, helpless in front of this beautiful girl who is trying to be so nice to me. I want to do whatever it takes to make her happy. I'm just not sure how to do that.

I shrug and take the small metal square. It's warm from her hand and for some reason that makes me blush a little.

"Thanks." I close my palm around the player. It reminds me of holding her hand. I wish I were, right now.

"You don't have to like it or anything. I mean, I can take criticism," she says as she spins the dial on her lock. "And there's other stuff on there. It isn't just me."

"That's..." I search for a word that isn't going to hold me to anything. "Great. I mean, not that you added stuff. I mean, I want to hear your music." Saying the words almost makes them true.

"Then come to our show on Thursday night." Her words are a challenge and she knows it. She puts her hands on her hips and waits for an answer.

"Your show?"

"Yeah. I've been sitting in on a friend's band from … from my old school. Frozen Polar Bears. We're doing an all-ages show at the Metro."

I tighten my hand around the MP3 player. I can feel its edges digging in my palm, working its way into me just like she is. I know where the Metro is, but, like I tell her, I have no idea how I'd get there.

"Maybe Luke would pick you up? Or maybe your brother could drive you?"

The idea makes me smile. Kevin and I do a lot together, but it's been a long time since we went out and did something fun.

"I don't know. I'll ask him."

"Good," she says, reaching back into her locker. "You know, I never did show you those pictures I took of you. But I printed this one off."

She holds out a black-and-white photo of me from when she snuck into the locker room. I'm ducking down and my hair is flopping halfway across my face. She caught a ray of sunshine flitting across the room behind me and there are specs of dust in the light, looking like the reflection of stars glittering in a pool.

It's been a really long time since I've seen a photo of myself, except for shots from games when I'm in uniform. This is different. It feels more real. I wonder if this is how she sees me.

"Can I keep it?" I ask.

"Of course. Do you like it?"

I try to figure out who the last person was who cared about my opinion. Mom, maybe? I'm not sure.

I wonder if Sarah has any idea how good she is.

I want to kiss her. I bite my bottom lip, hoping I can keep myself from just leaning toward her. I force myself to look back down at the photo. To try to stop thinking of how much I want to feel the weight of her arm around me again.

"Do I really look like that?"

She smiles as I put the picture between the pages of my geometry book. "Are you, like, a vampire? You can't see yourself in mirrors or something?"

"No," I say, looking down at my shoes so that she doesn't see how embarrassed I am. The white toes are scuffed on the top and the laces are tangled again. "Of course not. I guess I just don't pay much attention."

"Boys," she scoffs. "You're all alike."

I know she means it as a jab. But there's something in her words that I like. Something that says she sees me as normal. I never think of myself as being like anyone else.

I wonder if she'll be disappointed when she figures out I'm not.

NINETEEN

Someone way smarter than me would have figured out that making plans is asking for trouble. Assuming that things will be okay is a sure-fire way to disaster. Thinking I could possibly be happy is like flashing a beacon to the universe asking for everything to suck as much as possible.

I give up on going to the rink and spend the whole walk home working myself up to listen to Sarah's music. I pull the photo she took of me out of my book, shove it back in, and take it out again, just to prove that it's real.

I think about her hand in mine. And next year. And normal.

I'm still looking down at the photo when I get to the house. It isn't until I walk straight into the shrubs that I look up and see the front door open and the strange car in the driveway.

Regardless of what Sarah says, surprises aren't good. My mind blurs with ways to get back to school, the playground, the rink.

I read a book last year about how people cope after something happens to them. It said everyone falls on one end or the other of a fight-or-flight response. Some rush into danger, thinking they can head it off. Others try to get away as soon as possible. I just kind of freeze, like someone has super-glued my feet to the floor.

Kevin must have been waiting for me, because he flies out of the house before I can unfreeze and put any of my exit strategies into action.

"Who's here?" I ask, although I don't really want to know.

"DeSilva." He puts a hand on my shoulder and leaves it there. "You need to talk to her."

That doesn't make me feel any better. As much as I like her, Amy DeSilva is only bringing bad news these days.

"Crap. Why?"

His arm snakes behind my neck and pulls me forward. "I don't know. She wouldn't say anything to us until you got here."

Us. I swallow down the fear that rises in my throat. "Jim's here too?"

"Yup. Full house."

Jim is never home this early. He must have known she was coming. Worse, he must have known she was coming and didn't tell me.

I imagine that the roots of the trees are coming up through the ground and tying my feet down. I'm not sure I can move, but Kevin's arm is strong and pushing me forward. Their voices, Ms. DeSilva's and Jim's, float out of the house.

Everything goes quiet when Kevin pulls open the screen door and pushes me inside.

I put my backpack down and head toward the dining room, where they're sitting at the paper-covered table.

Ms. DeSilva gives me a hug. "Sorry for doing this so unexpectedly, Gordie, but I just picked up this paperwork and it didn't seem like it should wait."

"Just tell me." I'm not trying to be rude so I reluctantly add, "Please."

My skin feels electric. I need to keep moving, but there are too many people in the room. No escape.

Kevin must see me starting to panic because he comes up behind me and puts a hand on each of my shoulders. "Let's go sit down and hear what she has to say."

He leads me to the table and we take two seats in the middle. Jim is at one end and Ms. DeSilva is at the other. I have a very quick flash of memory, one I've never had before.

We're in the old house and sitting down to dinner. All of us together, which is rare. My father's not around much and things are usually too chaotic for regular dinner times.

It's my birthday. The twins aren't born yet, but Kayla is. I think I'm seven or eight. Mom made me a cake shaped like a hockey stick. We're all eating dinner. Like this. Around a table. There are cake crumbs everywhere. My father is yelling at Kayla for getting frosting on the tablecloth.

My arm shakes and Kevin's hand squeezes my wrist.

"Sorry," I say, turning to Ms. DeSilva. I wish I knew how to explain to her that I'm okay. I mean, I'm not having a seizure or anything. It's just a spin. I'm not going to bite my tongue off.

She takes a deep breath and shuffles the papers in front of her. It feels like it takes a million years for her to say anything.

"Gordie, what do you remember about us trying to reach your father after the ... incident?"

What I remember the most is that word. "Incident." It was the one she always used. "Accident" was never right, and no one was going to come out and call what my mother did "Murder." Not around me, anyway.

I search my brain for something else. There's ... nothing.

"I don't remember," I say. "Just being here, I guess. At Jim's. I remember the ... " In my head, I see my father at the funeral, all in black. Staring at me. Mom and the kids are in boxes and ...

I shake my head hard.

"He ... " This is also something I'm missing a word for. I don't like to think of him as my father, but I have no other way to refer to him. "He didn't want me, after."

I don't say out loud that my father not wanting me is the thing I'm most grateful for in the universe, because as much as it makes me happy, it also hurts like hell. I've never really understood how that works.

Ms. DeSilva's face falls a little. I get it. This sucks. This all sucks. I was just a little kid and no one can go back and change the past and now I'm all fucked up. That still doesn't mean I want to deal with those damned looks.

"It isn't necessarily true that he didn't want you, you know," she says, oblivious to the pressure that's building in my head. "It's just that after the funeral we couldn't locate him.

We figured he was dealing with everything that happened in his own way and that he'd come forward eventually."

She pauses and waits to see if I'm going to say anything, but there are no words in my mouth at all. All I'm aware of is that the thing in my stomach is starting to tighten.

There's no one to bail me out. Even Kevin is sitting rock-still and looking a little green.

DeSilva continues. "After a while, when we didn't hear anything, I petitioned the court to award guardianship to Jim so that you and Kevin could stay together. And the judge agreed." She looks from one of us to the other. I can tell there's something big to come. It's a good bet I don't want to hear that either. "Do you have any questions so far?"

We all shake our heads.

I realize I've been holding my breath when I try to let it out and it feels like it's sticking in my lungs. I lean over and grab a pen off the table. I'm sure I look like an idiot, but clicking that pen is the only thing that's going to keep my heart from exploding.

I close my eyes and focus on the clicks until I'm breathing kind of normally again.

Kevin knocks into my leg and holds his hand out for the pen. I'd tell him to fuck off if DeSilva weren't here, but I'm not going to cause a scene over a stupid plastic pen.

When I hand it over, he puts it on the other side of the table.

I glare at him and start twisting the bracelet. I know he's happy because it doesn't make any noise, but it doesn't help as much either. Not that he gives a shit.

It sounds like everyone exhales at once, and Ms. DeSilva starts talking again.

"Because your father never stepped forward, and because we just didn't want to put you through anything else at that time, we chose not to pursue any more formal arrangements. We would have had to go to court to charge him with neglect or abandonment."

"And?" I know there's something horrible lingering somewhere on the tip of her tongue and if she doesn't spit it out soon, I'm afraid that not even the stupid band on my wrist is going to be enough to keep me from losing it right here.

"Jim never officially petitioned to adopt you. You need to understand that it isn't because he didn't … doesn't care about you. There were no other relatives in the picture, and we just didn't think it was necessary. Instead he was granted guardianship."

I look over at Jim, who is examining the wood grain of the table like he's never seen it before.

"Which means?" This time Kevin beats me to it. I don't have to look at him to know his teeth are clenched together.

"It means, Gordie, that while it won't necessarily be granted, your father is within his legal rights to step forward and ask to play some role in your life."

I open my mouth, but nothing comes out. I know that I'm rocking, embarrassingly, back and forth in my chair, but it feels like every atom in the room is pushing me in a different direction. One more word about him is going to make me break into so many pieces that not even Kevin, not even Sarah, could put me back together.

I don't want to cry. I don't want to give him the satisfaction, even though he'll never know that his dumb kid, who is meant to be dead, sat at this table and sobbed. But the tears are stinging the back of my eyes like the boric acid Kevin uses in his cooking and I don't know where they can go but out.

As they start to spill down my face, I clench my hands as tight as I can, one pulling the leather of the bracelet hard enough to dig into my wrist. I know it should hurt, but all I feel is numb.

Everything and everyone in the room fades away until, finally, Jim asks the only question left in a voice that sounds sad and guilty and filled with more emotion than I've ever heard come from his mouth. "Is that what he's doing? Asking to take Gordie back?"

"He's ... " Ms. DeSilva starts and I close my eyes, waiting for her answer. "Considering it," she finishes just as the bracelet snaps and breaks.

Kevin tries to grab at me as I launch out of the chair, but I swerve around him, snatch my bag, and pound up the stairs.

I'm gasping for air. For a minute I think about breaking the window, but even I'm not stupid enough to trust myself right now.

Jim is always telling Kevin to give me space when I'm upset, but my brother never listens. I'm not sure why he's listening now, or if I want him here, or if I want to be alone, or ...

I rub the back of my neck, hard, wishing that everything in my head would stop screaming.

I rip open my backpack. Papers fly everywhere. I rummage around until I find Sarah's MP3 player, and then I remember I don't have any headphones because I don't listen to music.

But Kevin does.

I rifle through his desk drawer. I move some receipts, coins, and an unopened pack of condoms around until I see the wires peeking out from under a photograph of us. Of all of us.

Kevin never lets me put pictures of Mom up on the walls, not even on my side of the room. He says he can't look at them, and that they'd just screw me up, and maybe he's right.

Actually, I'm not sure if it's the condoms or the photo that freaks me out the most. It feels like my brother's been lying to me in more ways than one.

I pick the photo up. Finding it is like discovering a present under the Christmas tree you didn't even know you wanted until you took all the wrapping off.

I know where we are.

The backyard wasn't big, but there were a couple of old trees and a swing set. There was enough room for me and Kevin to play catch.

We're sitting on a blue-and-red-plaid blanket. The twins are propped up in the front, near the lilac bush. Kayla is sitting on Mom's lap. Kevin and I sit next to each other. I'm tucked under his arm, which is draped around my neck. I'm holding a hockey puck in my hands even though it's summer. There's a picnic basket off to the other side and Mom is smiling, happy. I wonder who took the photo. I wonder who was there with us to witness and preserve her happiness.

I try to remember that day. I try to remember the smell of lilacs, but all I can think of is the smell of Sarah's hair. I try to remember the feel of the puck in my hands, and, more than anything, the feeling of Mom sitting next to me, us all being together.

There is a question in my head. One I try never to ask. I squeeze my eyes closed and try to push the question out, but it won't leave. It knocks, knocks, knocks on the side of my brain, demanding to be answered, but I can't answer it. The question is, "What if?" What if Mom hadn't done what she did? Where would we all be? Would she be better? Would she still wear her hair long? Would Jason like hockey? What would it have been like to grow up normal? What would *I* be like?

I reach down to snap the bracelet, but then remember it broke. I need to find the other one. I need air. I need these questions without answers to be gone. They make me feel like I'm drowning again. I...

I take the picture and sit on the bed. I can't stop looking at Mom's smile. At how relaxed Kevin looks, grinning wide for the camera.

I even look at the kids. I remember how they were all so quiet in the back of the car until they weren't anymore and how I just left them there. Sometimes I wish I'd stayed inside the car with them like I was supposed to.

I shouldn't, but I miss my mom. I can't help it.

Tears are pouring down my face like rain, like the river. My shirt sleeve is soggy and full from trying to wipe them away. I give up and just let them flow and spin me around like a whirlpool.

Somewhere a door opens, but it sounds far, far away.

The bed dips as Ms. DeSilva puts her arms around my shoulders and pulls me toward her.

The way she's holding me reminds me so much of Mom, I forget I should be embarrassed to be falling apart like a terrified little kid. I lean into her warm arms and close my eyes. I can feel myself shaking and crying at the same time.

Somewhere, far off, I hear that Sylvia Plath poem Mom used to read. "Aquatic Nocturne," it was called. The music of my mom's voice wraps around me and I'm five again, curled up on the chair next to her, sucking my thumb and imagining life under the water. The edges of my mouth curve into a lazy smile as I drown, drunkenly, in the moment of a memory I never want to end.

I can picture the sea creatures, shining in the light, floating weightlessly. I want to be like them. Free.

My hand clenches around a section of the bunched-up comforter like it's a life raft. If I can hang on tight enough, maybe I can stay here where it's warm and safe. Where everything in the water is beautiful, and friendly, and not crying or praying. Where it's okay that I didn't run for help on The Night Before. Where it's okay that I didn't save the kids. Where it's okay that I didn't die.

Somewhere under the words of the poem I hear soft *shhh, shhh* sounds that make my breathing slow down and most of my tears go back to wherever it is in your body they live.

The arm around my shoulders tightens and then releases. I surrender and open my heavy eyes, which drop a fresh set of tears onto my shirt.

I want to apologize for acting like this, for being like this, but I don't trust my voice to work or my tongue to form any of the tangle of words that are bouncing around in my head.

Instead, I wait for her to tell me that I need to grow up, that I should have stayed in that car, that my father will be doing the right thing if he just tosses me into a hospital and throws away the key.

But here's the thing. She doesn't.

"You have your mom's eyes, you know," she says, staring at the photo she's taken out of my hand.

I've heard that since I was a kid. That my eyes, which are the green of worn sea glass, are just like my mom's.

But for the last five years, everyone has expected me to hate my mom for what she did. Even Kevin. It's like his own feelings are so complicated he can't put them into words, which means we rarely talk about her. And when other people talk about her, there's always something snide and sharp behind their words.

Even when I've tried—just because it seems to be what everyone wants—I've never been able to hate her. Instead, I just miss her a whole lot. And thinking about Ms. DeSilva's words, thinking there might be something left of my mother in me, actually makes me try to smile a little.

"It's going to be okay, Gordie. I promise," she says.

I want to tell her not to say that. She can't possibly know. But I want to believe her so badly that I'm shaking with it.

Nothing I could say will change anything that's happening, but I hear "It isn't fair" coming out of my lips.

Even I know it's the worst kind of whiny complaint and

doesn't even come close to scratching the surface of anything. I've tried so hard to roll with the punches, but I don't understand why they keep coming. When does it all stop? When does it not have to hurt anymore?

I expect her to tell me more of the legal stuff, and how getting my mom pregnant entitles my father to all of the terrible things he's done and all he has yet to do, but she doesn't.

She just tightens her hold on me and says, "You're right. I know that. So much of what's happened to you isn't fair."

We sit in silence for a few minutes as she rocks me like a little kid, back and forth on the bed.

"I bet you get angry sometimes," she says.

What's really strange is that I usually don't. I leave all the anger for Kevin. Sometimes I feel like I'm a sponge, soaking up all the sadness for both of us.

I don't know how to say that to her, so I shrug.

"You know what, though?"

I shake my head, because I really have no idea about anything right now.

"I think you're very brave," she says.

A laugh pushes out of me. Kevin is the brave one, not me. There's nothing brave about what I did The Night Before, or when I swam out of Mom's car and left the kids there. There's nothing brave about not being strong enough to keep myself from cracking into a million, sobbing pieces.

"I mean it," she says and strokes my hair. "And some day you're going to realize it too."

If she believes that, maybe she's the crazy one.

The room is silent except for the sound of the blood

racing through my head, my shuddering breaths, and the squeak of the bed. Time passes.

"The law is very black-and-white," she says in a far-away voice. "But the court is set up to look out for kids like you. We're going to take this one step at a time, together."

I look up at her and blink to refocus my eyes.

"In the meantime," she continues, "will you do me a favor?"

She removes her arm from my shoulder and I'm as cold as if I'd just stripped naked in the middle of an ice rink. She holds out a card to me.

"This is my business card. It has my cell phone number on the back. I want you to promise that if you need to talk, or if anything happens that you can't deal with, you'll call me."

I take the card, and it feels a little like the way Kevin's hand feels on the back of my shirt when we're up on the walk.

"Sometimes people put a phone number in their cell and instead of listing a name with it, they put the initials I, C, E. 'ICE,' for 'In Case of Emergency.' Just think of me as your emergency number."

I think it's kind of funny about the initials and all, but really, it feels surprisingly good to know there's someone besides Kevin who gets what a mess I am and still gives a shit.

She takes my chin in one of her hands and looks right into my eyes. "I know it might not feel like it, but you're going to be okay, Gordie. Just hang in there for me. Promise?"

My eyes follow as she gets up and heads to the door. What I really want is for her to come back and put her arm around me and just let me cry some more, but saying that would make me sound like a nutcase, so I let her go.

After she leaves, I pick up the photo again. Staring into Mom's eyes is kind of like staring into a mirror, but at the same time I try to see something in there that says "I'm going to kill my kids," and I just can't read that in her expression.

I give up and put the photo down, along with the business card.

Sarah's MP3 player is still on the bed, so I plug the headphones in and push them into my ears, finally getting them to stay and not fall out. I'm not sure I really want to listen to anything, but after a few minutes of spinning the wheel, I see a playlist with my name on it and curiosity gets the best of me.

I push "play" and the music starts. At first it makes me uncomfortable. It isn't like I haven't heard music in five years, it's that I haven't heard it being shot right into my brain like this. I squirm and sit on my hands to keep from ripping the headphones out. Then I can't help it. I have to reach up and take one of them out. I have to walk over to the door and open it and listen to make sure nothing horrible is happening downstairs. That I'm not making the same mistake I made The Night Before.

Everything downstairs is pretty quiet. All I hear is the soft murmur of voices. So I put the buds back in and sit down on the bed and close my eyes. I try to focus on the music. Sarah's music.

I don't know what I expected, but this isn't it. I thought flutes were supposed to be gentle and floaty. There is something gritty about this. These notes have teeth.

Sarah told me she learned to play from an old British guy that lived down her street who was in a rock band a long time ago. She stood and watched him playing on his porch one day and begged her parents to pay for lessons. It gave her something to do when they were fawning over Luke, she said. Playing took the place of parents, friends, everything.

There's a guy singing and his words aren't angry. But Sarah's flute behind him is. It makes sounds I'm not sure I've ever heard before. They're beautiful and ugly all at once. I let them wrap up around me and try to understand why she's so angry. I guess it's her parents, but really, I know nothing about normal families.

I let myself slip off into the middle of the songs. They circle around me and carry me to somewhere else. Listening to her play makes me feel like she's next to me. I wonder what it will be like to watch her show, to see her playing these angry and dramatic notes. I wonder what I'll see in *her* eyes.

I don't know how much time passes before I feel a tug on the wires going into my ears. I open my eyes to see Kevin sitting on the blue comforter. He leans over and gently pulls the headphones out.

The sudden silence in the room is like coming out of a spin.

"What are you listening to?" he asks. I can tell he's split between asking whether I've lost my mind and trying to hide his surprise that I'm listening to anything at all.

"Sarah's in a band," I say. My voice is hoarse, like I've been screaming. "She wants us to come see them play on Thursday."

I hope against hope we'll just sit here and talk about music, and plans, and whether he has enough gas in his car to get us there and back. That we can pretend that nothing else is going on. But I know that's impossible, given that I'm sitting here covered in old tears and teetering on the edge of crazy.

He picks the photo up off the nightstand and stares at it for a million years.

"You look like her, you know," he says, not taking his eyes off it. I peer over his arm, trying to see her like he does. Then he crashes his shoulder into mine. "And you might be just as nuts."

"She wasn't..." I start, but I can't finish the sentence. I grab the photo out of his hand and put it back on the nightstand.

"Do you want to talk about it?" he asks.

"What? Sarah's show?" I'm only half being a smart-ass.

"No joke, Ice. I think we need some sort of a plan here."

A plan? Plans are for people who have options, who can choose A instead of B. No one is letting me choose anything. I lean back into the wall and wipe my face off on the bottom of my shirt. I search my head for options. I can't find any. My hand starts jerking and since it's only Kevin, I let it. It feels like an out-of-control drummer is playing against my leg.

"Like, leaving?" I ask. It's the only thing we've talked about.

Kevin leans up against the other wall and wraps his arms around himself. "I don't know. I don't think leaving really makes sense."

"We could hitch to Canada," I offer. We're about twenty minutes from the border. Sometimes Jim talks about how he used to cross it for dinner. I always thought it was cool to imagine going all the way to another country just to eat.

Kevin runs a hand through his hair. "We have no money,

Gordie. And no passports. What do you want to do? Live on the street?"

"Maybe if we ask Jim, he'll give me access to the money in the bank," I say, but even as I say it, I know there's zero chance of that.

Kevin looks at me like I've finally lost it. "That's not happening. Wouldn't it just be easier to kill him?"

There's a challenge in his eyes. I think he actually believes that killing my father is a good option.

"Kill him." I roll the words around in my mouth. It would end this whole thing once and for all. But as much as I might want to, I know I wouldn't be able to do it. Not because murder is wrong or anything as moral as that. What's keeping me from committing patricide is actually far more selfish. "We can't," I mumble. "You're too close to eighteen."

I can see in his eyes that he doesn't get it.

"If we got caught, they'd send us to different prisons. I'd never see you again," I explain.

Kevin squints, staring at me. I can see him fighting against a smile as he shakes his head. "You *are* nuts. You know that, right?"

I know he's just kidding, but then his body tenses and he slaps the wall hard enough to make me jump. "Damn, I don't know what to do."

"I don't know either," I say. My voice sounds small and far away, like it's coming from under water. I'm suddenly so tired, all I want to do is sleep for a long, long time. "You don't have to do anything," I add, but the words take so much effort that I'm not sure I've even said them until he replies.

"Right. It's much better to sit here and just let everything go to hell?"

"It isn't your problem," I mumble, and I'm not at all surprised when his response is, "Since when?" I don't remember a time when Kevin hasn't been looking out for me.

Taking a breath feels like too much work. I don't want to think about anything except the notes of Sarah's flute calling to me. But Kevin wants to act, to keep me safe, and he isn't going to give up until he's confident he can do that. I just don't feel like being his cause right now.

My hands shake as I put the headphones back and will myself to let go, to leave my brother and float away to a place where there are no lawyers, no evil parents, and nobody I have to let save me. A place where there's only Sarah, and her flute, and her kisses, and her questions.

TWENTY

I'm not sure who first looked at a lobster and thought it might be food. I don't know why anyone ever thought that algebra was important. And I'm seriously trying to figure out what drugs have been dumped into the water system to make anyone think that my spending a "trial" week with my father is a good idea.

Ms. DeSilva says she tried to fight it. She says we got unlucky with the judge we were assigned, who is all about the rights of biological parents. She says I'm not being sent there tomorrow because I'm being punished. She says it's the law. She says it'll be okay.

Jim says he's sorry. Kevin doesn't say anything at all; he just keeps cooking things that foam and smoke and make us stay clear of the kitchen. When I look in the mirror, all I can say is "Fuck," over and over.

We're off school for two days of teacher training, which gives me too much time to stare in the mirror. I can distract myself for a few minutes by thinking about Sarah, or skating, or classes, but there's nothing strong enough to keep the realization of what's happening from lurking around the corners of my thoughts like a ghost.

I swear Jim's grandfather clock is ticking too fast. The hands spin around the dial, counting down my time. My fingers drum against my jeans as I try to figure out how to slow it all down.

"Knock it off," Kevin says, throwing a pillow at the back of my head. "You're wigging me out."

I don't turn around. He's just going to have to deal with it.

It's Thursday night and if I had my way we'd be getting ready to go to Sarah's show, but all of a sudden Jim decided to get all parental and tell us we had to stay home.

Yeah, that worked out well.

Kevin pulls on the back of my shirt and sighs. "I can't take this anymore. Come on."

He's holding out the key to the window like it's a biscuit for a dog. I should be offended, but suddenly I want to get outside more than anything in the world.

I follow him through our room and out to the walk. If I had any doubts about how freaked out he is, it's clear now. He isn't even bothering to make sure I'm pinned to anything.

I pull myself up so I'm standing on the wall. I can feel how the breeze would carry me. How it would feel to slip off the edge. If I jumped, it wouldn't matter anymore if I was normal or not. It wouldn't matter if I was still a freak. I'd just be the kid who jumped off the roof. Maybe everyone would even forget what Mom did and this would be the new big Maple Grove story.

I throw my arms out wide and close my eyes. I already feel like I'm in flight.

"Ice?"

I try to ignore him. I'm feeling so much lighter already. All I need to do is take one more step.

"Sure, let's do it," he says, pulling himself up next to me. The breeze is blowing his hair back and I don't recognize the expression on his face.

"What do you mean?" I ask.

"Is the altitude making you stupid?" His voice is calm and matter-of-fact, like he's giving me a hard time for not blocking an easy shot. "We're brothers," he says, as if that makes everything simple and clear. But then I guess it always has.

I want him to leave, so I ask a question I know he doesn't want to answer. "Why didn't you ever tell Jim about the things my dad did to you?"

His eyes flash. "Why?"

I hear all of the reasons he doesn't want to tell me in the tone of that one word. But he doesn't go away; he just teeters a little on the wall.

"Look. I didn't see my dad all that often back then, and . . ." All of his bravado seems to leak out with his next words. "Your dad threatened me. What do you think Jim would have done? He would have gone ballistic and called the cops."

"Maybe they could have protected you."

Kevin's eyes narrow. "Yeah, and they would have split us up, and then where would you have been? What do you think he would've done to you?" He crouches down and sits on the wall, pulling on the leg of my jeans. "Sit down."

The lights of the nearby houses are sparkling, calling to me, but I want to hear what he has to say, so I do it.

"And now..." Kevin wipes the back of his hand across his forehead and starts ticking reasons off on his fingers. "It's too late. We were too young. It was too long ago. We can't prove anything. Talking about it would just cause even more problems. Besides," he says, lowering his voice, "my dad doesn't need to know about all that."

I grip the brick under my leg and run my fingers along the edge of the wall. It sucks that my brother went through all of that for nothing. He got hurt and now that I'm being sent back there... it doesn't mean anything.

"You shouldn't have kept quiet just for me," I say. Thinking of what would have happened if Kevin and I had been split up as kids is threatening to send me somewhere else. I wipe my suddenly sweaty palms on my jeans.

He sighs. "Maybe we should go to Canada after all. What do you think?" He's trying to smile, but it's forced. His hands are clenched in front of him.

I watch as his knuckles turn white with pressure and say, "It could be like those road movies. We could get motorcycles and ride through the desert together."

I hope he'll smile a real smile, but he just looks at me. "I'll kill that bastard if he hurts you," he says softly, like it would be no big deal. Like it would solve all the problems in the world.

There's nothing I can say to that, so I watch as the streetlights flicker into life and let the silence hang around us.

"Have you talked to Sarah?" he asks, breaking the quiet. The question feels bigger than just a couple of words.

"About what?" I ask sharply. Thinking about her makes me feel guilty, since I promised her we'd be at the show and we aren't.

"Hmm," he says. The sound of it hangs in the air between us, fluttering like a moth.

Kevin wraps one arm around his legs and looks out somewhere in the distance. I can't tell what has his attention.

"After Mom did ... what she did, all I wanted was the chance to talk to her one last time," he says. "You know, to see if there was something I could have done. At least to say goodbye."

His eyes are so dark and piercing when he turns to look at me that I jerk back, and he has to reach out and grab my wrist to keep me from tumbling off the wall. He doesn't let go.

"Do you think it would have made any difference?" This is the first time we've really talked about That Day in years.

He shrugs. "Maybe not. But maybe it would have helped me."

I shake my head. "I was there, and it didn't help."

He tightens his grasp on my wrist. "That's not the same and you know it."

I try to shrug off both his hand and the uncomfortable somersaults in my stomach. Something moves out of the corner of my eye and I look down to see my other hand thrashing away. *Great. That's a new one.*

Kevin doesn't know that I've turned the ringer off on the house phone. Regardless of the fact that I'm trying to pretend

I don't care, everything in me is screaming to talk to Sarah. To see her. To hope she can think of some way to get me out of going tomorrow. To hope she can give me the courage that enabled her to run away.

But I know I wouldn't be able to hold it together with her. She makes me feel exposed in a way I don't feel with anyone else. Normally, I like it. But I can't imagine what she'd think if she knew I was just going along with this without putting up any real sort of fight.

"Ice." Kevin's voice is harsh. He thinks I'm off somewhere, only I'm not lucky enough for that to be true.

"Sarah should just forget about me." The thought makes me sadder than I thought was possible.

"Like that's going to happen," he says sarcastically. "Have you forgotten Mom? You know better than anyone that it doesn't work that way."

I can't imagine Sarah thinking of me in the same way I think about my mom. I can't imagine she'd let me haunt the edges of her thoughts until I was somehow a part of her. But I like that maybe I won't be able to forget her now, that maybe in a really small way, she's a part of me because she's a part of my memories.

I stashed the bird charm in my nightstand so that I know something will be here, waiting for me to come back. But maybe she will be too, and I don't think she'd want to remember me as the kid who jumped off the roof.

I shrug. "I'll see her in school on Monday, anyhow."

The muscles in Kevin's hand relax and then clench again. "Monday. Yeah. Sure, you will."

It seems insignificant. The act of getting through three days. But I know how quickly tides can turn and decisions can be made.

"I'll see her," I say, because sometimes when you say something it makes it more real.

"Just be careful," Kevin says into the wind. When I look at him to ask him what he means, he's already pulled himself off the wall and is standing at the window, waiting to guide me in.

———————

Big surprise. I can't sleep. The room feels too hot, and now it's too bright even though the sun is barely up. Besides, I'm not even sure I want to sleep. It would just make the time go faster and that's the last thing I want. But flopping around in bed isn't helping either so I get up and pad downstairs in the half-light, my bare feet slapping against the wooden steps.

I walk through the living room, looking for something new to capture my mind, but nothing ever changes in this house.

In the corner of the kitchen is a wooden broom. I take it back into the living room and lay it on the couch. As quietly as I can, I move the coffee table to a safe place.

I pick up a piece of paper, crumple it up hard, and throw it onto the floor. I can almost hear the roar of the crowd as I stand in front of it, imagining that I'm in goal at the end of some championship game.

Sliding on the wood is kind of like being on ice. I hold the broom in front of me, batting the paper puck back and forth. It's freeing to be in goal without the weight and constriction of padding. I make save after save, over and over, although on one I come close to taking out the lamp standing at the side of the room.

I think about all of the years I wanted to hate hockey because my father loved it. But I never succeeded. When I'm on the ice, my body listens to me. It does what I need it to do. When I'm on the ice, I usually don't spin. I don't shake. When I'm on the ice it's like I'm moving so fast the memories don't know where to find me.

I wish I could live there.

"What are you doing?" The whispered words come at me out of the dimness and I glance up to see Kevin standing in the doorway to the den with his arms crossed, looking tired and annoyed.

"I couldn't sleep," I say as I pull myself out of my goalie's crouch.

Kevin runs a hand over his eyes. "Yeah," he says and comes over on unsteady legs, like he's trying to walk on ice in sneakers. He sits on the couch.

I flip the paper up in the air, juggling it with the broom, which is actually harder than juggling a puck with a stick. Kevin reaches out a hand and catches it. I stand, staring, while he flattens the paper out and reads it.

His face breaks into a huge grin and he laughs. "And everyone says I have anger issues."

I shrug. Yeah, so I'm using one of my father's legal letters as a puck. That doesn't mean anything.

I lean the broom against the coffee table and sit down

next to him on the couch. I remember what Sarah said about everything being easier to talk about and wonder if she would still say that if she knew my brother.

I turn sideways on the couch so that I can lean back against the arm and draw my knees up.

When my brother finally talks, I expect him to say something about my father. Maybe even something about Mom. But that isn't what's preying on his mind.

"You're really into her. Sarah."

We stare at each other while I let his words sink in. Between other brothers, this might be a casual comment. A congratulatory one, even. Kevin's tone says otherwise, and the silence that was already uncomfortable has just gotten all jagged. I look away and pull at a loose thread hanging from the edge of my shirt. It feels like if I pull hard enough my whole life will unravel.

I roll Kevin's words over in my mind, trying to figure out his agenda. If he didn't already know how I felt, he wouldn't have said anything.

"Yeah." I look at him, daring him to find fault with my answer.

Kevin clenches his hands into fists, like he's testing out his muscles, and then releases them. "Really?"

"Yeah, really," I say. "Why?"

"And she knows everything?" he asks. His brown eyes get even darker.

I pull the blanket off the back of the couch and wrap it around my legs. I know he likes to make me uncomfortable as a joke, but something about this feels different. Something about his voice sounds wrong.

"So she knows how you just zonk out sometimes? And the pens? I'm sure that doesn't bother her. Have you told her about the spins?"

It doesn't matter whether or not she knows. I know whatever is going on with him isn't about her. That makes it worse. Way worse.

His voice, suddenly, is my father's voice. My father telling Kevin that he'll never amount to anything. Telling him he should be grateful to even have a place to stay.

My chest gets tight and I cross my arms and duck my head. Kevin always says not to show it when you're afraid— that way no one can use it against you. But this is him, and when I look up, his eyes narrow.

The sides of the room start to close in around me. Like a box. Like the car. Like a coffin.

He doesn't stop. "How about…"

I press my arms against my ears so I can't hear him anymore.

Kevin can be many things. Angry. Protective. Stubborn. But he isn't cruel. Not to me, anyhow. Not ever. But now his face is hard as stone.

He leans over to grab my arms away from my head and I catch a whiff of alcohol. He smells like he's taken a bath in it.

I wrench my arms free. "God, what did you … You're drunk!" I've seen Kevin drink a beer or two with his friends before. But he's never drunk. Not really. Not when that was part of what made my father a monster.

He breaks into a wide grin, but there's nothing happy in it. "Whoa, baby brother. When did you get so smart? Yeah. I'm hammered. So what?"

My mind races with emotions, so quickly I can't name them all. "Does Jim know?" I ask.

Jim may not be the most involved parent in the world, but he has rules, and I'm pretty sure that messing with his liquor cabinet would be breaking one.

"Yeah, I asked him before I downed his whiskey," Kevin says sarcastically. "No, Jim doesn't know. But that bottle was so dusty I could have written a novel on it. I don't think he's going to miss it."

I can see it in his face now. That strange glowing darkness in his eyes and how his cheeks are flushed red. For a minute I'm really worried about him. Worried that he's so upset about me going that he's resorted to this. Worried he doesn't know how to handle it either.

Any sympathy I might feel disappears with his next words. "But maybe Sarah knows. She knows everything right? Even how to change your piss-stained sheets."

My fists tighten around the blanket. His words make my teeth clench so hard it takes a minute before I can force anything coherent out of my mouth. "Once. Only once."

It was during a spin, a year after That Day. It was horrible and he promised he'd never mention it again.

"I'm sure she's got her own ways of distracting you, anyhow."

My balled-up fists fight for release. I want to hit him so badly. "Shut up. Please. Just shut up."

Kevin stretches his legs out and places them on top of mine. They feel like they weigh about a thousand pounds. I want to push them off, but I'm afraid of making any sudden movements. I don't know this angry, drunk kid sitting in front of me.

"You should drink with me, Gordie. I bet it would relax you," he says, getting right in my face. His breath is sour and sweet enough to make me gag.

I pull back as far as I can on the couch, but his legs are pinning me in place. Everything in me wants to scream, but I don't want Jim coming down here. I'm afraid if I open my mouth, I won't be able to stop, so I just shake my head from side to side.

"Yeah," Kevin says. "Didn't think you had the balls for that."

I want to ask him what he's doing. What he wants. But I can only manage, "Why?"

Kevin reverses himself on the couch and throws an arm casually around my shoulder. Nothing makes sense. My brain says to run, to get the hell away from him as quickly as I can. But my body thinks he's still my big brother, the one who has always been there for me.

I'm at war with myself and the smell of whiskey makes my stomach flip upside down. I swallow hard, over and over, to try to keep the contents of my stomach and my emotions inside.

Don't show them you're afraid. Yeah, right.

"I'm not angry, Gordie," my brother says, in answer to a question I never quite asked. But I know that tone of voice. It's one that used to get him into trouble at school until he learned to control it. It's a tone that means he's ready to let everything out. In fact, he's ready to explode. "Why would I be angry? I mean, the stupid-ass judge thinks it's a great idea to send you back to that prick and really, it's okay, right?"

I know better than to answer that question, which is fine because it isn't like he gives me time to say anything.

"And why? Because Sarah is going to swoop in and save you, that's why. Because she's the one thing that will keep you from flying off that edge. Maybe I've just been wasting my time anyhow. You don't need me at all, do you?" he asks, driving a finger sharply into my chest with each word.

"What?" I choke on the word and push his hand away. "What the hell are you talking about?"

I look at him. Really look at him. I can see that his eyes are wet with spit-thick tears that he's making no effort to hide.

"I need you," I whisper. It's admitting something I really don't want to say out loud. I think again of what Sarah said about talking in the dark, and I think about how Kevin has been the only one there for me my whole life. But I don't want to admit anything to this monster in my brother's body.

I stare at a worn spot on the wooden floor.

"But it doesn't matter," he says, in a voice that sounds like he's chewing glass. "And it doesn't matter what I've promised you. I can't save you from this. So what kind of a loser does that make me?"

I want to reach out to him. To say something that will make him feel better, but none of the words in my head form the right response. I've never really tried to picture a life that Kevin wasn't a part of, but for the first time, the idea of not needing anyone like that, not needing him, sounds like a goal to shoot for.

The silence stretches out so long that I think I might be spinning before Kevin bends over and puts his head in his hands and lets out a sigh. "What am I going to do, Ice?"

A million smart-ass comments race through my brain, most having to do with showers and sobriety.

I want to tell him that he'll go to college. That he'll be a chef and have his own restaurant and meet a girl. But I'm tired and sore and drained, and the thoughts are just clanging around inside me.

I place my hand on his back, which is spewing off heat. "Wait for me to come home. Be here."

In trying to comfort him, I've let some weird wall down, and now all of the feelings I've dodged start ganging up on me. They're running out of my mouth before I can stop them. "I don't want to go. Don't make me. Please."

And then I can't stop trying to tell him, to tell the universe, how badly I don't want to go to that house.

The next thing I know his arm is back around me, pulling me into his shirt, which is soaked with alcohol sweat and I don't even care. He's telling me that it will be okay. That we have a pact. That he's going to find a way to bring me home.

And because Kevin is somewhere in that body I try so hard to believe him. Harder than I've ever tried before.

Once I'm calm enough to stop talking, we sit there wrapped in silence.

"Lord, my head hurts," Kevin says eventually, sounding totally like my brother again.

"And you stink," I add.

His laugh is low and quiet. "And I stink. And I remember why I don't drink that stuff. Why do people like it anyhow?"

I shrug and stand up, letting the blanket fall to the floor. I feel wobbly. Numb and prickly all over. Like when your foot falls asleep and you just start to get the feeling back.

Kevin sticks his hand out so I can pull him off the couch. I hesitate, but then stick my hand into his and pull him up.

His voice is small and hurting when he says, "Jim isn't letting me come to drop you off. I think he's afraid I'll do something stupid."

I take my hand out of his and wrap my arm around his waist, draping his arm around my shoulders as I start to lead him toward the stairs. I try to make a joke. "You? Something stupid? Can't imagine."

Kevin snuffles and it almost sounds like a laugh except I know it isn't. "How can I keep you safe if he doesn't let me come with you?"

Our room is quiet, with the exception of the old clock ticking away the seconds. And the sound of my heart beating in time to it. And the soft sobs of my brother as he pulls me into a whiskey-scented embrace.

TWENTY-ONE

Jim pauses on the porch as we head to the car. I turn when I hear a window open, but have to shade my eyes against the afternoon sun. Kevin pours himself out of the window and leans on the wall.

My brother and I stand there for a minute, staring at each other like we're both wishing the Earth would open up and swallow us.

Finally, Jim tugs gently on my jacket and guides me to the car. I fold myself into the passenger seat. My hand is shaking so hard he has to fix the seat belt for me.

As we pull away, I look back. Kevin is already gone.

———

I'm handed over like something dirty and illegal.

I'm sure there are things said between Jim and my father, but I don't hear any of them. All I'm listening to is the roar of blood through my ears and the slight clinking sound that my keys make as my backpack shakes on my arm.

Every time my eyes skim across the surface of the house—

a brick, doorknob, window frame—a thousand images flip in front of my eyes like an old movie.

Jim stands in the doorway and pushes me forward. He can't meet my eyes as he backs away.

I have no choice but to go in. My hand rests on the splintered wood of the door frame as I steady myself and the door closes behind me.

"Place hasn't changed all that much, has it?" My father actually sounds proud of the fact that he's kept things so close to the way they used to be.

My head is clouding. Words, pictures, and memories are skating around each other, tying themselves in knots, threatening to pull me down.

Focus. Kevin's voice is also in my head, although after last night, it isn't the comfort it used to be.

My hand spasms as I clench the strap of my backpack.

My father's footsteps echo as he walks across the wooden floor.

There used to be a rug here. It was green with braided edges; Mom made it at the class at the community center. I remember Kevin and me running our toy cars over it. We built elaborate ramps that came down the side of the couch. My brother was always better at making his cars jump through the air. But I didn't care. We weren't competitive like that as little kids.

Looking around is like being in a museum. *Step right up and see where the freak lived.* My father's old hockey jersey is even still hanging in a frame over the fireplace. I have no idea why he'd want to be reminded of how he ruined another guy's life every time he looked up.

"Grab yourself a pop and come get reacquainted with your old man," he says as he settles himself into one of the armchairs next to the couch.

I glance toward the kitchen, but my throat is dry and closed. I think I'd choke if I tried to drink anything.

I sink into the other dusty chair, holding my backpack in front of me like a bulletproof vest. It's stupid, I know. Nothing is going to stop his words from shooting toward me.

"You're what? A sophomore now?" he asks as he runs a hand through his grayish hair. I can't believe he wants to play catch-up after all this time.

"Yeah," I force myself to say as I shift around in the chair. I feel itchy, like spiders are crawling all over me.

"That lawyer of yours tells me you're a good student," he says, tapping an unlit cigarette on the end table. "I guess you got that from me."

I have an overwhelming urge to take a knife and cut out every bit of DNA I got from him. I hate the thought of being linked to him in any way. I look down at my bag and fiddle around with the zipper to avoid doing anything stupid.

Breathe. Breathe. Breathe.

"Look, it's just the two of us for now, so you're going to have to carry your weight around here," he says.

I've only started to wonder about what he means by "for now" when he reaches out and grabs my chin, turning my head toward him.

"The first rule is that you need to pull yourself together

and move forward. All that stuff with your mother was a long time ago. The past is the past, do you understand?"

My eyelids flicker. It's like a spasm, only more annoying. "Yes," I force myself to whisper through my gritted teeth as he lets go. I wonder how in the hell he expects me to move forward.

Don't show that you're afraid. Don't show that you're afraid. Don't show that you're afraid.

I let Kevin's words play over and over in my head as my father keeps talking.

"I know it isn't your fault. I blame that brother of yours. He always babied you. You're going to thank me some day for getting you away from him."

"Leave Kevin out of this." The words fly out of me like a swarm of bees. It doesn't matter how pissed off I am at Kevin—my father has no right to say that.

He laughs; it sounds like sandpaper rubbing at a spot on the wall. "You have something to say to me, son? Let's hear it."

"I'm not...don't call me that." I pull the bag even closer to my chest. I can feel my heart beating against it. Racing, racing, racing.

"You have some of your mother's spunk. That's good." He looks me up and down. "Hopefully you didn't get any of her craziness."

Tears sting at the back of my eyes, but I'm damned if I'm going to let him see them. "Mom wasn't..." I start, and then catch him looking down at where my hand is beating against my leg. I guess I know what he thinks on that front too.

I bite the inside of my cheek and watch the tree limbs

blow against the window. I don't know why I'm talking to him at all.

Finally he says, "Why don't you go on upstairs and unpack."

I don't wait for a second invitation. I grab my backpack and suitcase and bolt up the stairs, glad to be away from him. Just like it used to, the fourth step creaks like it isn't going to hold me.

The walls of the upstairs hallway have all these dirty, rectangular faded patches on them from where Mom's photos used to be. I wonder if he just took them down, or if they've been gone all this time. I wonder what he's done with them.

The doors to all of the rooms, except the big one that the kids shared at the end, are open. Mom's room, which was my father's too when he was here, was across from it.

My room was the first at the top of the stairs.

I stand in the doorway. My old bed, desk, and dresser are there under a coat of dust. My old Wings poster is still up on the wall, but a couple of the corners have come loose and it's just hanging, waiting to fall.

I take a half-step in but can't go any farther.

The sun shines off something on the floor. I can see bits of broken glass. Some of it is tinged black-red with old blood, but I don't remember why. It makes my hand shake harder.

I continue down the hall.

Kevin's room has been stripped of everything that made it his. I used to love being in here, but it doesn't feel like my brother's anymore. He used to draw pictures of Mom, me, the kids, everything, and he'd hang them all over the room. After what happened, he stopped. I don't think he's drawn since.

I walk in and close the door behind me, checking to see if the locks are still there. My father put one on the outside to keep Kevin in. Mom let my brother put a hook lock on the inside to keep my father out. We knew it wouldn't take much strength to break through it. But we could pretend.

My father didn't like that. But it was one of the few things Mom stood her ground on. And he knew he could break it if he wanted to. It was mostly that he wanted Kevin to obey him, I think. And Kevin has never been very good at obeying anyone.

I latch the door behind me. I'm disappointed that the red corduroy bedspread doesn't smell like the laundry stuff Mom used to use. I only inhale dust when I put my nose to it. I empty my bags, shoving things into the bottom of the closet in no real order.

It isn't like I want to stay, anyhow.

Then I crawl into the closet next to my socks and jeans and T-shirts and shut the door.

My head is crowded with thoughts and memories, all scratching at me. But I can't seem to hold on to any of them for longer than a breath, so I just let them all pour out of me at their own speed.

I put my head down on my arms.

I'd rather be anywhere in the world but here.

Even in the river.

Being here makes me miss Mom a lot.

It's easy, in here, to pretend she's sitting next to me, holding me and reading to me.

But it doesn't help.

I need Kevin to tell me that everything will be okay. I wonder when I'll see him again.

I wonder if he'll be okay, or if the monster that came out last night will come back.

I'm pretty sure my father has to let me go to school on Monday. I mean, it's the law or something.

I want someone to tell me that I'm not drowning.

I'm scared.

I know I'm chewing on my sleeve, which I shouldn't do. I didn't bring that many clothes with me. And I love this shirt. It's the one I was wearing when Sarah talked to me in class the first time.

I wish Kevin were here to tell me to stop.

Dark things at the edges of my mind claw at me. I don't care about fighting them off. I offer myself up to them. To be food for nightmares.

Somewhere far away, I hear pounding.

Let him break the door down. I don't care.

I don't care.

———

I run out of memories.

Or they just get tired of me.

My muscles are sore from sitting, cramped in the same position.

At some point I realize that I'm me again, instead of just someplace for all the memories to hide.

I stand up slowly and stretch. First one side, then the other.

I open the closet door and step into the dark room. I flip on the light, which makes my eyes hurt, and look at my watch. Three hours. He let me stay up here three hours. I'm not sure if I'm happy about that, upset, or just surprised.

Listening at the door is like holding up a shell to hear the ocean. But I only hear silence.

I run my hands through my hair and pull on my sleeves. The right one is still damp, but I can't change. I don't want to run out of clothes. I'm not sure if there's even still a washer in the house. I almost wish I could go check. I'm afraid that if I stay in this room, I'm just going to lose my mind and spin for the rest of my life.

I try to figure out what Kevin would tell me to do, but I come up short. I try not to worry about him, but I still can't shake how he looked last night.

I don't want Kevin to be crazy like me.

I don't know what I'd do if he was.

As I stand near the door, I hear the creak of the staircase, of the fourth stair he's never learned to avoid. Like he expects it to listen to him and not creak just because he tells it not to.

I take a step backward as he tries the knob.

"Open the door, son."

The latch won't keep him out anyway, so I do what he says.

My hand starts to shake and I pull it up into my sleeve, wrapping my fingers around the damp cuff.

"Come on downstairs." He turns around before I have the chance to respond.

My feet follow my father's trail down the stairs. It's always been a fault of mine, Kevin says, that, unlike him, I can't help but follow a direct order.

He settles back into the same old ratty chair. I hold my breath, hoping it will keep me from pacing, because all I want to do is to keep moving.

"Sit down," he demands.

I sit as far as I can get from him. I shove my hand under my leg and try to figure out where to look. I don't want to look at him, but everything else in the room has a million memories attached and I don't want to get sucked down by them either.

I rub my eyes and wait for the next set of instructions.

My father pulls out a pack of cigarette and offers me one, like everyone gives their kids smokes. I try to shake my head, but I don't think I actually move.

He lights one and takes a long inhale. The smoke circles around me and threatens to rip my stomach out through my nose. I part my lips to breathe through my mouth.

"You're fifteen now," he says, like it's some revelation.

I nod, trying to think about what milestone might be set at fifteen that he would care about.

"Almost a man." He leans back in the leather chair and watches the smoke rise.

I hold tight to the undersides of the couch cushions, hoping I can keep still.

He taps the cigarette on the edge of the heavy glass ashtray and the ash falls onto the table. Mom always hated when he did that.

"You have a girlfriend?" he asks.

I bite my lip. I don't know if Sarah is my girlfriend, and I don't want to talk about her anyhow. I don't want him even knowing about her. But it seems unfair to her to say she doesn't exist, so I don't answer. I just let my eyes dart around the room, hoping that nothing will have time to send its memory into my head.

"It's Friday night. We could go catch a movie or something. I'm afraid I'm not much of a cook."

A movie? Is he serious?

"Or ... is there something else that you want to do?"

"Go home," I say before I can think better of it.

He narrows his eyes and takes a long drag on his cigarette. "It's good that Jim took you in and gave you somewhere to live. But it's been a long time and we're family. Let's just see if we can't make this work."

I get up and go to the window. I feel so trapped in here. I can't even imagine how insane he must be to think there's any chance of anything "working" between us.

"That isn't going to happen," I say into the window.

"I understand you're angry with me for not being here. But I'm back now. Boys need their dads."

My legs quiver and I lock my knees to steady them. And then I turn around and shove my hands into the pockets of my jeans.

"I don't need anything from you."

His laughter sends shivers up my back.

"It's going to take time. I get it. We'll do this in small steps then. Help yourself to whatever you want in the kitchen. I'm going to go watch the game. You can join me or not. Tomorrow I have something special planned. Maybe you'll feel differently then."

He walks into the other room and the sounds of a hockey game on TV seep out. I kind of want to watch it, but not with him.

It feels strange to be standing here alone.

But then I don't really feel like I'm alone. Every time I blink, I can see them. The kids in their playpen over in the corner. Kayla running down the stairs and Mom yelling at her to walk.

Shaking my head doesn't help to clear it.

Someone in the other room scores a goal.

I head to the kitchen and open the fridge. There's not much in it. Some cheese that looks hard, some raw meat.

My stomach heaves and I gag into the sink. I reach for a glass out of the cabinet and my hand starts to shake.

"Feed the kids, Gordie."

"No," I whisper under my breath. "No. It isn't real."

I steady myself on the side of the sink and look out the window. I can see into the kitchen next door. A woman in a pink apron is at her own sink, washing dishes. I move out of the way before she can see me.

I reach again for a glass, fill it with water, and take it upstairs, whispering to myself, "I'm fifteen. That was a long time ago. They aren't here." Anything to block out the voices that seem to be floating out of the walls.

When I get to Kevin's room, I lock the door behind me, hoping it will keep them all out.

It's just the hook latch. But it's all I have.

TWENTY-TWO

According to my watch, it's Saturday morning. I'm still dressed in my rumpled clothes from yesterday and my sneakers are still tied.

I don't know what happened to Friday night. I don't remember anything except needing to be away from him. Away from all of them.

The walls are still intact. There's no blood on my pillow. I run my hands over my arms. My legs. My chest. Nothing seems bruised. I've never lost time like that before when I wasn't spinning.

I always remember my spins, and I thought that sucked.

I was wrong. Not remembering them is worse.

I circle the small room.

The door is still latched, and that makes me feel a little better.

The house is quiet.

Not a comforting quiet, but an edgy quiet. A quiet like cemeteries.

I look out the window. There are no cars in the driveway,

which is strange. I'm surprised he left me here on my own. I could just leave, but I know if I went back to Jim's, they'd only drag me back here, where the court says I have to be.

And who knows what Kevin would do. Maybe we'd both end up in prison or something.

And then I'd really be alone.

I open the bottom compartment of my backpack and take out Ms. DeSilva's card. I still can't call her Amy. I've already memorized her number, but I don't have a phone.

I haven't seen one in the house either.

I really need to pee, but when I pull on the door, I can tell he's locked it from the outside.

I lie back down on the bed and try not to think about it.

Instead I think about Sarah. I pretend she's lying next to me with her arm heavy on my chest. It holds me down like an anchor. I can smell lilacs.

I think for a little bit about her running her hand through my hair. I do it myself and it doesn't feel the same, but the longer I think about her, the closer I come to feeling that same dizziness.

Then I think about kissing her. It makes me so hard, I'm pretty sure I could come just from thinking.

I'm going to need to kiss her on Monday when I see her at school, if she doesn't hate me for missing the show.

I close my eyes and think about Sarah until I'm almost shaking.

I hate this house.

I wonder what Kevin is doing. I wonder if he's really Kevin or the monster from the other night.

I try not to wonder where my father is, with his vulture voice. I don't want him to come back. I need to get out of here.

I also still need to pee really badly.

I get up and open the window. The maple tree has grown a lot in the past five years. I'm pretty sure I could reach out and catch a branch and lower myself down.

I'd leave if I didn't think that it would get Kevin in trouble. Somehow.

And Sarah. Although I almost think that Sarah would tell me to go. She always seems to want to be somewhere else.

But I don't know where I would go. Maybe Canada really is an option.

At least I could play hockey there.

I feel like I'm trapped in my head. Too many thoughts are soaring through it. It feels like my hand does when it's spasming. Like electricity.

Standing by the window, I take my shirt off and hold it over my lap as I unzip my jeans. I'm glad Kevin's room overlooks the back of the house. I pee out the window, hoping that no one can see me.

I zip back up and do homework that probably won't be due for a week. I lose myself in conjugating French verbs until his car pulls up.

Everything in me tenses in reply. My thumb starts moving. I know he's going to hate that. I sit on my hand. I don't want to; Sarah would be angry at me for hiding it, but I can't stop trying. Not around him.

The front door opens and I hear his creak on the stairs. I hold my breath and wait.

He unlocks his side of the door with a deafening click. "Open this now or I'm going to have to take that latch off."

I have no choice. I open the door.

He looks me up and down, like he can tell that I've peed out the window.

Like he knows what I was thinking about Sarah.

My hand gets worse. I forgot to grab the other leather band and I'm sure he'd kill me if I start clicking a pen.

I hide my hand behind my back.

He holds up a paper bag. "Do you still like salt bagels?"

I shrug.

"Go get cleaned up and then make yourself something to eat."

I grab clean clothes from the closet and force myself down the hall into the bathroom. I used to have to reach up to see myself in the mirror. I don't have to anymore.

It's strange to see this version of me looking back at me. I was expecting to see myself the way I looked when I was ten.

I change clothes and wash my hands and run them, wet, through my hair. I'm waiting for him to tell me I need to cut it, but I don't want to. I like the fact that it's longer than Sarah's. And Kevin and I look more alike when my bangs are shaggy.

The T-shirt I'm wearing is my brother's and has the name of a band on it that I've never heard of, much less listened to. The shirt is dark gray and rumpled. Kevin never lets me iron. He's afraid my hand will start acting up or something.

I go back into his room. It doesn't matter how long they force me to stay here; it will always be his.

I pull out DeSilva's card and stick it in my sock. With the bottom of my jeans covering it, you can't tell it's in there. But I can feel it rubbing against my ankle. It feels like a reminder of the rest of the world. It feels safe.

Then I head downstairs.

———————

I skip the bagel. My stomach is so clenched up, I'm scared to eat.

He tells me to get into the car, but I have obvious issues with that. First, I don't want to be in this small space with him. Second, who knows where we'll end up? Third, the car smells like stale beer and anger.

I sit so far over that the armrest is digging into my side.

For all I know, he's taking me to the river to finish the job that Mom started.

He looks me up and down out of the corner of his narrowed eye. "You look like you slept in a gutter."

I slide my hand under my leg.

"Stop that," he says, taking his eyes off the road to glare at me.

I pull my hand out and it quivers in my lap.

"I said stop it."

I try to will my hand to stop, but it doesn't listen to me. It never does.

"I can't," I say, waiting for an explosion, but he just har-rumphs.

Outside the window, the trees fly by. I take a deep breath

at the start of every block, feeling like I might forget to do it otherwise. I think about Sarah holding my hand. I think about kissing her on Monday.

He pulls the car down a bumpy unpaved street, the kind I imagine are found out in the country with empty lots and broken-down pick-up trucks rusting in the yard. I didn't know there were streets like this in suburban Michigan.

He turns and pulls down another, then stops at a house. It's unremarkable. Just a red brick house, really. Just like the ones on either side of it.

"I have to pick something up," he says, and laughs like there's some inside joke I don't get. "Stay in the car."

He lets himself into the house and I see a flash of blond hair before the front door closes. Then I roll the window down and let the fresh air dance around me.

My lungs struggle to remember how to breathe without the reminder of the blocks of trees.

I close my eyes, but even with the window open, it smells too much like him. I can feel the memories starting to come and I can't let them.

I bite down on my lip and open my eyes.

There's a little kid standing in the yard. Watching me.

He's the image I expected to see in the mirror in the bathroom.

He isn't me. But he looks a lot like the picture of me that was in all the newspapers when I was ten.

We stare at each other.

He slowly limps over to the car. There's something wrong with his legs. One is shorter than the other.

I look at his eyes, because focusing on his limp seems rude. His eyes are so dark brown they're almost black. And they're frightened. And something else. Like they're too empty and too full at the same time.

His worn jeans have been patched, but his shirt looks like it's just been ironed. Like he'd get in trouble if he got anything on it. When he gets close, I notice fading bruises on his pale arms: purple and green and yellow against his perfectly ironed blue shirt.

When I close my eyes, it's Kevin standing there instead. I don't say anything because Kevin will just get mad and say he doesn't want to talk about it. And that means he won't talk to me about anything for a long, long time.

Good thing I've learned how to say "I'm sorry" with my eyes. That's as much as he can take.

But when I open my eyes again, it isn't Kevin. It's this strange boy who looks like me.

"Hey," I say.

He looks back at the house and then at me. He smiles and his eyes light up, but both the light and the smile fade from his face quickly. He puts an arm over his face. Like he thinks if he can't see anything, then no one can see him.

"I'm Gordie," I say. "What's your name?"

He pulls his arm down and inches closer to the car. His voice is so soft I can barely hear it.

"Jordan."

His arms cross in front of his chest and he pulls at his short sleeves like he's trying to cover the bruises before he looks back at the house again.

"He says I have a brother. Are you him?" Jordan asks the question out loud that I'm asking in my head.

Now it's my turn to stare at the house. I don't know what's going on. But I know my father wouldn't like me talking with Jordan.

"I don't know."

The boy's eyes get sadder, if that's possible. I really want to say something to make him not look like he's going to cry.

"Maybe," I say, and nod. "I think so."

Jordan nods back and starts humming. His voice is high, like little boys' voices are. I know the song from somewhere but can't name it.

"Jordan." I call his name softly while I look over at the door to make sure it's still closed. I want to get out of the car, but I'm afraid of what will happen if my father comes out and finds me not doing what he told me to.

Jordan's humming turns into soft singing. I watch his lips move as he stares up at the sky. He takes a step toward the car, not watching where he's going, and stumbles.

"Hey," I caution him.

He looks at me, but his eyes are funny. It's like he's looking at something on the other side of me. "My leg makes me trip a lot," he says. "I'll never play hockey either."

His voice is sad, but it's his words that make me shiver.

"He doesn't like that. But it's okay, 'cause the dragon will look out for us."

I realize then that the song he's been singing is "Puff the Magic Dragon," which was my favorite as a kid, too. But Jordan hasn't been mouthing the happy verses, just the sad ones where the boy grows up and dies and the dragon is too lonely to do anything but hide in his cave.

"The dragon?" I ask him. "Puff?"

Jordan nods his head and comes over to the car. He leans through the window, putting his small bruised arms around my neck.

"Puff won't let him hurt you," he whispers into my ear, which makes all of the hair on the back of my neck rise.

I'm stuck for something to say. I want to ask if my father has hurt him, but I think I already know the answer.

"I have to go in before he gets mad," he says out of nowhere. He starts to walk toward the house.

"Wait," I call, and he stops. "How old are you?"

"Seven," he says.

I do the math as I watch him go through the door. Jordan is eight years younger than me. About a year younger than Kayla would be. Some of my father's absences make more sense now. I wonder if he was planning on leaving Jordan along with the twins when he took me and Kayla to California, or if Jordan would have come too. I think it's a safe bet he would have left him behind.

I open the car door and lean over to puke. I haven't eaten, so all I do is gag up that white stuff that seems to live in your stomach when there's nothing else there.

I don't hear my father return to the car until he's in front of me.

"I thought I told you to stay in the car."

Inside me, something unfurls. Some bird is beating its wings inside my heart, trying to get free.

"Didn't think you'd want me puking on the fake leather," I say, sounding an awful lot like Kevin.

I wince, waiting for him to lash out, but he doesn't. Instead, he just makes a sound in the back of his throat and slides into the car.

My mouth tastes like I've been eating one of Kevin's failed dinners.

I don't want to get Jordan in trouble, but I need to know. "You have kids with her?"

He gives me a sideways glance. I'm not really sure what it means and I'm not sure I want to.

"Yeah," is all he says.

I reach down and feel for the card in my sock.

I think about dragons and how much it sucks to be a little kid who feels all alone.

Then I run the corner of the card under my thumbnail and I realize it doesn't matter that I don't have any options. Kevin was right. I need a plan.

TWENTY-THREE

I assume we're heading back to the house, but at the last minute we turn. It's clear we're going somewhere else, somewhere I know almost as well.

A river of sweat collects on the back of my neck and runs down my spine.

I feel torn in two.

There's almost no place in the world I'd rather go.

Just not with him.

The Maple Grove hockey rink sits on the West side of town, near the high school.

"I've been looking forward to this," he says. "I want to see how far you've come."

You'd think he'd just come to a game this summer. I'm not sure how he thinks he'll see how I play goalie by watching me skate around in circles.

I wonder if Jordan is able to play any sports. I'd like to think that some of the bruises on his arms were from something that happened on a playground, but I know that isn't true.

I wonder what's wrong with him, though. Seven-year-olds aren't meant to have eyes like that.

The rink is usually one of the happiest places I can think of, but having my father here changes everything. It's like looking at something familiar through a glass. Everything is twisted and warped.

I don't have my skates so I have to rent the crappy ones they have at the rink. They're never sharp enough. The laces are all wrong. They smell like the hundreds of feet that have been stuffed into them before.

I think my father is just going to watch me skate, but I realize I'm wrong when he rents skates too.

Before he puts them on, he holds one in his hands and runs his thumb along the edge of the blade.

He's holding Kayla around her waist and the knife is so sharp in his hand. Against her throat. I can see the vein in her neck pulsing against it.

Mom is …

I'm shaking. That and the cold bring me back. I glance over at my father, who is chatting up one of girls who rents the shoes. Good thing he hasn't noticed me spacing out.

I finish lacing my skates up and dig my thumb along the sharp part of the toe pick. These are stupid figure skates. I already know he isn't going to like what I'll be able to show him in these.

I hit the drinking fountain and wash my mouth out. It still kind of tastes like puke. Then I slip onto the ice. Even though the skates are wrong and rub in strange places, it feels good to cut across the surface.

I'm forced to zigzag around the kids who are still learn- ing and the couples who skate holding hands, but that's okay. The catch of the ice against my blades fills me like something I've been hungry for. It's where I belong.

I inhale frosty air and think about taking Sarah skating, holding her while we move fast across the cold, hard ice. I know she's been to my games. But everything would be different if I had my arms around her while I was flying across the rink. She'd know for sure, then, that I'm more than just some spazzy freak.

I do a couple of quick turns and crossovers and let thoughts of Sarah replace all the others that are ricocheting through me machine-gun style.

I don't notice my father step out onto the ice. So I don't notice him make a run for me. When he checks me into the boards, I crumple like a rag doll.

Someone blows a whistle while I lie there.

I know better than to move.

My first thought is that you don't check goalies. All that padding is great, but we have no way of protecting ourselves in our catcher gloves. The rest of the team has to do it for us.

I'm not in a game now. I'm not wearing padding. Or a helmet.

I wait for the dizziness to ease up before I try to turn my head.

Someone is yelling, but I don't know who. Or what they're saying.

Slowly I stretch one arm, then the other. One leg. Other leg. I take a deep breath and my side screams in pain. I look down and the ice is still a pristine white. No blood.

There's a crowd around me.

Sue is the cute girl who sells popcorn. Bill is the guy who sells tickets. They know me. I've come here for years. I ignore the looks on their faces when I let them help me up. I steady myself against the railing.

Joe, the guy who manages the rink, is yelling at my father. I hear the word "police."

My ears are still ringing. I catch my father saying something about "accident" and "sorry," but I know this was no accident.

I'm equally certain that he isn't fucking sorry.

As I try to get the room to stop spinning, he talks his way out of it. As always.

It isn't until we've been escorted out of the rink that he says, "You're more observant in a real game, right?"

I don't answer. My head is still foggy and I can feel a pulsing in my side.

He knocks me hard on the shoulder and squeezes. "Don't worry. Next week I'll call your coach and make sure you get back into shape. That kind of thing isn't going to work if you're ever going to play for real."

———————

My father leaves me alone when we get back to the house.

I head upstairs and lock the door, peel off my wet clothes, throw on some dry ones from the closet, and climb under the covers.

I know if I fall asleep I'm going to spin hard. Everything hurts. Breathing. Blinking my eyes. Thinking. Even my hair hurts.

My eyes slither closed and all I can see is Jordan. Deep, deep inside, something is pushing me to help him. But how? I couldn't help Kevin when he was getting hit, and I couldn't help the kids, and now…

I sit against the wall, pick up the pillow, and hold it against my stomach so tight I think it might go right through me.

I want to sleep. I want to spin. I want to escape.

I want…

I'm so scared of what's in my head that every time I start to fall asleep, I poke one of the new bruises to wake myself up.

I sit there like that for a long time. Long enough that the room gets dark.

Something brushes against the window and makes me jump.

I think it's a branch from the maple, but then the window swings open and lets the night in. I shove my face into the pillow to keep from screaming.

"Lord, Ice. It's just me. I'm glad you're staying in here and I don't have to go wandering all over the house."

Kevin's long legs loop through the window. His bare feet, red with cold, land on the floor without a sound.

It's only been a day, but it feels like I haven't seen my brother in forever. He looks older. Or maybe it's just strange to see this grown-up Kevin here in his childhood room.

I rush over and throw my arms around him. I don't think I've ever been so happy to see anyone in my life. It's like what happened between us the other night was just made-up.

He hugs me back so hard I can't breathe, the pressure pushing against my bruised skin like a bandage, and then he holds me at arm's length, examining me the way he examines the result of one of his strange recipes.

"You okay?" he asks, eyes narrowed.

I shrug and untangle myself from his hands, wincing when I bend to pick up the shirts and papers lying around the room so that I can stuff them into my backpack.

My brother tugs on the back of my shirt and whispers, "What are you doing?"

"You're getting me out of here, right?" I ask, my socks slipping a little on the worn wooden floor.

"Ice … shit." Kevin sits down heavily on the bed, making it creak. I freeze, listening to make sure there isn't any sound coming from the hall.

He pats the bed next to him. "Come here. Sit down."

I sit next to him, trying not to wince again. I don't want him to know about the bruises.

Kevin puts a hand on my outstretched leg. "You can't leave," he says. "You know that."

"But …" I stop. I know that if Kevin had his way, I could. He isn't the one I need to convince.

"I just wanted to see you," he explains. "I wanted to apologize for the other night. I wanted to make sure you're okay. Are you okay?"

I let his apology sail away; it's enough that he said it, I guess. But I don't know how to answer his question. What does "okay" really mean, when I'm here?

"I'm hungry," I admit, even though I'm pretty sure food isn't going to fill up the place in me that feels so empty. Besides, everything else is just too big to talk about.

Kevin's shoulders fall. He'd make someone a great mom. Somewhere in his mind, eating equals being okay.

"I'll go get you something," he says, starting to move off the bed, back toward the window.

"No." I grab his arm and hold tight. "You can't. He'll smell it. Besides, you just got here."

My voice is too loud, but now that Kevin's here, bigger than life in his old room, I can't stand the thought of letting him go.

He puts his finger up to his lips and pries my hand off his arm. "Shhhhh..." he says as he walks over to the door and puts his ear against it.

A hundred thoughts fly across his face like a flock of birds.

He comes back and sticks his head out the window, looking in all directions. Then he offers me his hand.

"I have to bring you back. You get that, right?" he whispers.

I nod. The last thing I want is to get Kevin into trouble. But coming back isn't something I want to think about right now.

"Go," he says, pushing me through the window.

I shimmy down the tree. The air feels cool and fresh on my face after the staleness of the house.

When I hit the ground, I look up and watch Kevin make his way down the tree.

The moon is full and shimmery. I hold my arms out and spin around in all the open space.

"Come on," Kevin calls. "I parked down the street."

I tag him and we race without a sound to the car. Every muscle in my body is aching, but I don't care. I'm so, so, so glad he's here.

I think about Canada. Moose, and hockey, and maple sugar. It's starting to sound like a good idea.

Kevin starts the car. "Eggs okay? You shouldn't eat a ton on an empty stomach."

"Sure." I'm so happy I'd almost eat oatmeal.

I roll the window down and stick my head out like a dog. My hair blows back off my face. The car's clock on the dash reads one in the morning. We're the only ones on the road. It feels like the whole city belongs to me and my brother.

We pass the monastery and pull into the Starlight Diner parking lot. I've never been here before, but I've passed by it plenty of times. There's an old star-shaped sign out front that has little lights that glow in order, so that it looks like the star is shining. I think about making a wish on it, but right now the only thing I'd want is what I have, and that's to be here with Kevin.

The bells on the door startle me when we walk in and that makes Kevin laugh and shake his head. I bump into his shoulder and run ahead, sliding into a booth near the window with cracked blue vinyl seats.

Kevin slips in next to me and we both prop our legs up on the other side of the booth. Some happy 1950s music is playing from an old-fashioned juke box, and I can't help but bop up and down against the crinkly vinyl.

I'm exhausted and hungry and scared, and filled with all the happiness I can hold now that Kevin is here.

"Holy shit. There's actually some music you like?" he says with a half-shocked look on his face.

I know he gets that it isn't the music that's making me so

happy. It's just the first time since I got to the house that I've been able to breathe.

A couple with a baby pass by. I crane my neck and watch as they leave, the baby sleeping in one of those fabric things tied tight against the woman's body.

I'm not sure why, but it makes me think of Jordan. I know I need to tell Kevin about him, but I'm a little nervous to hear what he'll say. I think he'll be angry and I don't want to ruin our time together.

Kevin bumps his shoulder into mine to get my attention when the waitress—the tag on her shirt says her name is Janice—makes it to our table. I shrug and let him order for us. She asks him all the usual questions about what type of eggs we want, toast, meat. I don't even pay attention to what he tells her.

Janice looks at us with a big smile on her face. I don't know why she isn't wondering why two kids are sitting in a diner in the middle of the night.

When she leaves, Kevin picks up a packet of sugar and shakes it back and forth.

"How bad is it?" he asks, looking at the sugar like it's the most interesting thing he's ever seen.

I don't want to answer. But I do anyhow. I can't lie to Kevin.

"He's nuts," I say.

Kevin stares at me and waits for me to say more.

"I miss you." I know that doesn't answer his question, but really it does.

He puts the sugar down and his eyes get a little shiny. "I miss you too. It's really quiet in the house."

"I didn't know I made that much noise."

Kevin laughs. It makes me realize how long it's been since I've really heard him do it.

The waitress brings plates loaded with eggs, toast, and bacon. She asks if we want orange juice and I almost spit out my first bite saying "no," but other than that, it's some of the best food I've ever had.

We stay quiet for a while, shoveling food into our mouths as fast as we can and swaying along with the music.

Janice takes the plates all at once like a juggler and says, "You boys sure were hungry. Don't they feed you at home?"

I'm glad she doesn't ask why we laugh at her question.

Kevin holds his half-empty coffee cup in his hands and Janice leaves and comes back with a piece of cherry pie we didn't order. "You look like you could use it," she says as she puts it in front of me.

My mouth waters as I pick through the pie with my fork, looking for pits. It never seems like they get all of them out of cherry pies. When I find one, I deposit it into the ashtray.

"Tell me what's going on over there," Kevin says.

I slide the fork in my hand so that my palm folds around the tines. I move my thumb across each one, sticky with pie filling, in order. Pushing it deeper each time.

I don't know where to start.

Or what to tell him about Jordan.

"He's just…" I look into my tea, hoping the right words will float up to the top. "The same."

When I look up again, Kevin's face is twitchy and hard. His eyes are staring ahead at nothing.

"Have you slept?" he asks into the distance.

I shrug. Sometimes I'm not sure where spins stop and sleep begins.

"Next time," he starts, and takes a big breath. "Next time, maybe I'll come and stay for a few hours and you can sleep and I'll keep watch."

I move the fork, and it snaps out of my hand and spills some of the water from my glass. I reach over to grab some napkins, and my T-shirt must pull up because I hear Kevin gasp.

"What the hell is that?" he asks, pointing to my side. I twist my head to see what he's talking about. Thankfully, the way we're sitting, the really bad side is facing the window. I tug my shirt back down to cover the bruises.

"Hockey." It isn't a complete lie. Just more of one than I'd usually tell him.

Kevin scrunches his face up. He knows I'm not telling him the whole truth.

"The season's over," he mumbles.

A loud clap of thunder rattles the window next to me and makes me jump. When it starts to rain it feels like the sky is crying for us.

My brother's hands clench on the tabletop. And he goes quiet.

Janice brings the bill over and sets it down on the table. "You sure there's nothing else you need?"

I close my eyes. There are so many things we need that I can't even start a list.

"We're done," Kevin spits out, and I guess from his tone that he's talking to me and not to the waitress. That's confirmed when he slaps the table as soon as she walks away. "This is done. I'm calling DeSilva."

The temperature in the room drops a million degrees. "What? Why?"

"I'm going to tell her," he whispers through his clamped teeth. "Everything."

"Everything?"

My father hits Kevin so hard I can hear the slap through the wall that separates our rooms. He was late getting home from school again and didn't call to let us know. Maybe he had detention again. Or maybe he just didn't want to come home to this.

Through the wall, I hear Kevin whimpering, trying to hold the pain all inside. He doesn't want to give my father the satisfaction of hearing him cry. But the sound makes my eyes sting for him.

I blink the memories away and Kevin is still talking. Mumbling under his breath like I'm not even here.

"I know it won't matter. I know it's too long ago. I know she's going to think we're lying." He's breathing heavy and his eyes are glazed and scary. I have to do something.

"No." I shake his arm. "Just. No. There has to be another way."

I'm not sure Kevin stops talking because my brain is turning into a roller coaster of ideas. We need proof. Current proof. Proof he's still the same asshole he always was and I'm not sure that checking me into the boards is going to cut it.

And we need proof before Jordan gets really hurt. I have to save him.

"I think we have another brother," I blurt out, and Kevin stops rambling.

"What?" His mouth hangs open in shock.

I spit out the facts. "Well I do. My father has another kid. I saw him. His name is Jordan. He's seven."

"How do you know it's his kid?" Kevin asks.

"He told me."

"And you believe him?" Kevin's jaw is clenched and I wonder if I should just lie and take it all back.

"He looks just like me and he needs our help. He's just a little kid and his arms ... Jordan's ... there's something wrong with him."

Just saying that makes me feel a little sick. I don't know if he's as messed up as I am or not. Either way, it isn't fair. He's just a little kid.

"Don't you think you have enough to worry about already?" Kevin asks.

"But ... "

He reaches out and grabs my wrist so tight it hurts. "Tell me you're not spinning over there. That you aren't hearing things. Tell me you're okay before we worry about some kid we don't even fucking know."

I look down at the table because I can't tell him any of those things. But I'm not sure that my being a freak is a good excuse for not helping Jordan.

I grab my arm back and rub my wrist under the table. "It doesn't matter. I'm fine."

Kevin shakes his head, but his face is like a blank page. "Yeah. I thought so." After a beat he pulls his wallet out and leaves enough money to pay the bill and to give Janice a nice tip.

But he doesn't move.

Under the table, I twist the cuff of my shirt until it won't go any tighter against my sore wrist.

The music on the speakers is still light and happy. It's a strange juxtaposition to Kevin's voice. "I'm going to kill him one of these days."

I feel the words rather than hear them.

I know they aren't just words to Kevin. I know they're his idea of a solution. A plan. A way to keep me safe. To keep Jordan safe. A way to fight back.

It's what I want, but I know it can't happen like that. I don't want Jordan to end up like me, filled with so many memories that it doesn't feel like there's room for anything else.

"No," I insist. "Not that. But we have to do something."

I'm so tired.

"It's going to be okay, Ice. It's going to be okay," Kevin says, but something about the way he's looking at me makes me think he's saying it to make himself feel better.

We get up and head to the car in the rain.

Instead of getting in, he leans on the driver's door with his arms folded. The rain is bouncing off of his shoulders. I always seem to be standing in the rain these days.

"Do you want to come back home with me and sleep there for a few hours?" he asks.

I look at the rain-drenched sky and then at my watch. It's already two-thirty. I want to go with him, but I don't want him to get into trouble for me again. And I need to think. I need to sort this out.

"After all that food I can probably fall asleep anywhere," I say, only I can't look at him when I say it because he'll know I'm lying. He probably knows anyhow.

My brother looks defeated as he drives. We don't talk until he gets back to his parking space near the old house.

"I'll see you in school Monday, okay?" he says. "Come early. I'll meet you at your locker before homeroom."

I don't want to let him go, but I have to.

I throw my arms around his neck just like Jordan did to me. "I love you, Kev."

"Love you too, Ice. Try to get some sleep and...stay out of his way."

I nod and climb up the tree, back to my prison. But it's not until I go through the window that I hear Kevin's car door slam. And he only drives away when I'm on the other side.

TWENTY-FOUR

I pretend I have homework to do on Sunday. I stare out the window and watch the rain beat against the glass. My father leaves. Comes back. Leaves again. I stay in Kevin's room, afraid of what might be waiting for me in the rest of the house.

When I leave for school on Monday, my father is snoring off the ten bottles of beer he drank the previous night. I'd counted each empty bottle as it bounced into the yard, hoping that if I knew he was drinking himself into a stupor, I could fall asleep myself.

It didn't work.

Now I'm so tired, I'm seeing things move out of the corners of my eyes.

Kevin is waiting at my locker, but I can tell he's angry and restless. He's bouncing on the balls of his feet and his hands are fidgeting. I wonder how many cups of coffee he's already had.

"Look, I've been thinking," he says. "Maybe Canada isn't such a bad idea ... I saw a movie once ... "

I haven't seen my brother like this in a long, long time, and I'm not sure I can handle it now. "It's okay. I'm okay," I tell him.

He scowls like he doesn't believe me.

"Really. I'm okay." Maybe he doesn't believe me because I don't believe myself, but it doesn't matter. I need Kevin to pull himself together, or I'm going to fall apart, and if I do that there will be no one to do the important stuff. "We need to find Jordan."

There are so many things I'm unsure of, but this is the one thing I know. I may have screwed it up before, but this time I'm going to get it right.

It isn't what my brother wants to hear, though. He doesn't even react; he just spins the dial of the locker next to mine, over and over until I have to look away. I can tell he wants to keep moving. I know what that looks like. I know what that feels like.

"I need to get you out of there," he says, like I haven't even spoken.

"You will." I shake his arm. "Just ... I need to do this. I can't leave Jordan there. And if I get busted for leaving, he'll be stuck there."

"You need to do what?" Kevin looks at me with wide eyes. I know he's surprised I'd do anything that would mean staying in that house even a minute longer than necessary.

"Look, first I need to talk to Sarah." Just saying her name brings up all sorts of thoughts that have nothing to do with either Jordan or Kevin.

"Sarah?" he asks, his jaw clenching tight.

"Yeah ... why?" I dare him to answer.

"Nothing," he says. But he won't look at me, so I know there's really something.

After a minute, he picks up a red-striped plastic shopping bag I hadn't noticed sitting at his feet.

"I brought you some food," he says. "It isn't much, but I figure you aren't able to run to the fridge every ten minutes." I peek inside hoping it isn't filled with solid soup, or egg-shaped peanut butter and jelly, or crystallized anything.

I get lucky. All I see are fruit, chips, and bottles of energy drinks. Nothing that looks like it's going to explode or like it was cooked in a chemistry lab.

I take it and stick it in the bottom of my locker while he says, "I thought that the empty bottles might come in handy."

It takes a minute for me to figure out what he's talking about. Then I get it. "I've been peeing out the window," I admit.

That, at least, brings a smile to his face. "I'm sure those fucking lilac bushes are appreciating it."

His smile fades, and I look over my shoulder to see Sarah heading toward us with a huge grin on her face. The picture I had of her in my head while I was locked up wasn't even close to how she looks as she comes our way.

I turn my back on Kevin and stand there like I'm made of stone.

It takes her hours to reach us, from the other end of the hallway.

And then suddenly she's next to me, right in front of Kevin, when she puts her arms around me and squeezes.

Part of me registers that it hurts like hell when she pushes against the bruises on my side, but the rest of me doesn't care. The rest of me feels like I'm flying.

"Why didn't you call me? I'm so glad to see you. Are

you okay? Is it horrible? I called, and your ... Jim told me where you were. Are you free for lunch?"

I don't want to pull away, but her questions circle like seagulls pecking at me on a beach. I don't know which one to address first.

"Sarah..." I try to free my arms, even though I don't really want to.

"You must be the famous Sarah Miller," Kevin says from behind me. His voice is forced, but he's polite enough to shove his hand in her direction.

"In the flesh," she says, and curtsies like Cinderella.

"Great. That's just..." Kevin locks his arms tight around himself as he leans against the locker.

Sarah looks at me, confused. I don't know how to begin to explain how squirrely Kevin's acting because I don't even get it.

"I'll see you later," I say to him and start to move back toward Sarah, but he grabs me in a headlock with a muscled arm, my throat lodged in the crook of his elbow.

A searing mix of hurt and anger floods through me. I can taste it, bitter on my tongue. My hand clenches, not because it's in a spasm but because I want to make him stop.

I know he's already all wound up and if I'm not careful, he'll stay that way for a long time. But I'm too pissed to care.

"So... Sarah..." His words blow past my ear. I try to pull away, but he tightens his arm around my neck and I can't move.

Sarah narrows her eyes and looks from me to him, unsure of what to do.

I feel Kevin take a deep breath as his chest expands against my back.

"Are you for real?" he asks, digging his chin into my shoulder. "I mean, you're cute and all. Why are you bothering with my brother?" His voice is full of acid. "This better not be some sort of game or something."

I elbow him in the ribs and push away.

"Fuck off, Kevin," I say, or think. I'm not sure that I've made a sound, because Sarah doesn't really miss a beat.

She steps right up to him and, in a steely voice I've never heard her use, she says, "You know, Gordie says you're his best friend. Do I really need to tell you how smart he is or that he's one of the sweetest guys I've ever met?"

She's standing so close to Kevin they're almost touching, which isn't something I'd recommend when he's like this. Meanwhile Kevin is clenching the bottom of his T-shirt in his fists, which means he's trying not to punch something.

Then she goes in for the kill and says, "If you don't see that, maybe you're the one playing games."

My heart stops in shock. Shock that she stood up to him and shock at her words. I'm just stuck in place, waiting for Kevin to explode all over the hall.

There's only silence and I hold my breath, waiting for it to be broken. I'm not even sure which of them I'm meant to be rooting for.

I guess my brother can still surprise me, though, because after all that, he laughs. I can actually see the tension seep out of his shoulders. "I might actually learn to like you, Sarah in the flesh."

He winks at me before he turns and walks off down the hall.

I close my eyes and press my back hard against the door until the combination lock hits a bruise on my rib and I jerk forward.

"Gordie, are you okay?" Sarah asks.

She's standing so close to me that I can smell her shampoo. I wonder if Kevin could smell it when she stood next to him. I wonder if it turned him on like it's doing to me.

I shake my head to clear it. "Yeah, yeah, I'm fine," I say, but it doesn't ring any truer when I say it to her than it did when I said it to Kevin.

"Is he always that jumpy?"

"No. He's just … I don't know." I don't want to think about why Kevin is being so weird in front of Sarah, because then I'd have to think about the other night, and there are other things I'd rather think about now.

"Did you … " I ask, forcing myself to turn toward her. "Did you mean what you said about me?"

She smiles and it makes my stomach unclench, but she doesn't answer. Instead, she puts a hand on my arm, and I can feel its heat burning through the long-sleeved shirt I'm wearing to cover up my bruises from the rink.

She leans over and kisses me, and the hall explodes with whistles that make me flinch. When I spin around, it's some of the guys from the team.

Someone pats me on the back.

"Go for it, Gordie," Walker says as he walks by, then "Ouch" as Luke elbows him in the ribs and says, "Hey, that's my sister."

A couple of the others laugh and walk backward so they

can watch us. I'm relieved that Cody isn't one of them, but still I turn a million shades of red and come close to collapsing against the lockers.

Sarah gives them the finger and then turns back to me like nothing happened. *This girl is amazing.*

"So seriously... are you okay? Is it horrible being there? With your father?"

I look into her concerned eyes and think about lying yet again, but I don't. "Yeah, it's pretty horrible. Plus... " I don't know who else is going to walk by and I'm not sure if this is the place to talk to her about Jordan, or if I should tell her about him at all. I just can't think of any way to try to help him that doesn't involve her.

"Look. There's other stuff. And it's complicated. And I'm not sure what to do. I mean, I think I know what I should do, but I don't think I can do it alone and I'm not sure I can ask you to help me, but I don't know who else to ask."

My words are coming out tangled, and I know there's no way in hell she's even got a clue about what's going on. I need her to understand. I just don't know if I can say it to her, and now my damned hand is starting up so I bend my arm back between me and the locker. But I know she won't like that, so I pull it out again and then the first bell goes.

"Gordie, do you want to just skip first period and go somewhere and talk?"

I didn't know that was what I wanted, but now I realize it's exactly what I need, to go somewhere with her and talk. And maybe even kiss her.

"Yeah," I say again, relieved. "Want to go to Jim's house? I mean, mine...you know."

She nods, and we slip through the crowds and out of school. We don't say anything the whole way to the house. I don't want to tell her anything while we're out on the street and she somehow knows that, so it's okay.

Jim's car isn't there, which is good. I really hadn't thought about what I'd do if he was home. I let us in and it's like I haven't been there in forever. Everything is just like it was on Friday morning, only now, for the first time in five years, it feels weird to be here.

"Hang on, okay?" I say to her. She nods as I go to the kitchen and rummage through the drawers. I find a beat-up butter knife and put it in the back pocket of my jeans. It will have to do.

When I come back into the living room, she's holding a photo of Kevin and me that has been living on Jim's bookshelves so long that it leaves a perfect square in the dust when she picks it up. Long enough that I've been able to forget it's there.

"You guys were really cute kids," she says.

I look over her shoulder at the photo. It was pretty soon after we moved here. We're at the playground in matching striped shirts that Mom bought us. Kevin has a fake smile plastered onto his face, but I look empty, like I'm not there. Kevin's arm is around my shoulders. I can see he's holding me so tightly that it must have hurt, only I wasn't feeling much back then, so who knows.

Looking at the photo makes me feel a million things at once. It makes me miss Kevin and think how I've always been able to take for granted that he'd be there looking out for me. And it makes me realize how hard it must have been for Jim to suddenly be saddled with two screwed-up kids when all he wanted was to travel and see the world.

Before I push myself too close to a spin, I take a deep breath and force myself to look away, to look at Sarah, to try to forget.

"Come on. I'll show you my favorite place." I reach over and take her hand so fast I can't scare myself out of it, and lead her upstairs.

My first thought when I open our bedroom door is that I'm glad Kevin didn't leave underwear or that pack of condoms lying around. I hadn't even thought of all the embarrassing crap that could be sitting out for anyone to see. Then I go to the window and, after a few attempts, open it with the knife.

And then the air. All the fresh air comes rushing in and wraps around me. I can't help but close my eyes and sigh even though I know we don't have a lot of time.

I climb out first and help her through. The first thing she does is walk around the whole perimeter of the widow's walk, a smile on her face.

"Cool. This is great. I wish my house had this."

I'm at war with myself as I head to the safe side and sit, pressing my back hard against the wall of the house. I'm not sure when I was last up here without Kevin. I wonder if Sarah being here will be enough to hold me if I feel like I have to start moving closer to the edge.

She comes over and sits down in front of me. She leans back between my legs so that my chin rests on the top of her head.

I'm pretty sure she'll be enough.

I close my eyes against her hair as she takes one of my hands in each of hers and wraps them around her.

I'm drowning in lilacs.

"I'm getting my driver's license this summer," she says. I can feel my arms around her, but it sounds like she's so far away. "When I have it, we could leave. Just the two of us."

"You mean, like a vacation?" I ask.

Her hands tighten on mine but she looks straight ahead when she replies. "No. I meant we could really leave."

I feel the world spin as I think about being with her all the time. But just like going to Canada with Kevin, I know it can't really happen.

My hand starts to tremble as I tighten my grip on hers. I can hear my voice shake when I answer. "You could just leave Luke, and your parents, and everything?" I think about how much I don't want Kevin to leave and wonder whether it would feel the same if I was the one to pack my stuff up in a car and disappear.

She presses her back into my chest and for a minute I think everything I could ever want is right here.

"There's so much out there, Gordie. So much more than we have in this little hick town. It isn't just that I want to get away from my parents, but there are places I want to go. I want to visit New York and London. I want to kiss someone at the top of the Eiffel Tower. Don't you ever think about that?"

I've never really thought about traveling that far. I figured it would just happen someday, like not having spins and being normal. But now I'm thinking about kissing her in Paris and I can feel my heart pounding against her back.

Before I can answer, I lean back too hard and hit one of my bruises. Suddenly, I have to untangle myself from her, and it's the most painful thing in the world to have to pull away.

"I . . . Sarah," I say. "My father. It's just . . . he's . . . " I don't know where to start and my thumb is moving and I can't stop it. I'm freaking because I don't want her to think I'm some weak, defenseless kid who lets himself get beat up and doesn't fight back. But I'm not sure she'll understand how much danger Jordan is in if she doesn't know what my father does.

Before I can talk myself out of it, I pull my shirt over my head. She gasps, reaching out to gently touch the bruises on my side. It doesn't hurt. In fact, it feels like the best thing ever.

"Oh, Gordie. You have to tell somebody."

Her words are a whisper on my cheek. Her hand is still hot on my skin, and my shirt is balled up tight in my fists.

"I can't. Not yet anyhow." My eyes trail along the edge of the wall. I feel the pull. But I won't do anything that will make her take her hand off my skin.

"Why not?" she asks. "You can't go back there."

I take a deep breath and tell her the whole story—about the weekend, and going to the house, and about Jordan and how scared his eyes were. I tell her I think he's been hurt in some really, really bad way.

"That poor little boy," she says, only the sad expression on her face makes me wonder if she's talking about Jordan or about me.

I slip my shirt back on. I don't want her thinking that way about me.

"What do you think he wants?" Sarah asks.

I rifle through the possible answers in my head. What I want and what Jordan might want gets all knotted up. So I shrug. "Jordan? I think he just wants … "

She shakes her head. "No. I mean, your father. My parents … they want Luke. They want some golden child who is great at everything and has his whole future planned out in a way they can understand. They want someone who is going to get a scholarship to a good school and move down the block and give them lots and lots of grandchildren. They hate me because I'm not like that."

I can't imagine anyone hating Sarah.

"You're asking what my father wants?" I know that's what she's asking. But I have absolutely no idea, and this sets my hand off bad. I stop myself before I sit on it. I rest it on my knee instead and Sarah reaches out and puts her own hand lightly on top of it. It feels like a butterfly or a sparrow.

"I don't know," I tell her. "All he ever wanted from me was for me to be really good at hockey. I'm supposed to do all the things he wanted to do but screwed up. But it's like nothing Kevin ever did was good enough for him because Jim's his dad, I guess. But Jordan's just a little kid."

My hand shakes under hers and I grab it away.

I realize, as I say it, that Kevin was just a little kid too when my father was beating him up. It makes me feel really bad for my brother and washes some of my anger away.

"Why is Kevin so upset about you seeing me?" Sarah asks suddenly.

I picture him standing against the lockers, clutching the bottom of his shirt in his fists. "I don't really know. I think he's scared." His drunken words come back to me. What if Kevin is as afraid of leaving me as I am of losing him?

"Scared of me?" she asks.

"No, of ... of himself, I think."

She nods like she understands, and we just sit there lost in our own thoughts until she breaks the silence. "So what do you think we should do?"

The way she says "we" makes it the most beautiful word I've ever heard.

"I need to find Jordan, but I don't remember where the house was."

"Maybe he'll take you there again."

"I don't think I should wait."

"Okay. Do you think you can remember how you got there?"

I close my eyes and try to remember the path the car took. But all I remember is tree after tree after tree.

"Maybe a little. I wasn't really paying attention."

"Do you have a computer? We could look at a map." She's all business now. It must be wonderful to be used to finding solutions for problems.

"Kevin took it to school, but I was thinking we could look in the library."

"Gordie ... " She links her arm through mine and leans her head on my shoulder.

I lean my head back on hers. Her hair tickles my cheek and for a minute I forget that she's asking me something. "What?"

"What are you going to do when you find him?" Her voice is quiet, like she's afraid to hear the answer.

I lift my head and look at her. "I haven't really figured that out yet." I bite my lip, my breath coming faster as I try to gear myself up to tell her what I *have* figured out. "I thought..."

I stop myself from saying I thought she could come with me and take Jordan's picture. Somehow I know, even though it scares me, that this is something I need to do on my own. Well, mostly anyhow.

"I think I know someone I can tell," I finish.

Even though it isn't still in my sock, I reach down to my ankle for where Ms. DeSilva's business card was. Somehow, I hope she'll be able to do something, and I tell Sarah about her. "She's a lawyer, and...I'm not sure what else. But she's kind of looked out for me. I think I need proof, though. I think I need all the proof I can get."

"That's good, Gordie. That's really good." She stands and brushes off her jeans, and then she's smiling at me like she did when we were under that willow tree.

Her smile makes me shiver.

I get up so fast my head spins a little. I know that if I think too much I'm going to scare myself into doing nothing.

"Sarah..." I want to tell her how I was thinking about her this weekend. How those thoughts were pretty much the only things that kept me together.

"What?" she asks and moves closer.

My teeth are chattering even though it isn't cold. "I just want..." I can't think of any words that are right, so I just lean in to kiss her.

It isn't quite like it was under the tree.

For one thing, I'm not really as scared of it this time.

And for another, being up here and kissing her is like stepping over the edge and getting stuck on a cloud.

She pulls back for a minute and I think she's going to tell me to stop. That I'm doing something wrong, that she didn't mean it. But then she leans forward again and so, so, so gently brings her hands up under my shirt. Her fingers dance across my bruises and I feel my legs start to shake.

She turns and backs me up to the wall of the widow's walk. We aren't kissing, but her face is so close to mine that I can see myself reflected in her eyes.

In some ways this is more intense, more frightening, than kissing her.

I have to force myself not to turn away from the interrogation of her eyes. To swallow. To breathe. I'm surprised to find that my blood is still flowing through me because it feels like my brain has shut down and is just stuck in this one perfect and terrifying moment.

Her fingers are still moving so softly against my skin. I wonder if I might be imagining it. I know I'm not. Nothing my brain has ever come up with has ever felt this good.

I can tell she's worried about hurting me, and I want to say that nothing she could do would ever hurt, but I can't find my voice.

My heart is pounding. Everything in me wants to be touching and kissing her until I can't feel where I stop and she starts.

Somehow my hands are steady. But it's like they move all on their own as they crawl under the edge of her shirt and my fingertips skate across her soft skin. For a few amazing minutes I don't care about anything other than the feel of her tongue on my lips and her body pressed against me.

She pulls back, her breath coming in fast gasps too. I knot my hands behind my back to keep from drawing her back toward me. Just the few inches of wasted space between us are making me feel empty and alone.

She reaches up a hand and rests it on my cheek. "Will you hate me if I say that we need to get back to school?"

I'm glad to hear that her voice sounds as raw and odd as I'm feeling. I have to search my head for words that sound like English. And even once I find them, I have problems getting them out of my grateful, bruised mouth.

"I could never hate you."

She smiles and takes my hand to lead me back toward the window, but I stumble, dizzy and shaking, feeling like I've been turned inside out.

I've only barely recovered when, as I lock the front door of Jim's house, I realize that I never once seriously thought about flying over the edge of the walk.

————

When I see her in the library at lunch, she blushes.

I wonder if she's thinking about us kissing on the walk like I am. Probably not, since it's all I've been able to think about. It's almost like a spin, but not. It's just something I want to do again really, really badly.

I stand there like an idiot, staring at her.

"Sit down," she says, grabbing my sleeve and pulling me out of it. "I have a map."

I'm grateful to have a task to focus on. We pore over streets. I try to remember everything I can, but my mind is a frustrating blank.

My hand starts to cramp so I massage it. It doesn't help. I let it sit in my lap and do its thing.

Sarah ignores it.

"Maybe we can find Jordan on the Internet," she suggests.

"He's only seven." I'm surprised to hear the anger in my voice.

"You'll find him, Gordie. We'll find him." I'm glad she knows I'm not angry with her.

She chews on the end of her pen and I watch her teeth make tiny indentations in the plastic. Her mouth forms words and I have to struggle to listen to what she's saying because watching her mouth only makes me want to kiss her again. "Maybe if you talk to that lawyer now, she can help too."

She's probably right, but talking to Ms. DeSilva seems like something I need to do *after* I have something to show her. Maybe Jordan isn't there and someone will think I'm making it up, or Kevin will pipe up and say that it's all in my head because he doesn't want me to get involved.

"I have to wait until I see him again first," I say.

"Maybe there's something in your dad's house that has the other address on it?"

That stops me. Of course.

I can't take waiting anymore, so I lean over and kiss her. Once. Quickly. With my lips closed because I know that if I feel her tongue inside my mouth like before, I won't be able to stop.

"You're a genius," I say, gasping for air.

Sarah laughs and starts refolding the map. "You would have thought of it eventually."

I pause and swallow hard when I think of the other favor I need from her. I regret not asking her when we were at Jim's.

"There's something else I need you to do," I say before I lose my nerve.

"Sure. What?" She's distracted by the paper she's shoving into her bag when I grab onto her hand.

"I need you to take pictures of me. Of the bruises."

Her eyes open wide and she goes pale like a ghost.

"Oh, I don't know." She shakes her head and her voice is small and squeezed. "Maybe I could loan you my camera and Kevin could..."

"Please," I beg. There's no way in hell I'm letting Kevin see my back. I'm pretty sure he hasn't been joking about killing my father, and that would send him over the edge. "We have to do it now. Before they fade." I don't say I'm pretty sure that if we wait long enough, my father will do it again.

She chews on her pen again as she considers the idea. "Now... like, this minute now?"

"Yeah."

We walk in silence to her locker so that she can get her camera, and then I lead her to the closet outside the entrance to the gym. It's never locked. It just has brooms and stuff in it.

We sneak in one at a time, but no one is paying any attention to us anyhow.

After we close the door, I tug on the string to turn the light on and start to pull my shirt over my head.

She turns away from me and looks at the wall, which is silly because she's seen me without a shirt before.

"Are you sure about this?"

I hang my shirt on a broom handle and think about turning around, locking the door, and kissing her until my lips are sore again. "Yeah."

She turns toward me and flinches. Then she bends down and pulls her camera out and attaches a lens and flash.

When I twist around, leaning against a stack of boxes so that the worst of the bruises face her, she sighs. "Oh Gordie..."

My fingers curl into the cardboard and I force myself not to move.

I hear the click, click, click of the shutter and she directs me how to turn, and stand, and after a few minutes that feel like hours, we're done.

After I put my shirt back on, she puts her arms around me. "Gordie?"

"Yeah?"

There's silence and all I can feel is her hair against my chest.

"I meant what I said to Kevin. I really like you a lot. I just want you to know."

Suddenly the room is hot and my shirt feels sticky against my skin. I don't want her to like me just because of what my father's done, and I'm not really sure what I'm supposed to say back.

"I like you a lot too," I say, but I can't meet her eyes even though it's the most honest thing in the world.

"Promise me you'll try not to let him do that to you again."

I'd promise her anything, but it would be a lie to say I have any control over my father.

"I'll try," I say. But I know I'll fail. If I can do what I'm trying to do, he's going to want to kill me.

TWENTY-FIVE

After school, I walk back to the old house. Maybe I shouldn't. Maybe I should just run away, but I have nowhere to go and the thought of leaving Sarah now makes me almost as scared as thinking of Kevin leaving.

My father's car is in the driveway, black, shiny, and long, like a hearse.

It's kind of weird that he's not picking me up from school. I guess he knows I have nowhere else to go without getting someone I care about in trouble.

The garbage is out near the side porch, which strikes me as funny because I don't think it's garbage day. It isn't even bagged up right. I walk over and reach down to pick up some bit of red fabric, to stuff back in, but the minute my hand hits it I fall to my knees. I remember this dress. Mom's dress.

I can't breathe and the fabric is just running through my hands like water, like blood, like... no... I'm surrounded by a hundred million memories. I swat at them ineffectively as they swarm around me.

I'm shaking. My stomach heaves as my head fills with picture after picture after picture after...

"Mommy."

No, I don't call her that anymore. I'm ten. I'm big now. I don't want to sound like a baby. Even Kevin is going to make fun of me if I do that.

I bury my face in the red. It smells like the perfume she wears when she goes out to do something special. But I don't want her to go. I don't want her to leave me here all alone again.

"Stay. Stay. Stay. Stay. Stay." I hear myself say, over and over and over, and...

"Sweetie, what are you doing out here?"

I curl myself into a ball, pull my arms over my head, and try to block out the voice. The movement makes my muscles ache in the spots where my father slammed me into the boards.

I know the voice is coming from inside my head. I know it is. However much I want her to be here, she isn't.

"My sweet boy..."

I should open my eyes to prove to myself that I'm alone, but they're glued shut.

There's a soft breeze against my face as I rock my head back and forth into the side of the concrete step. I'm pretty sure it should hurt, but I don't feel anything no matter how hard I push.

"Z. Y. X. W. V." I recite the alphabet backward, hoping that will push the voice out of my brain.

"Gordie."

My name is like a whisper on the wind. Like the wings of a bird beating against my ears.

I try to pick up where I left off with the alphabet, but the wings have blown all of the letters away.

The very worst thing is that I'm not really stupid enough to think my mom is here. I just wish she was. I want her to be. A part of me thinks it might even be worth it to be crazy if it means I can see her again.

"Mom." The word escapes my lips even though I don't want it to. I bite my cheek until I taste blood. But now that I've let a sound out, I can't stop another from following. "Why?"

"Because I love you," says the voice, only I don't understand. How could she do what she did if she loved me?

"But..." I start to ask the question, then force the back of my hand to my lips to stop myself. I bite down on the skin, the fabric in my hand grazing my cheek like a caress, and try to make myself stop rocking. I can't do this. Kevin says that if anyone finds out how much I'm spinning, they're going to force me to go back to the counselors or even worse. And lately it's been so, so bad.

What if I'm like Mom?

I know that talking to people who aren't there is a whole other kind of crazy from spinning. I've read about those hospitals. If I end up in one, I'll never get out again.

I struggle to pull myself up against the wall of the house. My head is heavy and falls backward against the cool brick. I can hear my breath coming in little gasps.

I focus on that. On my breath. On trying to take long pulls of air, trying to get my heart to stop beating a million times a minute.

I slam my hand onto the concrete of the porch. I'm so tired of being a freak.

At least I can feel the pain this time.

When I'm able to pry my eyes open, I look around and make sure I'm alone. I knew I would be, but there's a small little sparrow of a thing inside me, crashing against my heart because my mom isn't here.

I pry the fabric out of my hand and shove it deep into the bag, trying not to touch anything, terrified of what else I might find.

I'm just tired. I know that's it. Tired and stressed. Tired and stressed. Tired and stressed. That's all this is. I'm not expecting dragons to come save me, like Jordan is. I'm okay. I'm fine.

I'm not ten, I'm fifteen. That means I can take care of myself. I can make this better for me, and for Kevin, and for Jordan.

I'm okay. I'm okay. I'm okay.

My legs are shaking, but I pull myself up on the side of the wall and dust off my jeans.

A car speeds down the street. I want to flag it down and beg whoever's driving to take me far, far away from here, but Ms. DeSilva says I have no choice. I have to spend the week here, which means that even if I tell someone, all they're going to do is ship me back. Or to a hospital. I can't imagine Sarah would ever want to kiss someone who's locked up in a loony bin.

I want to kiss her again so badly.

And that means getting through tonight, finding Jordan's address, and holding it together until I see her tomorrow.

I'm okay.

I put my shaky hand in my pocket and walk around to the front door. I try to make it up the steps without looking at anything.

A voice stops me as I enter the house. I have no doubt this one is real.

"Come here, son."

I don't have the energy to tell him, again, not to call me his son. I make the mistake of staring at him, though, and feel a pull of memory so strong it makes me stumble. It's so hard to stop spinning once I start.

"Sit down," he says.

I fall onto the sofa and rub my temples. My head feels like it's going to break into two.

"Are you sick? Do you need me to find a doctor?"

"No," I say, too loudly. "I don't need a doctor."

He looks through me. "You see that mantel there?" he asks, pointing toward it.

My eyes follow his finger to the wall and I nod.

"Starting next week, you and I are going to be doing some intensive practices. You're going to fill that mantel with trophies."

His words are so wistful and unexpected that I parrot them back. "With trophies?"

I get up and walk over to the mantel and run my hand across it, picking up a coat of dust on my fingers. In spite of myself, I picture all my hockey trophies lined up next to each other. An endless assembly line of successes. Of normal.

His breath on my neck makes my skin crawl. He reaches out and puts a beefy hand on my shoulder, squeezing until I wince.

"You were in line to be great when you were a kid. Do you remember? 'The best young goalie in the Metro area' they all said. So, fine. You've slacked off for a while. But from now on that changes. From now on, you will breathe, eat, and shit hockey. Do you understand?"

Only my father could turn something I love into a punishment. But that's how it always was, from the time I could walk. Practice. Practice. Practice. He didn't care about school, or friends, or anything else I wanted to do. He didn't care about me.

"You still have a year," he continues, "to get up to speed. The scouts will start coming and then we'll talk about scholarships and advances. You're going to get all the money that people donated when you turn eighteen, and we'll be able to move away from here and all of this."

I dig my nails into my palms and clench my teeth until my jaw aches. Whatever happens, I'm not leaving with him even if it means I never see a cent of the money.

He shoves something into my hand as his face breaks into a wide smile filled with razor-sharp teeth. "Open it."

I turn it over in my hand. It's just a white envelope. I don't want anything he'd give me, but I don't know how to get out of this, so I do my best to plaster a bored expression on my face and pull the flap.

Two tickets fall out of the envelope and flutter like dying moths onto the floor. Tiny print covers them and I see a red and white symbol in the corner. I can't stop myself. I bend down, pick them up, and flip them over.

Before the thought even embeds itself in my head, he explains. "Season tickets for the Red Wings. For you and me."

Fuck. I never get to go to real games anymore. Tickets are so expensive that I pretty much only ask to go as my Christmas present from Jim and Kevin. I've never dreamed of having season tickets.

His hand returns to my shoulder and he squeezes again, with enough force to crumble brick. "I think 'thank you' is the phrase you're looking for."

I put the tickets back into the envelope and place it on the mantel. Then I shove my hand deep into my pocket.

"Why did you want to take us to California?" I ask, without planning to. I can't even believe my dumb mouth is letting these words out.

He's silent as he lets go of my shoulder and brings out a packet of cigarettes and a lighter. I can't tear my eyes away. It's like when people watch a car crash on the freeway. I don't want to look, but I can't help it.

He lights up and I watch the smoke rise, bracing myself for his answer.

"What are you talking about?" he asks.

"California," I whisper. "You were going to take me and Kayla to California." My hand jerks hard. I know he knows what I'm talking about. He has to. It was what caused everything.

He sits down and picks up a newspaper like I'm not talking about anything that matters. "You must have been dreaming. I've never even been to California."

I want to scream. I want to hit something. He's lying. I know he's lying.

But what if he's not? If The Night Before didn't happen, then why did Mom...

The smell of smoke is suffocating.

Either he's just being a dick and screwing with my head, or I'm nuts and Mom hated us. Hated me. Wanted me dead.

The newspaper covers his face and he isn't looking at me. I clench my hands to stop myself from grabbing at it and ripping it up into shreds of confetti.

I want to force him to admit everything.

My mouth won't work. I can't feel anything. I chew on my sleeve until I can feel my tongue again and force out, "knife."

The paper rustles as he brings it down.

"Get a hold of yourself, son. You know what happens to boys like you who make up lies, right?"

Kevin was right. He's going to have me locked up.

His stare forces me backward and I just keep backing away until I hit the banister.

I turn and run upstairs, leaving the envelope perched on the mantle like a white heron.

———

It's dark.

I don't think I've slept. But I haven't really been awake either.

I can't help it. I've been lying here in a pool of sweat, replaying The Night Before over and over and over.

He has to be lying. He has to be.

Otherwise I'm never going to be normal, and next year will be the same as this year, and last year, and every year to come.

I need one normal day. One normal night. No spins or memories. That isn't going to happen so long as I'm anywhere near him.

I hope it's close to morning. Close to school, and Kevin, and Sarah. Close to getting the hell out of here.

I look at my watch.

11:23.

I rip my watch from my wrist and throw it across the room.

I hate 11:23.

Even though that was a.m. and this is p.m., it's the same.

I see the numbers typed on the form. Each digit in its own box.

1

1

2

3

They couldn't tell what time the kids died. But they knew Mom died around then. And that's the time they chose for them all.

11:23 would have been typed on my death certificate, too.

It's strange to know what time you were supposed to die.

I never look at the clock during fourth period.

Once the numbers get in my head, that's it.

They're in attack mode now.

I get up and tug on my T-shirt, damp with sweat and stress. I pull it off. It takes a while because my hands are shaking and I can't get a grip on the thin fabric. My boxers follow.

I touch my face. I feel like I'm on fire.

I crawl over to my backpack and pull out the other leather band. I put it on before pushing myself against the cool wall. It feels good against my naked back, but even though I'm snapping the band against my wrist as hard and as fast as I can, the numbers don't go away.

I unzip the bottom compartment of my bag.

Ms. DeSilva's business card has other numbers on it. I run my fingers over them and imagine them holding up knives, fighting the clock's numbers.

11:23 falls over. Bloodied and bruised. Gasping.

I wonder if numbers can die.

I wonder why I didn't.

———————

The chattering of my teeth wakes me up.

The floor is hard and cold, and it's dark, and I'm lying here naked and cramped.

I groan when I try to get up, then clamp my lips together. The very last thing I want is for him to come in here.

I pull myself over to the closet and layer shirt over shirt until I can almost remember what warm feels like. Jeans follow, before I lean my ear against the door to listen to the silence.

I turn the knob as quietly as I can, holding my breath so even that won't make a sound.

The door to Mom's room is closed. I hope he's on the other side of it as I make my way down the steps.

I avoid the fourth one.

Mom had an old sewing table in the living room. She

used to throw bills and letters and receipts and other bits of random paper in there.

I pull it open, hoping it won't squeak.

The stacks of envelopes in the drawer are too new to be hers. Every single one of them is from a law firm downtown.

They've been opened. I scan one of the letters. Something about child support payments for Jordan.

And there's an address.

I wonder if I survived the river so that I could save Jordan. My brother.

Sticking the letter into my jeans pocket, I take it back to Kevin's room. The fact that I'm wearing almost every shirt I brought here isn't keeping me from shivering.

I pull out the letter and DeSilva's card.

I hold them close to my chest and rock back and forth on the floor, watching the red numbers on the clock change, one after another after another after another.

Waiting for morning.

TWENTY-SIX

Mr. Brooks is always in his office before homeroom. He says it's the quietest part of the day. When he was teaching middle school, there were full weeks that he'd find me on his beat-up old couch every morning, waiting for him.

Sometimes we'd talk. Sometimes I'd just sit there. He always let me be the one to decide.

I don't remember the last time I did that.

His door is open and, as usual, he's stretched out on his couch reading some dog-eared paperback. He smiles when I come in and goes back to his book.

I set my bag down and stumble over my feet as I make my way to the rocking chair.

The chair has a perfect view of Mr. Brooks' letter-filled wall. There's stuff from old students and collages of photos detailing his years of teaching. You wouldn't think it would be relaxing to look at, but it is.

It would be easy to sit here until class, but that isn't what I came here for. When I start to doze off, I force myself over to the air hockey table and push the puck back and forth.

Mr. Brooks is suddenly next to me. "Do you want to play?" I nod. He closes the door and fires up the machine.

Mr. Brooks always plays to win. He says that kids need to learn to be graceful losers as well as graceful winners. He doesn't believe in mercy rules.

I like that about him.

He always wipes the floor with me in foosball; I can't get my hands to do that many things at once. But usually I can beat him at air hockey. Today he scores three straight goals against me. My reactions are sluggish. I always seem to be moving the wrong way in response to his shots.

I don't really care about beating Mr. Brooks. I just don't know how my father could have lied to me about The Night Before.

Crash. I beat the mallet into the side of the table.

Then again, maybe he's telling the truth and I'm just crazy and making everything up, like hearing Mom's voice.

Crash. The mallet hits again, harder this time.

Maybe I was always nuts and that's why Mom tried to kill me. Who would want a crazy kid anyhow?

Crash.

Mr. Brooks covers my hand with his own and gently pries the mallet away from me. He guides me over to the couch. I sit in the corner of it and pull my legs up to my chest. Mr. Brooks doesn't care if we put our shoes on the cushions. This couch is already like a hundred years old.

I run a hand through my hair. It's damp. My hands are shaking.

Mr. Brooks sits on the arm and says my name, but nothing more. I came here to talk to him, but I don't know where to start. Anything I say is going to sound demented, so I just spew out all the words at once. "How do you know if something you remember really happened or if you're making it up?" My thumb starts up, so I shove my whole hand under the cushion, where it wraps around a nickel.

He answers carefully, like he always does. It's one of the ways you know he's really thinking about what you've asked. "If you remember something, it probably did happen. Maybe not exactly as you picture it, though. Memories are like that sometimes."

Mr. Brooks rarely answers a question in a way that just gives you an answer. I think he likes to make you figure it out on your own.

I like that about him, too.

So I think that means there was a Night Before. But what if my father didn't really want to take us to California? What if it was some grown-up joke I didn't understand when I was ten?

Still, Mom was crying and there was the knife; I know I saw the knife. There's no way I could have made that up.

"What is it?" he asks.

I let go of the nickel, leaving it there for someone else to find, and pull my hand out from the cushion.

"How do you know if you're crazy?"

Mr. Brooks pauses, and I'm pretty sure he's going to tell me that I am and that I shouldn't move because he's going to call the counseling office. Or that someone from the hospital will come and get me.

"I'm going to guess that if you're thinking straight enough to ask the question, it's a safe bet you're okay." He pulls on my sleeve. "You aren't crazy, Gordie. You know that. Well, not any more than the rest of us, anyhow."

I take a really deep breath and try to relax.

"Do you want to tell me what's bothering you?" he asks.

"I have a little brother," I blurt out. I know, I know, I know I shouldn't say anything to anybody, but Mr. Brooks always seems to know what to do, and I'm hoping he can tell me now.

He cocks his head. "You do?"

I nod. I'm just about to tell him that I think my asshole father is hurting Jordan when Sarah comes flying in through the door with a paper in her hand.

She stops and smiles when she sees me. I have to hold onto the cushions to keep from launching myself over to her.

"Sorry I missed the deadline yesterday, Mr. Brooks. Here's my paper," she says without taking her eyes off me.

"Hmm..." He takes it from her and I feel all the blood rush to my face. "Thanks, Sarah. See you in class."

We kind of stare at each other for a minute before she leaves. My eyes stay glued to the doorway until I feel a tap on my shoulder.

"Sarah Miller? That's why you've been so distracted in class lately?"

I cross my arms in front of me. Have I been distracted in class? I've tried really hard to pay attention, but with all this stuff about my father and all the spins...

"Gordie?"

Crap.

"Yeah. I mean, no. I'm sorry," I squeak out.

He puts his hand on my shoulder and smiles. "It's okay. That's … interesting." He gets up and walks to his desk and sits down, which is strange because I'm not sure I've ever seen him use that chair. He's usually on the couch, or playing a game, or sitting on top of the desk.

Just as he sits, someone else bursts through the door.

This time it isn't Sarah, but a junior girl with a paint-covered skirt and long disheveled hair. She looks like she was playing paintball and forgot to change clothes. I think it's possible she might need to talk to Mr. Brooks even worse than I do.

I start to get up, but Mr. Brooks waves me back down.

"Lizzie," he says with a sigh. "Do I even want to know what happened to you this time?"

"This is the second time in a week that those f … " She glances at me and shrugs.

I'm surprised to find that something in her half smile says *kindred spirits*, something says that she gets it, and I wonder if maybe we could be friends or something one day. Assuming I don't get locked up or have my brain fried in some hospital.

The girl pushes down her painted skirt and says, "I'll just come back," and then we're alone again.

Mr. Brooks rolls his eyes and lines a couple of pens up on his desk. "So, what were you saying?"

I know he isn't going to let this go, but now I'm kind of regretting that I said anything about Jordan, so I just shrug and stare down at my shoes.

He doesn't say anything for a minute and then sighs. He's

good at waiting for me to want to tell him stuff, instead of trying to pull it out of me like Kevin.

"Well," he finally says, "I have a secret of my own that I need to talk to you about."

I look up at him and my heart flutters. I wish he didn't have something to say if it's going to make him look so serious, like a typical teacher.

"I'm taking a sabbatical next year. I'm going to do some studying of my own, in theaters in England."

Mr. Brooks is head of our drama club, so I guess this makes sense, but ... "For the whole year?"

He smiles and leans forward. "Yeah. I leave a week after graduation."

I get up and walk over to the window. He has this cool feeder that suctions onto the window and it's always crowded with hungry birds and the occasional squirrel.

The room is silent. My head is silent. Not in a good way. I just feel empty and confused. Mr. Brooks was there from the beginning. He's the only one who ever treated me like I wasn't some nutcase.

"Gordie?"

I know I need to tell him to have a nice time, that I'll see him when he gets back. That's what normal people would do, right? But my heart is pounding and I'm stuck here watching the birds crack the little seeds with their sharp beaks.

His shadow fills the window as he comes up behind me. "I have email, you know. You can always write me. Or even call, if you need to."

I lean my forehead against the cool glass. A couple of the

birds fly away and then come back to finish eating. I'm jealous of how birds get over being frightened so quickly. I want to get over it too; it's just that everything feels like it's changing at once. And sure, some of it is good, but I don't know why bad stuff needs to happen at the same time.

"Gordie."

I turn, but my eyes are stuck on the ground. I don't want him to know how upset I am. Even though I'm sure he already does.

"Sounds fun," I say as I grab my backpack and head toward the door. "I have to go. I have to … " I don't know what I have to do except not make an ass out of myself in front of Mr. Brooks, which is all well and good until I walk right into the air hockey table.

"Crap," I say, kicking it, which just makes my foot hurt.

"You're going to give that table a complex if you keep beating it up," he says.

I feel like a total idiot. "Sorry," I mumble again. I let my bag slip down my shoulder and lean against the table.

Mr. Brook leans next to me. "You're going to be okay. This is all good, right? I mean, finding out you have a brother, and Sarah Miller?"

"It's just … I don't know … confusing."

"All of it or just the part about Sarah?"

I snap the band against my wrist a couple of times. Something about seeing Sarah and having Mr. Brooks say he's leaving makes it hard to talk about Jordan again. "All of it, I guess. But Sarah … yeah. That too."

"It isn't you, you know. Relationships are always confusing. Girls are confusing." He laughs. "Take it slowly and you'll be fine. Just be yourself."

"Like I have any choice." I think I just say it in my head, but then I realize I've said it out loud.

"From the look on her face, she obviously likes you. What are you afraid of?" Mr. Brooks' question flies around the room like one of the birds at the feeder. I could make him a list of a hundred things that scare me, but I know he's asking for something more specific.

I shrug and snap the band on my wrist again a few times. This whole conversation is making me edgy and I know there's still enough time before the first bell that I'm not going to be able to escape it. "You're leaving."

"You have other people you can talk to, Gordie. You have Kevin and Jim, and now Sarah."

"It's different though. I can't talk to Jim like this, and Kevin . . . that's just different. Sarah . . . that's really different."

"You can always talk to someone else," he says softly. He knows how I feel about the whole idea of talking to someone who is just paid to listen, someone who doesn't get me at all.

"That didn't work out so well last time."

"You aren't ten anymore. I think you'd find it a completely different experience at fifteen."

I really want to just lose it and tell him he can't go, that I'm not sure how to do this growing-up thing. That everything with Kevin is changing and I don't know how long Sarah is going to stick around; she always seems to be talking about leaving. And Mr. Brooks has always been there for me to count on, and now that I think about it, I'm terrified of being left alone by all of them.

I would have said all of that when I was ten.

I know better than to say it now, but I think maybe I was better off when I was just a stupid kid.

I drag my sleeve across my eyes to make sure that I'm not crying like I really want to.

"Just think about it, okay?" he asks.

My bag feels a lot heavier when I pick it up to leave.

Mr. Brooks leans over and clasps my shoulder. "You're going to be fine."

I wish "fine" didn't seem to mean "alone," the way that everyone says it.

TWENTY-SEVEN

"Watch where you're going, freak."

I've almost walked into Cody, and now he's standing in front of me, his usual smug expression plastered onto his face. This is the last thing I'm up for.

"Sorry." I move to step around him.

"You sure are," he says.

Normally, I'd walk away and figure I got off light. But there's a powder keg of pissed-off inside me and Cody's just lit it. I let my backpack drop to the floor and try to imagine what Kevin would do.

"You're graduating in a few months, right?" I ask. "I mean, you aren't going to be held back again or anything?"

His smirk narrows into a straight line. "Why, honey? You gonna miss me?"

I try to remember everything Kevin ever tried to teach me about fighting. Action is better than reaction. Throw a punch with your body, not just with your arm. Keep your thumb out of your fist or you'll break it.

I wish I'd actually tried it out and not kept it as just a

bunch of words. I take a deep breath and tighten my fists. Maybe I am nuts, but, at the moment, I don't really care.

"Yeah, we're all going to miss you keeping the penalty box warm and leaving us short-handed," I say. "In fact, why don't you stick around because really, we'd love to miss the playoffs again and I'm not sure we can do that without you."

He's such a moron that I can see him trying to figure out my insult.

"You know what I don't get?" He takes a step forward and I fight every urge I have to back up.

"What?" I ask, although I could write a book about everything Cody didn't get.

"Why haven't you just gotten over it? I mean, your mom was probably nuts too, right? So at least you didn't have to deal with her. I think she did you a favor."

I don't even take a breath before I move to punch him. But like a blur, Cody is jerked away and Kevin has him pushed up against the lockers.

"You have a death wish, Bowman?" Kevin asks, his face about an inch from Cody's.

Cody looks at me and then at Kevin. "Hey man, your whacked-out brother started it."

Kevin pulls Cody's shirt up so that it rests, wrapped around his fist, just under Cody's neck. "Yeah. Sure he did, you piece of…"

"Mr. Allen, do we have a problem here?" Mr. Brooks appears out of nowhere and stares down at Kevin.

My brother takes a step back and lets go of Cody, but I can see the anger still pouring off of him, and I still feel it churning inside me. "No," he says. "Everything is just fine."

I stare at Mr. Brooks, hoping he can feel how badly I need Kevin not to get hauled off to the principal's office.

But when Cody straightens himself out and stalks off, everyone takes a breath at the same time.

"Watch yourself, Kevin," Mr. Brooks warns, and then gives me a little nod before he leaves.

Kevin leans against the locker and looks at me like he's never seen me before. "Did you really start that?"

I swallow hard to try to contain my anger. Try to focus on what I need to do. "I'm going to go see him. Jordan. I found his address."

"I know you want to." Kevin pauses and takes a deep breath. "Sarah and I were just talking, Ice, and maybe this isn't the best way to handle things."

"What do you mean?" I'm not sure what's freaking me out more—that they've been talking, or that they agree on something.

His mouth tightens. "What are you going to do? Ride in there like the cavalry and kidnap him?"

The urge to slug something returns. But I see Sarah coming down the hall and work on letting my fist relax.

"No." I draw a sharp intake of breath and let my words flow out as I release it. "No. I need to talk to him. I need to make sure . . . I just need to see him. Then I'm going to let DeSilva know what my father is doing to him."

Sarah comes over and puts her hand on my arm. "Can't you just tell Jim now?" she asks. "Or a teacher or someone?"

I want to tell her I will, because that's what she wants to hear. I want to do whatever she wants me to. But if I'm right, I can't leave Jordan there one more day than I have to. And there's no way I'm telling anyone that. Not her, not Kevin. And if they wouldn't understand, then there's no chance of Jim or Mr. Brooks getting it.

No one is going to get why *I* have to do this.

I can't do nothing. Not again.

And the idea that maybe it *isn't* my father who's the crazy one is starting to take over my head. And if that's true, then maybe I'm imagining it all.

I need to be sure. I need to be sure of everything.

Kevin must be able to tell that a bunch of stuff is rattling through my head because he says, "I don't like this. I don't want you to get hurt, Ice. This kid is nothing to you. He isn't your problem."

Without thinking, I do something I've never, ever done before. Just like he did with Cody, I grab the front of Kevin's shirt, push him into the wall, and get right up into his face. "How. Can. You. Say. That? You, of all people?

Sarah gasps and Kevin's eyes cloud over. I tense up, bracing for the punch. I'd almost welcome it. But then Kevin spins away, slamming his hand into the locker hard enough to draw the attention of half the kids in the hall.

When he turns back to me, his eyes are sharp as daggers. "Fuck, Ice. You trying to grow up to be like your dad?"

I don't say it's more likely that I'm turning into *him*. I'm too busy feeling each of his words as they slice through my skin, each syllable sharper than any blade.

I want a fight, but this hurts worse than any blow ever could.

Maybe my father is crazy. But what does that make me, aside from the kid who inherited it?

———————

"Wait. Gordie, wait."

Sarah's voice chases me as I storm out of school and across the parking lot. At first I think I'm imagining it, but then she's right there, matching me step for step.

"Stop. Please," she pleads as first bell goes off.

What else can I do? I stop like I've walked into a brick wall.

She reaches out to touch my shoulder. I can't help it when I jerk away from her.

"Are you angry with me?" she asks. She's upset, and I hate that I'm the cause of it.

"No," I say, but I don't think she believes me. My hand is clenched again and I can't open it. The muscles don't loosen when I try to massage it so I let it fall, limp and useless, to my side.

"Gordie, I'm worried about you."

A part of me wants to put my arms around her and lay my head on her shoulder. But I can't get Jordan's eyes out of my head and I won't let anything, not even Sarah worrying about me, keep me from doing the right thing this time.

"Go back to school, Sarah. I don't want you to get in trouble," I say. I force myself to walk away.

She runs up again and grabs my sleeve. "I want to help you."

I look into brown eyes that seem like they can see right through me, like Kevin's can. "I know," I whisper.

She takes the backpack from my shoulder and puts it down on the ground. Her arms circle around me. I'm surrounded by lilacs and warmth as she breathes into my ear, "Then let me."

I give myself a few seconds to enjoy being so close to her before I pull away. It takes me a minute to get my hand into my pocket, but when I do, I tug the crumpled letter out.

She takes it from me and stares at it for a long time. "Is this his address?"

"Yeah."

"Won't he be in school now?"

It's like I'm standing on the wall at Jim's. Do I go over, or do I stay put? Do I tell Sarah the truth, or do I keep my unspoken promise to Kevin never to talk about what my father used to do to him? I need to give her an explanation but I can't do that without … without …

"I don't think so," I say crossing a line I never thought I'd cross. "When things were really bad, and he thought it would show, my father made Mom keep Kevin home from school. There's only so many bruises you can hide from the teachers." The expression on her face changes as the meaning behind my words sinks in and I silently pray that Kevin isn't going to hate me for telling her this.

But I'm pretty sure he will.

"You're just going to talk to him, right?"

For some reason the question sounds different coming from her than from my brother.

I nod.

"I could come with you," she says, glancing back at the school.

My heart races. I want her to come with me so badly. But she already skipped first period yesterday because of me, and I really don't want her to get into trouble.

Also, what if my father is there? What if Jordan is fine and it's all in my head? What if I'm nuts and she decides she doesn't want anything to do with me?

I take her hand and squeeze it.

"I'll be okay," I say.

She nods, but I'm pretty sure neither of us thinks that's true.

TWENTY-EIGHT

I look out the bus window, at tree after tree after tree. The houses get really big and then really small again as we drive through various neighborhoods and then they end up in the middle, just like Jordan's.

Cody's words ring in my ears. *Over it?* Do other people get over shit like what my mom did? Sometimes I wish I'd lost a leg or something. Everyone can understand that. They never get it when what's been broken is inside your head.

I close my eyes and focus on the hum of the engine beneath me, trying to let the rhythm calm me, and the next time I look up, the bus is stopped and the driver is impatiently calling out the street name. I pull on my cuff and realize I've been chewing on my damned shirt sleeve again. I'm glad Sarah wasn't here to see.

I think of turning around and going back, but all it takes is a glance at Jordan's house to know I have no choice.

Everything is dark and quiet. There are no cars in the driveway. I poke my head around the back, but there's no one there, only a grizzly looking dog who growls when he sees me.

I go back around and ring the doorbell. I don't know what to expect. Jordan's mother, maybe?

Something shuffles inside and I start to panic. Then the door swings slowly open, like it's been blown open by the wind.

If he looked sad last time, Jordan looks absolutely terrified now. But as he realizes it's me, the fear seeps out of his face and he rushes to throw his arms around my waist.

I put my hand on his shoulder and try to keep my voice from shaking so that I don't freak him out. Or myself. "Is your mom here?" I ask.

What I want to know, really, is that my father isn't, but I know from my own experience that the longer I can avoid bringing him up, the better off we'll all be.

"I'm not supposed to open the door," Jordan says.

"That's pretty good advice," I say, but he lets me in anyhow.

I look around. It's one of those houses where the couch is covered in plastic, where everything looks unused and dead. There isn't a single light switched on or anything to even suggest there's a kid living here. I don't see a toy or a book or a stray article of clothing.

"Are you alone?"

Jordan looks down and, for a minute, I'm pretty sure he isn't going to answer me.

"Puff is here," he says. I don't know how to respond, so I just go for facts.

"And your mom?"

"I think she's gone again," he says in a dry voice.

I sit down on the floor next to him. "Again?" I ask.

He nods.

"You mean she left you here alone? When?"

He shrugs. "After the other day, I guess."

I hope he doesn't mean the other day when I was here. "Three days?" I say, trying to keep the stress out of my voice. "You've been here alone for three days?" Even when my mom was at her worst, she wouldn't have left us alone like that.

"I have cookies," he says, as if that somehow makes up for it.

I try to keep my hand from shaking as I reach up and push Jordan's sleeve back. The bruises I saw on Saturday are still there.

I know that the plan that's been hiding in the back of my head—the one I haven't told anyone about—is the only option. And I know that what I'm planning to do is going to piss Kevin off. I know my father will want to kill me. I don't even know what Jim or Sarah would think, but I don't see any other way out.

"Are these from your dad?"

I can feel the tension running through his little body, down his arm and into mine. I remember hearing my father tell Kevin that if Kevin ever told anyone how he'd beaten the crap out of him for "saying the wrong thing" or "having a bad attitude" or breaking one of a million other rules we didn't even know existed, he would kill him. And then, when Kevin got pissed off about that, my father would threaten to hurt me or Kayla or Mom.

So Kevin never told Jim and he didn't tell anyone else. Even now.

"You don't have to say anything. Just nod, okay? I won't tell."

There's a huge pause as I wait and bite at the inside of my cheek. The pain sort of distracts me from the pictures in my head of Kevin lying silent in his room while I tried to get him to play with me, to race cars or read, to do anything but lie on his bed, his tear-stained face directed at the ceiling as he cradled a new set of bruises.

"I'm sorry about your mom," Jordan says.

My whole body shudders before my brain even registers his words. I hear myself stutter when I answer, hoping I haven't heard him correctly. "My m-m-m-om?"

He nods and tightens his grip on my hand. "He took me there. To the river."

The room spins and I can't breathe.

"Why?" I barely can force the word out.

Jordan reaches up and puts his hand on my cheek. "He said he wanted me to see what happened to bad kids who didn't listen to him."

My stomach knots tighter than anything I've ever felt. If I could, I would run and run until this pain flowed out of me. I close my eyes and press myself against the wall. I pray silently for a spin.

"Are you okay, Gordie? You aren't sick, are you?"

I force my eyes open. He's staring at me like what he's been told makes sense. His own eyes are wide and worried and that makes me feel even worse. I force myself to take a deep breath and try to hide the burning panic that's awakened inside of me.

"I'm okay," I say. I'm sure even Jordan knows I'm lying.

He sits down and settles into my lap while I wrap myself around him like he's a teddy bear.

"You miss her, huh?" he asks.

I lean my head on his and feel his hair soft against my cheek. There's no way for me to explain to him how much I miss my mom and how sick it makes me to hear how my father has threatened him. "Yeah. I miss her."

"I miss my mom too. She used to be different," he says, sitting within my shaking arms.

I know it's wrong and even illegal. I know everyone is going to be pissed at me, but I don't know what else to do.

"Jordan?" I take another deep breath and it feels like I'm jumping off the roof. "Do you want to come with me?" Then I add, "Until your mom comes back?"

Jordan lifts his serious face up to me. "Where?"

That's the question, really. But when I think about it, there's only one safe place to go.

———

While Jordan goes to get his backpack so I can help him pack some clothes, I stand at the kitchen counter and write a note to my father on a pad of paper with kittens printed across the top. I tell him everything. How I know The Night Before really happened. How I remember what he did to Kevin. And how I know he's hurting Jordan and that I'm going to tell people about it. Tell everyone. I tell him that he was right. I'm fifteen and that means something. I'm not going to let him hurt us anymore, even if I end up going crazy for real.

Jordan comes back downstairs just as I see the cell phone sitting on the table.

"Is this your mom's?" I pick it up and turn it over, praying that I'll see a camera lens. I'm not disappointed.

He nods.

"Can I take some pictures of your arms?" I ask, holding my breath.

For a minute I think he's going to say no, and there's no way I'm going to force him into anything, even if he's only seven. But eventually he pushes his sleeves up and starts to hum.

Damn. I'm never going to hear that song again without my stomach ripping itself to shreds.

I snap some photos of his bruises. The pictures aren't up to Sarah's quality, but I think they'll do what I need them to do. Then I send a text and the photos to Ms. DeSilva, telling her where I am and about Jordan.

For the first time in weeks, I feel like everything really is going to be okay.

And then a car door slams. Jordan tries to pull me upstairs, but I gesture for him to go without me. I need to end this one way or the other. If it's his mom, maybe I can talk to her. Maybe she'll call Ms. DeSilva and get some help. Or maybe it *is* Ms. DeSilva and we can just walk out of here.

The front door bursts in. My father couldn't have known I'm here, but he storms over like he's not even shocked to see me standing in Jordan's mom's living room.

Before I can say anything, he takes a swing at me, hitting one of the bruises on my side from the rink. The pain makes me slump down, but he grabs at my shirt and holds me up.

"You crazy little bastard. What do you think you're doing here?" His eyes are wild, just like they were The Night Before. Looking at him makes my brain feel buzzy, as if I'm about to spin.

I struggle out of his grasp, pressing my arms close to my side, trying not to pass out. Trying to remember Kevin's fighting rules again.

"I'm not going to let you hurt Jordan anymore," I say, wincing through the pain. Talking hurts. Breathing hurts. "I'm not going to let you hurt any of us again. I have proof now. The police. Ms. DeSilva. Jim. They're all going to know what you've done."

In spite of the pain, I'm spring-loaded with adrenaline, ready to hit back, but then I hear shuffling upstairs. Jordan doesn't need to watch our father kicking the shit out of me.

So instead I circle around until I'm at the other side of the breakfast bar. Somehow I'm sure that this was on Kevin's list: *When all else fails, put something between you.*

"What makes you think that anyone is going to believe you?" my father sneers. I can smell the smoke on his breath and it makes the buzzing in my head get louder.

I want to tell him what I've done, but I don't know if that's a good idea. As far as I know there's no way to unsend something from a phone, but maybe he knows something I don't.

"I know I didn't make up what happened the night before

Mom..." Even now I can't say it. "I know that really happened."

"You don't know shit," he yells.

All I can think about is Jordan upstairs. I don't want him to hear this, but I have to guess he's probably already heard worse.

I glance around the kitchen. There are scissors on the table. A block of knives—not like the huge ones that Kevin uses, but still dangerous. I don't want my father anywhere near them, so I slowly come around the counter to block him.

"I know you're hurting Jordan. That you were. But you can't anymore."

My hands are shaking like crazy. I try to form fists, but I can't keep them closed. Jordan makes a sound upstairs and my father moves toward the staircase. I reach out for his shirt, but the fabric just slides through my hands.

When he turns, I brace myself for his next swing, but instead he pushes me away hard. While I'm stumbling back, he reaches into his pocket, takes out a cigarette, and slowly lights up.

For some reason this is worse than him hitting me. I can take the punch, but I have no idea what he's planning to do now. I should run. Instead, I'm frozen in place, watching the lit tip of his cigarette.

It feels like a million years before my father takes a long drag and laughs his ugly laugh. The shuffling from upstairs stops and I hold my breath, which hurts more than it should. "It's really a shame, Gordie. All your wasted potential," he says, like he's really concerned. "Did you know they still do electro-shock to kids in those hospitals? I mean, I thought you had more of me in you than your mother. But I guess I was wrong."

My eyes fall closed. It's finally come to this. What if the photos never got sent? What if Ms. DeSilva doesn't believe me? What if I screw this up and get sent to some stupid hospital?

"And really," he continues, "what could I do when I came in to find you hurting my son, my little Jordan?"

"What?" I stumble from the shock of his words and back up until I'm against the wall.

"I had to defend him from you," he says, as casually as if he's talking about the weather.

"No," I gasp, grabbing at my hand to keep it from spasming. Every time it moves, it pulls something in my side that hurts like hell. "I'd never hurt Jordan."

His eyes narrow. "You're sick. Dangerous. You don't even remember the things you do." He moves to the phone on the wall and rests a hand on it before breaking into a wide vulture smile. "In fact, I think I'm going to call the police now. To protect my little boy."

My thoughts tangle. I'm screwed. They're never, ever going to believe me. I sink down to the floor. I want to check out and just let go. Maybe he's right after all. Maybe I'm just too fucked up to help anyone.

And then the sirens start.

TWENTY-NINE

Everything happens at once. The police come in and Kevin is only two steps behind them and I'm scanning the room for Jordan and it's loud. The dog is barking in the yard and my father is screaming and Kevin is screaming and I hear my father say, "Of course you were behind this" and Kevin says something about a knife, and all I can do is put my arms over my ears and try to block it out before my freaking head explodes.

One of the officers yells, "We can sort this out here or at the station," so loudly that the whole room goes quiet. At first I think I've gone deaf, but then she offers me a hand up and tells me to sit on the couch next to Jordan while two other officers pull my father and Kevin apart.

Jordan is just staring at everything and I'm trying to catch my breath. Kevin is clenching his fists like he's about to blow. I'm glad not to see a knife or anything near him. My father just looks annoyed.

"Are you Gordie?" the lady officer asks, and I nod.

"Did you email some pictures to a...?" She looks toward another officer who says, "Amy DeSilva."

I nod again and take a deep breath. "Of Jordan. My little brother." I glance at him and see him smile when I say that. "I know I'm supposed to be in school, but I had to help him before—"

Kevin jumps in and finishes my sentence. "Before that son of a bitch beat the crap out of him." He points at my father and takes a step in his direction, which makes the cop standing closest to him put an arm in front of my brother's chest to stop him.

"Yeah," I say, fighting hard to unknot all of the twisted sentences in my head. "And I'm supposed to be staying with him, but I can't stay in that house and I couldn't let him hurt Jordan anymore. He's the crazy one."

My father rushes around the officers, over to where I'm sitting, and puts his hand around my throat before I even know it. "You're even worse than your mother," he sneers.

He squeezes his hand and for a moment I can't breathe, but then everyone starts moving again and the police pull him off me and drag him outside while Kevin flies over and kneels down in front of me.

"It's okay, Gordie. It's okay now." He looks up at the officer and asks, "Right? It's okay. This is done, right? Right?" He starts crying and punching the cushions of the couch, and I'm scared they'll arrest him, but all the officer does is put her hand on his back and hold him there.

My neck is hot where my father's hand was, but I can still swallow, so that's good. One officer is talking to Kevin and another one is talking to Jordan, so I get up and walk over to the window. I pull back the curtains. The blue and red lights are still whirling on the cop cars and I snap my band hard, trying not to let the lights send me into a spin like they sometimes do.

Everything behind me has gotten soft and quiet and I catch my father's narrow eyes through the dirty glass of the police car window. They look far away, and trapped.

Maybe like my eyes looked when the car went into the river.

I let the curtains fall back and exhale.

"What were you doing there anyhow?" I ask Kevin as he holds a bag of frozen peas against my neck. Jim says it will help stop the bruising.

Kevin steps back and sighs. "Saving your ass as usual." He says it like a joke, but he isn't smiling.

"I didn't need you to..." I start, but it's a lie and we both know it so I go for the truth. "I'm glad you were there."

Half of his mouth twitches and he puts the peas on the other side of my neck. "Why didn't you tell me it was that bad?" he asks.

I want to tell him that I did and he didn't listen, but that doesn't matter anymore. "I was hoping his mom would do something, I guess."

Kevin gives me a complicated look and sits down next to me. "I don't mean with Jordan, Ice. I mean, why didn't you tell me it was so bad with you? With your dad?"

I stare at the floor. There's an ant that keeps trying to crawl up a piece of bread that someone dropped, but he's struggling. I guess when you're an ant, even a piece of bread can seem like a huge mountain.

"Hey," Kevin says, but I don't look up.

"You would have done something," I say. All the horrible things Kevin could have done scroll through my mind. He might have actually killed my dad, or even just called the cops before I had the chance to see Jordan, and who knows what would have happened then. "Look, I just needed to help my little brother," I admit. "The way you've always helped me."

I feel Kevin lean closer, and out of the corner of my eye I can see that he's hunched over with his elbows on his knees and his hands knotted together. "I took it for you, you know," he says quietly. "When we were kids. I figured if he was hitting me, he'd leave you alone." He pauses and I know what's coming, and it's enough to make my hand start up. "And Mom. I wanted him to leave Mom alone. But not like that really worked out."

I guess I always knew all of this, but it's different hearing him say it out loud. I don't know what to say back. "Thank you" doesn't seem to cut it. "I'm sorry" seems better, but still wrong.

So I rub my hand and try to guess what Kevin might need to hear. And I think about what Ms. DeSilva said to me. And I tell Kevin the truth. "Mom used to say you were the bravest kid she'd ever met."

Kevin makes an odd strangled sound, but then he looks at me, really looks at me, and I know that he believes me. And that, for once, I got it right.

THIRTY

Jim lets me skip school the next day because I need to get checked out by the doctor and because the police want to talk to me and Kevin about everything that happened with my father. Everything that *ever* happened. Even the stuff before That Day.

And I guess Kevin told them everything, too, because Jim's eyes were red when they came out of the meeting and it was a while before Kevin would even look straight at me.

Ms. DeSilva is waiting for us at the house when we get there. Kevin goes right up to our room and Jim tells me to give him space, so I curl up on the couch with my bag of peas and just kind of let myself drift off.

Every once in a while, some bit of Jim and Ms. DeSilva's conversation floats over to me. I hear terms like "preponderance of evidence," which has something to do with whether they think my father is likely to hit me or Jordan again, and she talks about a bunch of petitions she's filed to keep him away from both of us.

I try to ignore them as much as possible, but when she

starts talking about termination of parental rights, I can't help but listen.

I guess that means more petitions, because she says Jordan is in foster care and a ward of the court until they can find his mom, but they don't want that to happen with me so they have to move quickly.

I've already decided that if they force me to go back to the old house or anywhere with my father, I'm going to tell Sarah I'll leave with her. We'll go to Finland, or California, or wherever she wants.

Their muted voices mumble on for a while, and then they both come over to the couch.

I sit up and bite the inside of my lip. I hate this crap.

Ms. DeSilva sits on the edge of the coffee table, and I have to stifle a laugh because Jim always gets ticked when Kevin sits there.

"It's good to see some color in your cheeks," she says, which sounds positive, but I hold my breath anyhow because I wish they'd just take care of all this legal stuff and leave me out of it.

"I know you've had a hard couple of days, but there's one more thing I wanted to talk to you about before I file these papers tomorrow," she says.

I look at Jim and he smiles a little, but this is still bugging me out.

Jim takes a deep breath and says, "Yeah, um. So, one of the petitions. I mean we have to … " He looks at Ms. DeSilva to help him out.

"Gordie, Jim would like to petition to formally adopt you."

Jim looks at me long enough that I'm scared he's going

to change his mind. "Yeah," he says, and his voice breaks. He clears his throat. "I mean, yes. If that's what Gordie wants."

The words I want to say are sticky in my brain, trapped inside me. I think I'm going to be sick if I don't get them out once and for all.

"Are you sure?" I ask.

Jim leans over and rests his hand on my hair. It feels good. Not in the same way as when Sarah does it, but nice anyhow.

"I guess I deserved that," he says with a sigh. "But yeah, kid. If you'll have me, I'd like you to stay."

I look at him in disbelief. I think it's the first time anyone aside from Sarah has chosen to be with me. I mean, since Kevin is stuck with me as his brother and all.

"I'd like that," I say. My voice has holes in it, though. It's like it can't contain everything I'm feeling, and I worry they won't understand this is what I want almost more than anything.

Ms. DeSilva leans over and hugs me. I think I should try to figure out what this all means, but of course there's one more question knocking around my head.

"What happens now? I mean, is he back at the house? I don't have to go back there, right?"

"No, Gordie, I already have court approval for you to stay here," she tells me. "And what happens now is that I've got to go back to my office and tell my assistant I need her to work late with me tonight on all of this." She points to the stack of papers on the table. "We'll need to have a meeting with a mediator, and I'll let Jim know when that is. You don't need to worry about any of it, okay, Gordie?"

You'd think she'd know by now that I'm really not good at not worrying about things.

"Where's my father?" I ask, more directly. It isn't like I really care, but not knowing is making me nuts.

She leans forward and I can tell she's trying not to watch my hand shaking on my knee. "He's in jail, Gordie. Between what you and Kevin told us, and the bruises the doctors documented on you and Jordan, not to mention how he acted at the house, there's enough evidence to charge him with assault and child endangerment. And given how he disappeared, before, they're considering him a flight risk. It's up to the court to decide how long he's going to be in prison. I think we all agree that we don't want you to have to testify at a trial, so I'm going to try to get this all resolved as soon as possible."

That really isn't the answer I want to hear.

But I guess it's a start.

———————

I jump when the doorbell rings. For a minute I think I'm back at the old house and I can't catch my breath, but then I hear Jim's voice and it all comes back to me.

Sarah comes flying into the room and hugs me. She feels solid and real and I don't want to let go. I close my eyes and burrow my face into her neck. She smells like lilacs and warmth and everything good.

"Easy there, big boy," Kevin says from the kitchen doorway. I turn my head just far enough to glare at him. He looks tired, but I guess I'd rather have him giving me a hard time than shutting down.

Jim nudges him out of the room and down the hall.

Sarah and I pull apart and she reaches into her bag.

"I don't know if you still need these," she says, holding a folder out to me. "I was going crazy worrying about you and had to do something."

When I open it, I see the photos she took in the broom closet.

"Thanks," I say. I don't know if I still need them either, and I don't really want to think about her looking at them, so I start to close the folder, but she puts a hand out and stops me.

"There are other pictures in there too," she says. "I thought you might want them."

I flip quickly past the photos of my bruised skin and land on a couple of me playing goal in summer league last year. Also, one I didn't know she took of me that day when we were working on our *Moby Dick* assignment. That one I pull out.

I'm lying on top of the wooden train, the snowy sun behind me and a faraway look in my eyes.

"I'm going to submit that one for the school athlete calendar," she says. "I mean, if you don't mind."

I'm about to say no, that I don't want to be in the stupid calendar and somehow this picture is ... I don't know ... private. But the look on her face tells me she really wants this, and I don't want to disappoint her.

"I guess," I say.

It's the right answer, because she moves over and hugs me again.

"I'm really proud of you," she whispers in my ear.

I want to thank her, or kiss her, or something. I want to

keep her here and I want to learn how to be the person she thinks I am.

I wonder if it's always like this. If really liking someone means that you just want more and more all the time. If no amount of kissing is ever enough, and if no matter how much time you get with them, you always want more.

I think of asking her, because it seems she'd know the answer. But all I can do is hold her too tight and listen to the refrain in my head saying, *Don't go, don't go, don't go.*

THIRTY-ONE

A week later, we head to the courthouse to discuss custody. Ms. DeSilva has explained that there's a huge difference between Jim fully adopting me, the type of custody where I have to live with my father, and the type where I can live with Jim even though my father is still legally in charge of me. She says some judges might say "no" to the adoption and force me to see my father, regardless. So now we have to sit down and discuss all of it. The whole thing sucks and makes me feel dizzy, like I've been spinning for a week.

Kevin and I take the day off school again and Jim doesn't go to work. Instead he drives us downtown to this huge white-marble building that looks like a mini White House. When Kevin and I get out of the car, I can tell from the way he keeps fidgeting that he's on edge, which doesn't do anything to make me feel better.

Jim puts an arm around each of us, even though Kevin is almost taller than he is. Jim isn't usually touchy-feely, so I guess he's nervous too. That also doesn't make me feel any better.

None of us says a word as we walk up the steps. I shove my

hand in the pocket of my dress pants when I feel it start to act up. I think the last time I wore dress clothes was at the funeral. One more thing on the "doesn't make me feel better" list.

Ms. DeSilva hugs us and brings us into a conference room similar to the one at her office. She and Jim talk while Kevin and I stare at the clock. I'm not sure if he's trying to speed it up or slow it down. I'm not sure what I want either, aside from wanting all this legal stuff to be over with. I'm trying to act like I don't care, but I'm pretty sure I'm doing a crap job of it.

Ms. DeSilva calls us over and gives us a cell phone and tells us not to wander far. Trying not to disturb all the office people staring at their computers with frazzled expressions, we make it to the end of a hall where there's a window looking out onto nineteen floors of air. I press my forehead against the glass, but it isn't the same as being out there. I try to focus on the beating of my heart but it's making my head spin.

"Deep breath," Kevin says, squeezing the back of my neck.

"Easy for you to say," I mouth into the glass, watching the condensation form. "It isn't your future that's being decided."

"You think?" he asks, all attitude.

Okay. Fine. Obviously he's going to be affected by the outcome, but not like me.

I look down and watch myself snap the band against my wrist. It doesn't even feel like it's me. I feel disconnected from everything. I'm so out of it, I don't even notice the phone start to buzz until Kevin grabs it out of my back pocket.

"Yeah. Right. Okay. Sure." He rattles off these meaningless words while I'm waiting, waiting, waiting to hear what's going on.

"Come on," he says as he pockets the phone and tugs on my sleeve. "She wants us back there."

I know I'm not moving, and I know I need to move, but... this feels too big. Like everything is going to change all at once.

Kevin leans against the wall next to me. "Ice, come on, man. It's gotta be okay, right?"

"Why?" I ask. "Why does it need to be okay? It could just as easily suck. I mean, things go wrong all the time. They break, and people screw up, and then it all goes to hell, and..."

My voice gets louder and louder until Kevin covers my mouth with his hand.

"Shhh..." he says.

I take a deep breath and swallow the rest of the words that want to come pouring out. When I'm sure they're all contained, I nod and he removes his hand and stands right in front of me, blocking everything else out. "I promise. Do you hear me? I promise this will all work out somehow."

I nod again, but it's that last bit that kind of scares me. I don't even want to point out the number of promises that have been broken lately.

"Come on," he says, pulling my sleeve.

The walk through the hallways feels much longer than it did the first time. I think if I had to find my way back alone, I'd get lost in the twists and turns of offices that each look the same as the one before.

I close my eyes as we walk into the room and let Kevin guide me like a tugboat. I feel seasick, like everything is churning inside me.

Kevin stops short and I come close to walking into him, which makes me open my eyes even though I don't want to. I look around the room. We're here, obviously, and Jim and Ms. DeSilva, and a guy I've never seen before who looks kinda young and relaxed and not like a judge or anything.

There's an empty chair. My father isn't here.

I look over at Ms. DeSilva and bite my lip, nervous about what she's going to tell us. She comes up to me and puts a hand on my shoulder.

"Relax, Gordie. Your father isn't here. There was an altercation with another inmate and he's still in jail. At least until this is settled."

Kevin and I look at each other. His eyes are wide.

Jim said my father was going to be in jail a long time, but I've learned that things don't always happen like they're supposed to.

"Gordie?" I turn my head. The young guy says, "My name is Sam Harrison." He holds a hand out to me, which I shake, although I'm embarrassed because I'm sure he can feel how badly my own hand is quivering.

He shakes Kevin's hand too and explains that he's a mediator, not a judge. He's just someone who makes recommendations to the judge.

He gestures for us to take our seats. I sit down and, even though I know Sarah wouldn't approve, I jam my hands under my legs. I can't imagine that showing Sam Harrison what a freak I am will help my case any.

"This isn't court," the mediator explains, looking at me. "So you can call me Sam and we're just going to talk, if that's okay. I know this isn't much fun, but really, there's nothing to be stressed out about."

I hear Kevin let out a loud breath and feel my shoulders relax a little. This Sam guy seems okay.

"We'll just go through the few remaining issues one by one. And you should feel comfortable to say whatever is on your mind." He looks around the room. "That goes for all of you."

Jim gives Kevin a look that almost makes me laugh. I guess he doesn't want Kevin feeling too comfortable talking about what's going on in his mind.

"So," Ms. DeSilva starts. "Sam has reviewed all of your records, Gordie, but I'm officially going to present my recommendations here and if Sam agrees, he will take them to the judge."

We all nod.

"First," she says, "Jim would like to officially adopt Gordie. He's been living with Jim for the last five years. He's doing well in school, he's an excellent hockey player, and he wants to stay with his brother Kevin. I don't see any good that could come of disrupting that."

Sam looks at me and smiles. "Okay." He looks down at his pad again and scribbles some notes and then starts to say something else.

I can't help myself. "Wait. That's it?"

Sam laughs and his blue eyes crinkle. "Did you want it to be more complicated?"

I feel my cheeks get hot. "No, I just ... no."

"That's okay. Nothing is a done deal until we get the

judge's signature, but we all seem to be in agreement on what would be best."

He makes some more notes. I lean forward, trying to see how many things he has on his list, but Kevin pulls me back into my chair, which makes my still-bruised body ache.

"The next issue," Sam says, "is visitation. Should the judge not approve full legal custody—which I think is unlikely—and Gordie's father be considered rehabilitated, we might have to cross that bridge in the future. But I think we're best served waiting to see how things play out on that front. He isn't being terribly cooperative from what I've heard." He checks something on his clipboard. "Given Gordie's age, I think his father will be incarcerated at least until Gordie is a legal adult."

"But what about Jordan?" I ask. I can't stand the thought that I'm getting everything I've dreamed of and Jordan might be stuck in that strange plastic-covered house waiting for my father to get out of jail.

"Jordan is fine," Ms. DeSilva says. "The family he's with has fostered a lot of kids over the years. I've told them about you and they're happy to arrange a visit." She shuffles some papers. "He's been seeing someone. A doctor. Someone who can help him deal with everything that's gone on. And his mother is getting help as well, for a long-term drug addiction. We hope that eventually we'll be able to send him back to her."

"But what about when our father gets out?" I twist the band on my wrist and hold my breath. They can't have all these solutions for me and just let him have Jordan.

Jim moves over behind us and stands with one hand on

my shoulder and one on Kevin's, even though my brother is now staring down at the table like he wants to break it into two.

"When he gets out, he's going to have to deal with me."

Jim's voice makes everything in me stiffen up. Not only have I never heard him sound like this, but he sounds just like Kevin does when he talks about killing my father.

I look at Ms. DeSilva, hoping she's going to say something. She looks at Sam, who nods and says, "Like I said, I think it will be years before that happens. But you have my word, Gordie, that we'll look out for Jordan. For both of you, even after you're adults." Then he looks at Kevin and I'm relieved to hear his voice, so calm and quiet, say, "For all of you."

Sam tells us the rest of it is all paperwork that Jim needs to sign and that we don't need to sit there. I tug on Kevin's sleeve until he follows me out into the hall.

"You okay?" I ask him.

He's usually the one who owns that question, and I'm not surprised when he doesn't answer it. He just hangs onto his belt like a life preserver and takes a few deep breaths.

"Kev?"

It takes a minute, but then his shoulders relax. "God, I hope we're done with all of it now. I just want everything to get back to normal."

We stare at each other and laugh at the same time. What do either of us know about normal?

The conference room door opens. Sam comes out and says how glad he was to meet us, then heads down the hall.

"Come on. Let's go home," Jim says.

Kevin launches himself off the wall like he's been shot out of a gun. But I think of Mr. Brooks and realize I have something else to do before I can join them.

"Wait. Can you give me a minute?" I ask.

Both of them look puzzled, but that's okay. I head back into the conference room. Ms. DeSilva is gathering her papers and clipping them with those little black things that I'm always afraid will snap onto my fingers. I walk the length of the room, which feels like it's a million miles long.

She smiles like she knew I was going to come back. "I just wish I'd known earlier," she says. "We never would have sent you there. I'm really sorry. I hope you know that."

"It's okay." I know it wasn't her fault, and I can't really think of much we could have done differently.

I bite the inside of my cheek and pull at the band. My question is simple, but scary enough that I'm not sure how to ask it. I just know I can't do this anymore either. I can't keep living for the time between spins, which is never really living because all I'm doing is worrying about the next spin. And I certainly don't think I can take hearing Mom's voice again, even though I know it really isn't her.

Especially because I know it isn't really her.

Ms. DeSilva might not be able to help me. There may be no one who can really help me. But if anyone could, I think it might be her.

"You know how you said they'd found someone for Jordan to talk to?"

She nods.

"Could you ... I mean, maybe ... "

I can tell by her eyes that she knows what I'm going to ask, but she waits while I try to get the words out.

"Everyone keeps saying that I should, too. Talk to someone. I mean, if you know someone." I wrap my arms around myself and dig my nails into my skin. For some reason, just saying that makes me feel really strange inside.

"Yes," she says without hesitating. "Yes, I do." She pulls me into a hug and whispers, "See, I told you that you were brave," before she lets me go.

THIRTY-TWO

Jim's cell phone is warm in my hand. Kevin reaches from the front seat of the car and I just manage to delete the text before he swipes it.

He laughs. "My brother, the stud."

I ignore him, savoring Sarah's words saying again how she really, really likes me and that she thinks I'm brave for saving Jordan. I don't know why everyone suddenly thinks I'm so brave, but I pull Sarah's "really, reallys" around me like a blanket.

No way am I sharing them with Kevin.

I smile all the way home.

"I was thinking … " I say once we're back at the house. "Now that I'm really living here, I think I need a key to the walk."

Jim and Kevin look at each other and say "No" in unison.

Then Jim says, "You were always living here, kid. You just never believed it."

"Come on." Kevin tugs on my sleeve. "I've got to get out of these clothes."

We race upstairs and strip out of our stiff clothes and pull on jeans and T-shirts.

"I left all my stuff over at the old house, you know," I say, sinking down onto the bed.

"Anything important?" Kevin rips open a bag of chips and shovels some into his mouth. "Damn, stress always makes me hungry. Want some?"

I shake my head. I do a mental inventory of my bag and, aside from my homework, the only thing that mattered in there was Ms. DeSilva's card. But I guess I don't need that anymore. "Just a few of your shirts."

"I don't care about any of those. And why are you being so quiet?" Kevin asks. "I thought you'd be happy."

I know I should be flying-off-the-walls happy. I'm not sure why this thing in the pit of my stomach is telling me not to be.

I shrug.

"Everything that happened at that meeting was good. You get that, right?" he asks, trying again.

I tug at the band around my wrist. There isn't anything I can say to disagree. "Yeah, I guess."

"So?" Kevin isn't going to give up, I know that. But I also know I don't have an answer he's going to like because one thought keeps circling through my head.

"What happens when he gets out of jail?" I ask.

Kevin rolls his eyes and sits down next to me, wiping his greasy fingers on my comforter. "Crap, Ice, really?"

I shrug again, wishing I could just stop worrying and

enjoy things. Maybe that's part of what comes next year. Maybe that's part of normal. I hope so.

"If or when he does, it won't matter," Kevin says. "Jim is adopting you, right?"

"Yeah."

"So, what is it?"

I spin the band around my wrist, walk over to the window, and talk to the Kevin I see reflected in the glass. "Mr. Brooks is taking off for a year and Sarah is going to leave. She hasn't really come out and said it, but she is." The words kind of hurt as they rush out of my mouth. I don't want it to be true, but I know it is. It probably won't be over the summer, but it might be next year or the year after. At some point she's going to leave and I'm still going to be here. "And so are you, and—"

"Don't be an idiot." He drapes an arm around my shoulders and looms large in the window. "Brooks will come back and I'd put money on the fact that Sarah isn't going anywhere. And us? We have a pact. Don't you understand that means you can't really get rid of me? Whether I go to school or get a job or, hell, run away to Canada, we're brothers and we need each other, right?"

I turn and look at him for real. His expression is soft like it used to be as a kid before he got angry all the time. I'm not sure he's ever said straight-out that he needs me, and it's kind of funny to think that anyone could. Then I think of Jordan, and okay ... maybe it's possible. Just maybe.

I walk over to my nightstand and pull out Sarah's bird necklace and drape it over my head. Then I pick up the photo of me, Kevin, Mom, and the kids and stick it on my wall.

I expect Kevin to complain, but he doesn't. He just looks at me and nods.

Everything finally feels like it's where it belongs.

I can't help but let a smile stretch across my face as I look at my brother. "Tell you what," I say. "I won't leave you if you don't leave me."

————

My eyes flutter open and it's still dark. The room is silent except for the sound of Kevin's breathing. A soft breeze floats through the window. I pull the blankets around me and wrap up in their familiar smell.

I close my eyes again to keep the dream inside me. For the first time it really *is* a dream, too. Not a memory. Not a spin. But a real dream.

In it, I'm flying this huge mechanical bird. Kevin is there, and Sarah, and even Jordan. And we're charging through the sky, cutting through clouds, zigzagging across blue.

The wind is in my face, blowing my hair back.

Everyone I love is laughing.

I look down and we're over the river, only the water is so clean and clear that even from up here, I can see everything. Every rock and piece of algae. Every minnow and eel and fish. And just like in Sylvia's poem, it's the most beautiful thing I've ever seen.

I'm home.

Author's Note

This book is a work of fiction, and while I tried to be as accurate as possible when telling Gordie's story, each individual copes with trauma differently. It is a common misperception that Post Traumatic Stress Disorder is only suffered by members of the military. If you are having difficulties coping with a traumatic event, or you know someone who is, please educate yourself and consult your healthcare provider.

One good educational source is the National Center for PTSD: www.ptsd.va.gov/public/pages/fslist-ptsd-overview.asp.

Acknowledgments

There were people who believed in the viability of this book even before I did, and I'd be negligent if I didn't put them at the top of this list. So to Stephanie Cardel, Carmen Erickson, and Sue Kamata, I will always be grateful for your belief in Gordie's story. To Dana Alison Levy, who tirelessly read many many versions and threatened me into the correct ending, and to Lynn Lindquist, who very bravely told me when I got it right, I am forever in your debt.

To Melissa Jeglinski, for taking a chance on Gordie's story, and to Brian Farrey-Latz, Sandy Sullivan, Mallory Hayes, and the gang at Flux for letting me break their hearts and then thanking me for it, there are no words of gratitude large enough.

To the editors of the She Writes Young Adult Novel Contest and the folks at MidSouth SCBWI... on the surface, awards are only pieces of paper, but they sometimes give writers the courage to go on, so *thank you*.

To those who read drafts or bits of drafts, I can't thank you enough.

To Scott Sitner, for friendship without question and legal advice I've probably bungled, and to Beth Hull and Susan Gray Foster, who stepped in at the very last minute to teach me that I know absolutely nothing about semicolons, I owe you each vats of chocolate and endless champagne.

To the band Spring Offensive, who somehow appear on all of my playlists... this would have been a different and lesser book without your voices in my head. Thanks also to Chris Foster for all the sneak peeks and downloads.

And, of course, to John, who believed me and *almost* didn't flinch when I sat down one day and said I was going to write a book. With all my love.

© Stephanie Saujon

About the Author

Helene Dunbar usually writes features about Irish fiddles and accordions, but she's also been known to write about court cases, theater, and Native American Indian tribes. She's lived in two countries, six states, and is currently holed up in Nashville with her husband, daughter, two cats, and the world's friendliest golden retriever. *These Gentle Wounds* is her debut novel with Flux.